Praise for

D1496753

The Year ᴗ. ᴗᴗ

"The 'Tsunami' crashes onto your frontal lobe. It soaks you in diverse culture. A vacation for the mind and soul."

—Brad W. Cox, *Children of the Program* Trilogy

"In Derrick Credito's *The Year of the Tsunami*, the protagonist at one point cites the tried and true wisdom that it's best to 'think globally, act locally.' The philosophy applies not only to the character, but as a thesis for the book as a whole—a worldly journey that crosses national borders and oceans, but that ultimately centers on much more intimate human connections, for all of the sex, drugs, violence, love, and hope they entail. This is a novel of discovery, told from a unique voice at a unique time."

—Michael Chin, author of *My Grandfather's an Immigrant, and So is Yours*

"There's an old saying that half the stories ever told share a universal propulsion: *someone goes on a journey.* In Derrick Credito's *The Year of the Tsunami*, the journey is both literal and metaphorical. This adventurous first novel reads like a quest in itself, as though Credito had just told himself a crucial story, all the while keeping the reader entertained."

—Madeleine Mysko, author of *Bringing Vincent Home* and *Stone Harbor Bound*

THE YEAR OF THE TSUNAMI

Candace,

THE YEAR OF
THE TSUNAMI

All the best!

Derrick Credito

WANDERING BOHEMIAN
PRESS

Wandering Bohemian Press
Columbia, Maryland
wanderingbohemianpress@gmail.com

Set in Baskerville
Printed in the United States

Editor: Melissa Ringsted
Developmental Editor: Tracy C. Gold
Final Developmental and Technical Editor: Lexa Hayes
Author Photograph: Lacey Braden
Dutch Translations: Astrid van den Bold

LCCN: 2022911922 | ISBN: 979-8-9866419-0-4 (paperback)

First U.S. Edition, November 2022
Book design and imprint design by Jon Malfi

For my amazing wife, Miraf Abebe

CHAPTER ONE

On the first day of class, Wes Levine, an American English teacher in Bangkok, had asked the group of twenty Thai students to write a paragraph about themselves. Between pages of his sketchbook, Wes set aside Sao's response, hoping to later review it with Arthur, the retail language center's dyspeptic head teacher and former cattle hand from Australia who always looked shitfaced.

Sao didn't belong in that class. She wrote flowing, developed sentences while her classmates marveled at Wes spelling out the word "elephant" on the whiteboard. When Arthur returned to work after a bad case of food poisoning had laid him up in misery for a week, he was swamped and flustered. Arthur was quick to brush off Wes's valid concerns of Sao's erroneous placement in the lower intermediate speaking course. "I hardly see how it matters," Arthur said, waving a dismissive hand in Wes's direction. "They all come and go, anyway. You got paid, didn't you?"

Every Sunday afternoon in the classroom, Sao sat solitaire at a corner desk. Sometimes she rolled her eyes at the other students who jabbered in provincial, singsong tones. Most of them showed up for class wearing department store markdowns, while fashion-forward Sao comported with elegant, self-possessed poise. She never wore the same thing twice, and all her clothing choices commanded attention: the knee-high Louboutin boots, the velvet cashmere berets, the silky scarves looped in Parisian double knots around her bare collarbone.

Studying Sao became a dirty little habit as Wes picked up her paragraph on lonely nights in his studio apartment. With each word so carefully curated, the English class icebreaker read more like a dating ad:

I love adventure. I'm twenty-five and single, no brothers or sisters. My dad is Thai and lives in England with his new wife. My mom is a Jewish New Zealander, and we keep a kosher home in the heart of downtown Bangkok. I attended university in Paris and traveled all over Europe by train. My dream is to see all seven continents. Only two more to go.

As the class flitted into the lobby for break time, Wes snuck a peek at Sao's words, wondering how she ever got lumped together with a room full of Thai village people. Wes concealed the paragraph in his sketchbook as he noticed Sao sauntering to the podium in slow, fluid steps that turned the heads of a few interlopers speaking among themselves in rapid-fire hand gestures. As she approached, Wes watched as Sao slipped on a pair of dark sunglasses, turning her back on the busybodies cackling away in the corridor.

"Do you have a moment for a personal question?" Sao asked in a near-whisper.

4

Wes wet the whiteboard with a spray bottle. "Sure. What's on your mind?"

She backed away, shyly fingering wisps of her raven black hair. "Why Bangkok?"

Exhausted from a year of soupy, polluted air, Wes paused and sighed in resignation before responding. "My dad came here before I did. Now he's in New Zealand."

Sao smiled warmly at the mention of her mother's homeland. "Is he a teacher, too?"

"Isn't every foreigner in Thailand?" Wes quipped, cracking open his sketchbook to a page with *shalom* etched into a puffy cloud. "When I was a kid, he taught me how to scribe in Hebrew."

Sao leaned closely enough to turn the pages herself. "How come you never shared this with the class?"

"Better to keep a low profile," Wes replied bluntly, clapping the book shut as Sao's intro paragraph nearly slipped from the pages. "Some hateful people work here."

"That's what I've heard," Sao said, her voice dripping with suspicion. "I want to quit this so-called school. Students here spend way too much money just to practice their English with teachers who aren't even qualified."

Wes shrugged. "Well, my degree isn't in education. But I like what I do."

"I didn't mean you, Wes," Sao swiftly backpedaled. "You're the only good one here. And you can do much better."

"I appreciate that. But I just signed on for another year."

"Think about it, Wes." Sao let the sunglasses slip down her nose. "Live a little. You can do so much more than teaching English with bitter, old men."

"What are you saying I should do?"

Sao looked calm and radiant, speaking straight into his eyes. "I think you should visit New Zealand. It's the most beautiful place in the world."

"You've been there before?" Wes played coy, not wanting his student to know he'd committed to memory the personal details of her first-day paragraph.

"My mom grew up in Auckland. We go back to visit every year."

"My friend Dave lives there," Wes said. "You know, the former head teacher? He's always inviting me to stay at his house in Herne Bay."

"Whatever," Sao said, waving her hand in a graceful, sweeping motion. "See the world when you have the chance."

"It's *while* you have the chance," Wes replied with a wink. "As a teacher, I feel lucky that I can hold on to a traditional job."

Sao gazed at him as a sly smile tugged at the corners of her mouth. "Wes, it's 2004. Nothing is traditional anymore."

"I don't know," Wes added. "What if I leave and your next teacher's a jerk?"

"Look around you. This place is a revolving door. You can suspend your contract and come back whenever you want. It's what my last two teachers did."

"Maybe we can quit together," Wes said offhandedly.

Sao held an assured grin, stepping sideways to her desk as the other students shuffled back to their seats. "Now that, Teacher Wes? That's the spirit."

The very next day, Wes hopped a bus for Siam Square to revise the terms of his employment at the Head Office. There, a hurried receptionist handed off stapled pages with dotted lines awaiting signatures before turning her back to continue a conversation about "that fight." Shrugging, Wes exited, paying no mind to the gossip.

6

Back in the elevator, Wes bumped into another educator, Colin, who turned away and leaned over the handrail. His wrinkled shirt was tinged with drops of blood. Big bruises ringed both of his eyes.

"What) you?" Wes asked. "Are you

SECONL ITION BOOKS ing filmy, dried blood on his
BUY * LL * TRADE 1 from the company for two

04/20/2024 11:34AM 01 ists going on about a fight at
000000#8751 CLERK01

 right."

 T $14.99 s Heinrich. I confronted him
NEW ITEM $14.99 him with, and he went off."
MDSE ST $0.90 he scratches on Colin's nose
TAX1 ttle guy, five foot seven with
 10 chest. "I just hope that you
ITEMS $15. 89
CHARGE

Once I got out of the headlock, I bashed his head with a chair. He went to the emergency room and I didn't, so the company's blaming me."

"New topic, then. So, my dad's in New Zealand," Wes said as they walked off the elevator and into scorching central Bangkok. "I decided to suspend my contract to go look for him."

"For how long?"

"We'll see. Dave Sterling's setting me up with a room in Auckland. Sorry for always being too busy to jam with you."

Colin crinkled his battered eyes. "What are you saying?"

"If you're feeling up to it, let's play some music tonight."

Colin's practice space was a storage capsule planted into dusty ruins. On the fringes of a dark, dusty highway, Colin had staked out a dry piece of land between a patchwork of tin-roofed shanties and a sprawling outdoor market overlooking a muddy *klong.*

Before coming to Thailand to teach English, Colin had ended a three-year run in the world's financial hub. Everything he owned went into a shipping container on a big boat in the Port of Tilbury, thence floating an eastbound path around the world's continents from the Thames River to the Chao Phraya. Colin brought his entire rehearsal space from the UK and was forever going on about gigs he had lined up.

Tempting as it was to put another band together, Wes didn't relate to Colin all that well. He found it odd that the affluent Londoner had relocated on a permanent basis to Thailand for a teaching job that paid peanuts. Besides, they were from different sides of the tracks. Colin was third generation in his family to graduate from Oxford, while Wes went to a state university on full scholarship.

So that his mom could rent out his bedroom and catch up with the mortgage, Wes moved out after college and stayed at the home of Boone Somphan, his best friend since high school, and whose dad, Lek, was born and raised in Thailand. Bangkok jobs would pay better than anything out in the provinces, Lek advised, when Wes decided to set out to find his own father. Stanley Levine disappeared from Playa del Carmen "like a ghost in the night," as one neighbor had phrased it on the phone. After ten years on the Caribbean shoreline, Stanley pulled a midnight runner to Bangkok.

Colin turned open the padlocked door, leading Wes into the full rehearsal studio he'd imported into a developing country where flood waters knew not how to discriminate in the annual rainy seasons.

"Nice setup," Wes said, looking over a slotted rack of Fender Stratocasters. "Now that we're in a private place, can you tell me what's really been going on?"

8

Hiding his battered face behind the drum throne, Colin looked downcast, idly twirling a pair of sticks until one slipped from his fingers. "Maybe. Sure. What's on your mind?"

"Some of the teachers at the branch have been acting really strange lately." Wes strapped on one of Colin's electric guitars and, without plugging it in, strummed absent-minded chords.

"It's not only our co-workers," Colin replied as he stepped away from the drums. "Take a look out the door for a minute."

"Okay." Wes returned the guitar to its stand. "What am I looking at?"

"You see that girl by the Coke machine?"

Wes bit down on his lip. "She looks very young."

Colin leaned closer. "That's the kid I saw with Heinrich the other night."

"So why don't we get her some help?" Wes suggested, feeling for the Nokia in his pants pockets.

"Don't do that." Colin laid a firm hand on the cell phone. "Heinrich has connections."

"Would you consider leaving the country?" Wes asked. "Dave might even be able to hook you up with a room at his house Down Under."

Colin shook his head. "I've got too much tied up here in Bangkok."

Wes peeked through the crack in the door as Colin flipped a switch, bringing instant darkness to the rehearsal space. A wayward white man too tall and stout to stand upright wobbled out of the shadows and into incandescent red light shining from the Coke machine. As the looming giant deposited some coins, he helped himself to the pink spaghetti straps on the girl's loose tank top. Faster than the can tumbled to the dispenser, the man and the child disappeared into the murky field of shipping cubes.

9

"I've got to take care of some unfinished business," Wes said, patting Colin on the shoulder. "Let's jam another time."

It was time. Wes had to let Tely know about his plans to leave Thailand.

Ever since Wes moved into his seaside apartment by an industrial park, the forty-five-year-old concierge receptionist had acted like a second mom. In her younger years, Tely had arrived in Thailand by way of the Philippines. She had chin-length hair, a red rose tattoo that wrapped around her wrist, and two adult children from whom she was estranged. Wes, expecting that his decision to break the lease would incur a financial loss, approached the counter, picking at his fingernails. But Tely amended the pages of his written rental agreement with a red rubber stamp, and with a maternal, sad smile, she handed over the security deposit in full. Wes returned her smile with a quiet one of his own. He did care about this woman a great deal. When her mother died on Christmas Eve, Wes left a bouquet and a sympathy card on her desk, and Tely had never forgotten it.

Sitting on the studio floor with a packed trunk suitcase at his back, Wes scratched a dull pencil into an unfinished Hebrew chai. An old birthday greeting from his dad slipped from the sketchbook. Wes stared into the faded snapshot of the Playa Del Carmen shore. The same year on Mom's birthday, Dad sent another postcard that she ripped to shreds straight out of the mailbox. Wes taped the pieces together to find that Stanley Levine now lived in an overwater bungalow, and he was inviting his family to join him.

Mom said, "No way!" as Wes asked, "Why not?"

The postcard picture looked like a paradise deserted, too distant for Stanley's many creditors to find him. Since the twelfth grade, Wes usually kept the birthday message taped to his bedroom mirror. Over the years, the once sun-soaked photo faded to dusty gray.

Hi, Son. Can't believe my Bar Mitzvah boy is already seventeen. Say hello to Mom. I miss you both all the time. Happy birthday.

Wes dropped the room key on Tely's desk, remotely aware of the tears beginning to pool in his eyes. Tely made him promise he wouldn't look at the postcard in lonely times. Going out the double glass doors, she clasped his hand on the marbled front steps, wrapping him in a warm hug that sent his blood coursing. Tely, twenty years his senior, seemed more in touch with her sexual side than the shy university girls he'd notice at the mall, tucked carefully in skin-tight uniforms, giggling whenever they saw a man. And despite her motherly role, Tely's maturity turned him on. Sometimes, Wes imagined what she looked like under those sleek business blazers. In the tight embrace, Tely cradled Wes around the shoulders, holding him close enough that he could feel the firmness of her breasts. As she saw him out, Wes took uncomfortable steps through the door and into the public. Everyone on the street could see that Wes was hard, a Pinocchio's nose showing through the crotch of his khaki trousers.

He wheeled his clunky suitcase through the *soi* and turned around, waving to Tely one last time. Mournful harmonics rang out spacey, organic sounds. A tiny woman sat curbside on straw mat next to a smoking charcoal grill. She blew a disoriented melody into her bamboo pipes, holding her instrument between unevenly amputated limbs. Wes spared eighteen baht, dropping tiny coins into her tip cup, and he climbed the steps of the skybridge with his head down, as if ashamed he hadn't given more. But earlier that day, he'd exchanged nearly all his baht for traveler's checks, keeping just enough Thai currency for a taxi ride to Don Muang Airport, where a nominal international departure tax also awaited at the final checkpoint.

As he walked, Wes happened upon a merchant table outside of the mall. A man in a purple Indian pagari shuffled his cards. Wrapped upon the mystic's forehead, an embedded red ruby gem shone like a third eye. A straggling salt-and-pepper beard of biblical proportions forked into two trails down his chest.

"Hello, please come see me!" solicited the mystic, splitting the Tarot deck into three. "I can look into your future. I'm the chosen one."

"Now, how can I be sure of that?"

"For two hundred baht I'll give you a palm reading. If you pay a little more, we can use my crystal ball."

"Just palm," Wes returned, pulling the exact amount from his pocket.

"Yes, yes, that's fine," Chosen One said brusquely. He snapped the money into his hand, and Wes whiffed a peculiar, sour odor of nuts on the man's breath.

"Soon," Chosen One traced a thick fingertip across the long line on Wes's palm. "You'll hear good news from two people. This line is about communication, Wes."

Wes sharpened an eyebrow. "How do you know my name?"

Chosen One cracked a toothy, cocksure smile. "Tell me, what's my name, brother?"

"Um, Chosen One?"

"Now tell me who loves you the most?"

Stanley came to mind. That Stanley, the one who fled Maryland for Mexico, disappearing from his family to shield them from harm. *He did it from a place of love*, Wes told himself for the thousandth time.

"Love's a complicated thing," Wes replied. "Besides, you're the psychic. Maybe you can answer that question."

12

"I'm seeing a man and a woman in your life," Chosen One returned, his eyes widening with excitement.

"Really?" Wes asked, intrigued. "What do you know about them?"

Chosen One reached under his table. "We can look with my crystal ball."

"Sorry." Wes shook his head. "I only have enough for the palm reading. I'm about to catch a taxi. Is there anything else you can do for the two hundred?"

Chosen One nodded as he passed Wes a tiny slip of a blank paper. "Hold this and think of a number from one to twenty."

"Okay. Got it."

Chosen One rolled his eyes heavenward. "Now open your hands."

Wes unfolded the paper. Bewildered, he looked at the one and eight penciled fancily in freehand. Eighteen and the chai were his most favored number and letter, symbols of life and luck since Abraham.

"H-How did you do that?" Wes stammered, staring into the unfolded parchment. "It was blank when you gave it to me."

Chosen One smiled beatifically as sunlight beamed across his big-bearded face. "I didn't write on it, my brother," he whispered solemnly. "You did."

"No, I didn't," Wes snapped, as though offended by a serious accusation.

Recoiling from the table, Wes felt foolish for blowing his money on a palm reading. During Senior Week at Ocean City, Wes had stumbled into the boardwalk shop of a Latina beauty in a long, gilded dress who calmly told Wes that he'd go on to travel the world and write the greatest book of all time. Chosen One reminded Wes more of his dad's card reader, so hot-tempered and alarmist. Despite gambling debts spiraling out of control, Stanley managed to rack up thousands in phone bills so that he could spill his guts to a husky-voiced drama king who saw Mexico in the cards. On his last call, Stanley had been issued a warning: the closer he stayed to his wife and son, the graver the dangers they'd all face.

"Please come back," Chosen One cried to Wes, who had already sprinted across the street and was handing his suitcase to a taxi driver. "You're breaking my heart!"

As Wes slipped into the backseat, he rolled his eyes before flicking a peace sign. "I foresee that you'll get over it," he added, bidding the mystic farewell.

CHAPTER TWO

On his seat-back screen, Wes viewed a graphic simulation of the southbound aircraft hovering over the north Indian Ocean. The first few hours of the flight passed in blissful silence. Then, a soda can tipped from a trembling drink cart, jolting every seat on the plane.

Approaching the Equator, the pilot played favorites with the erratic wings, steering five second intervals of left and right. Everyone aboard had no choice but to trust in the pilot's strategy, which provoked the aircraft into a clockwise roll across the clouds. Wes gripped the Star of David pendant around his neck as the plane swirled with squeals of terror. In the middle aisle, a pair of veiled nuns clutched rosary beads as they mouthed prayers. By the time the pilot made an announcement on the intercom—Wes couldn't quite make out the words, though the voice sounded breezy and assuring—the plane had recovered equilibrium. The black-and-white clad sisters continued to pray, which gave Wes a twinge in his chest over thoughts of crashing into the ocean.

As the wheels bounced on the runway at Auckland International, Wes opened his porthole shade to glimpse up close the verdant expanse of pastures he'd previewed from New Zealand airspace. Flight attendants stood like guards beside the exit gate. A Māori powerhouse with bazooka arms in a too-tight uniform fist-bumped Wes and other relieved travelers who disembarked a plane that Wes was certain wouldn't make it in one piece onto the tarmac.

Wes collected his luggage, hauling it out of the airport and into a chilly Southern Hemisphere on the cusp of winter. With that first crisp taste of Auckland air, a gust of wind prickled his shoulders. Somewhere in the acres of cars, Dave was waiting in his yellow Jeep. Under the six-in-the-morning tangerine sky, Wes scanned the lot for an automobile close in color to the rising sun.

When Wes joined the company in Bangkok, he had instantly clicked with the head teacher, Dave Sterling, a New Zealander who got around by motorcycle and studied Thailand on folded maps. The company footed expenses for teachers to take day trips into the provinces. Wes and Dave had donned helmets and bandana masks, doubling up on a Honda Rebel. Instead of riding with their teacher colleagues, they trailed the chartered bus from downtown Bangkok into dusty villages where little monkeys roamed the streets and elephants sucked down unpeeled bananas as tourists with cameras around their necks snapped pictures.

Finally, Wes spotted Dave. "Thanks for getting up so early to come get me," Wes called, and they came together for a tight hug, more like a final goodbye than a hello.

"Can't believe you're really here!" Dave said in his Kiwi surfer drawl, hauling Wes's trunk suitcase into the hatch. "Arthur e-mailed me about the scuffle at work. Old chap means well but hasn't got a clue."

"Yep," Wes responded, shrugging in resignation. "His answer to everything is 'it's the culture.'"

"Culture my foot. Head Office was useless as tits on a bull. Whenever I asked for help, the staff all said the same thing. Take ..."

"Take what Heinrich says with a grain of salt," Wes finished Dave's sentence. "Give him the attention he craves just to keep him calm. Don't worry about him. He's harmless."

"I imagine this sort of thing would be taken more seriously in the States," Dave added, prompting Wes to nod tensely.

In highway traffic, Wes stared into the lucid horizon at little country houses speckled like dots on rolling hills where gold-dusted treetops swayed with the wind. From the exit ramp, the highway turned into a winding road. They arrived at Dave's house, a stony little cottage with a shaggy thatched roof. Olive green silvereyes perched under the eaves, chirping off to a nearby branch as the front door opened. A fresh coat of white paint gleamed in the living room. On the other side of a carved-out wall, pots and pans hung from a mounted rack. The small but wide abode was a study in contradictions: a rustic, natural exterior with clean, sterile lines on the interior.

Standing at the entrance, Wes could see everything in the one-story home, from the coat rack by the doormat to the telescope pointing out of a bay window beyond the kitchen. Dave showed him to the guest bedroom, where a gold-plated *mezuzah* sparkled in the door. Wes looked closely into the glass-encased parchment, squinting at hand-scribed Hebrew letters nearly too tiny for the naked eye. The scroll had belonged to the last tenant, Dave offhandedly mentioned, and he lacked the precise tools to uninstall it before moving out.

"It lends the place a little character, don't you think?" Dave asked.

"We never hung a *mezuzah* at our house," Wes said, dragging an uncertain finger across the glass.

"Why not?" Dave asked.

"Dad's Jewish, Mom isn't. We were the only family on our street with a Jewish name."

"With that *mezuzah* nailed into the door, I didn't expect the chap to up and leave so soon."

"Speaking of up and leaving, the last time I talked to my mom, she mentioned getting some mail about Dad renewing his passport in New Zealand," Wes said.

"What exactly was he doing here?" Dave asked, his tone suspicious.

"Wish I knew," Wes answered, handing over his Nokia mobile. "But I'd love to be able to make some phone calls again."

"And how did I know you'd come to me for this?" Dave said. The sarcasm wasn't lost on Wes as Dave dug his nails into the panel, popping off the back of the phone. Once inside, Dave flipped a latch to release a thumbnail-sized plastic chip, and, with a sigh Wes knew was exaggerated for dramatic effect, reached into his pocket for a small local SIM card, which Dave then inserted into the phone to replace the one from Thailand.

"There you go." Dave snapped together the phone and set it back into Wes's palm with a handshake. "We should get going. Mum and Dad made reservations."

On the drive to dinner, Dave briefed Wes on his family. Bill was an affluent subdivision developer and Nancy, a department chair at a small college. When Dave told them that an American friend was flying in from Bangkok, his parents jumped to make dinner plans. The family got their start in the old Herne Bay cottage Dave was now living in before moving to urban, upmarket Ponsonby when Dave and his brothers were teenagers. It was now just the two of them, Bill and Nancy, in a boxy, modern house overlooking downtown Auckland from a poolside hill. Dave's younger brother had left the nest to intern at a bank in Singapore, with the oldest brother studying marine biology in Melbourne.

At an Indian restaurant outside of the city's center, they gathered in an orange-tinted dining room. Bill and Nancy were all smiles as they greeted their son and his American friend. A hostess in a bright silk dress led the way to a table, where they took seats in oversized leather chairs.

"So, Wes," Bill said, pulling apart a piece of *naan* bread. "Now that you've had a chance to spend a little time overseas, have you thought about settling somewhere permanently?"

"Nothing's ever permanent," Wes replied without a moment of thought. "But the main reason I took a leave from work in Bangkok was because my dad is somewhere in New Zealand."

"North or South Island?" Bill asked.

"I'm not sure. I haven't heard from him. My mom received notice that he renewed his American passport at the embassy in Auckland. Neither of us has seen him in ten years."

"Such a long time," Nancy chimed in after a stilted silence.

Wes threw his hands into the air and inadvertently rattled the silverware set on the table. "Maybe he had an interest in New Zealand that I never knew about."

"Have you tried to contact him?" Bill asked.

"Sure," Wes replied tersely. It felt like a shameful secret, that his father had abandoned him beyond all points of contact. Besides the birthday postcard that

19

Wes kept in his Hebrew sketchbook, it was almost like Stanley Levine had died on the day he disappeared from his son's life.

"May I ask," Nancy began. "Is it something urgent?"

"Sort of. In recent years, my grandparents passed away, both of heart disease. My dad, Stanley, has no way of knowing that they're gone."

Bill cocked an eyebrow. "What's your last name, Wes?"

"Levine."

Bill turned to Nancy, cupping a hand over her ear. But the whisper was for naught. Nancy simply sighed and turned to look at Wes.

"Stanley rented the cottage," she said slowly.

"What? You mean Dave's place?" Wes confirmed, repeating himself for an uncomfortable minute that passed like an hour. "Really?"

"Wes," Nancy returned, her tone calm but firm. "A man by that name spent a year at the house."

"How did you meet Stanley?" Wes asked.

"The Internet. You know how it is these days. In *The Herald*, we placed an ad as a Jewish-friendly rental. Within a couple days, Stanley had snapped up the room."

From across the table, Wes shot Bill a mistrusting glare. "What makes it Jewish-friendly?"

"We're not religious," Bill quickly replied. "But Nancy's mum is Jewish, so we still keep some traditions."

Forcing a polite smile, Wes cleared his throat. "I just need a minute."

Wes tipped back his chair, almost knocking it over as he dashed for the washroom. Standing before the mirror, he splattered cold water on his face, staring himself down like a man possessed. An electric hand dryer did little to dry the mixture of sink water and tears, and Wes returned to the table with dampened cheeks and bloodshot eyes. Dave leaned forward in his chair, sending Wes a concerned gaze, which countered the straight-backed, funereal gloom of his parents' stone-cold Anglo faces.

"I just wish I knew what exactly he was doing here," Wes said, breaking another uncomfortable silence. "Don't get me wrong, I doubt there's a more naturally beautiful country on Earth, but why New Zealand?"

"He never told us, and we never asked," Nancy said. "Stanley was the most reliable tenant I've ever known. Sometimes he'd pay us months in advance. What did he do for a living stateside?"

"Oh, a little bit of everything. Over the years, he did well on some investments. We had a small family restaurant going for a while, too."

When times were good and Stanley Levine was still winning big on horse races, he walked out of the bank with the deed to Sal's Pizza & Subs, the carryout joint he'd opened on a subprime loan. Eventually, he had the walls knocked down to add a small dining room, a pinball machine, and a vintage jukebox that played modern rock. With the rest of the loot, Stanley helped Kathy finish the MBA she'd quit soon after Wes was born. But as his Midas touch slipped away, Stanley tried desperately to bet his way out of the hole, throwing more cash into the pockets of bookies. Meanwhile, Kathy kept on the straight and narrow, working for a financial firm. Neither of Wes's parents could discuss money without shouting or throwing things. Wes, a tenth grader teaching himself the guitar, strummed acoustic chords as kitchenware clanged or plates shattered not too far from his bedroom.

For years, Stanley was lucky. But once that luck evaporated, everything quickly fell apart. Wes was hiding behind his bedroom door on the day when two collection agents in black suits flashed wallet holder badges and entered the home, flanked by muscle-bound men who followed orders and lugged everything out to the front yard. Neighbors walking their dogs watched as the Levines stood like statues on the front porch while their house was emptied into a moving truck.

Losing the restaurant was another bitter pill to swallow, and Stanley tried to sweeten it by betting some more. Every time Wes saw his parents together, they barked like dogs until one of them broke something or slammed a door on the way out. After the last big blowup, Stanley Levine vanished from the house, the state, and the country.

"Sorry for dumping all this on you," Wes apologized.

"No worries. I just hope that you're able to reach him." Bill passed Wes a business card. In simple text, it stated only the following: Stanley Levine, Jack-of-all-Trades. Phone Inquiries Only.

"Great, so there's a phone number." Wes sighed in relief, securing the card in his billfold. "But 'jack-of-all-trades?'"

"He did do a little bit of everything," Bill added as the server returned with the cheque. "Stanley loved working on houses."

Driving home, Dave steered cautiously through a gravelly backroad, shining the high beams to cut through the dark of night. On the scenic route, Dave said he wanted to show Wes a glimpse of the real New Zealand. Within a minute, long grass brushes replaced tall buildings and asphalt streets, and the cityscape was gone.

"Did Stanley ever mention that he had a family?" Wes finally asked.

Dave took a deep breath. "Don't read into it too much," he started. "We didn't see much of each other."

"Come on," Wes pressed him. "You lived together."

"For a few weeks," Dave countered. "And I didn't know who he was. Like I said, we weren't close or anything. Stanley was always out working."

"I just can't figure out how he supported himself as a jack-of-all-trades."

"I think he painted."

"Painted what?"

"Houses, commercial buildings, picket fences. We gave him a rent-free month for touching up the walls of the cottage," Dave answered, turning to steal a glance at Wes. "You know, mate, you do look a little bit like him. I see that now."

The sheep came out of nowhere. Dave kicked both his feet on the brakes, cutting the wheel so sharply that the tires screamed across the pavement. The Jeep spun full circle while undeterred hooves went on clacking across the street like nothing happened. Wes stared through the windshield, counting the flock in stunned silence as an unconcerned Dave shifted the gearstick to park on the shoulder.

"That was so freaking close," Wes uttered, his mouth hanging open. "Almost a bloodbath."

"Out in the wild," Dave explained nonchalantly. "Near misses like that happen all the time."

"Have you ever had an accident?"

Dave didn't answer straight away. "No."

They chuckled at the gurgled mewling of a dozen oblivious sheep clearing the roadway at a leisurely pace. While the flock moseyed across the street to graze in the grass, Dave shone the high beams and hopped from the Jeep to scan the deserted street for any stragglers lingering around the figure-eight tire skids seared into the street. Wes watched through the windshield at Dave dancing with his own shadow, making all kinds of funky noises to interact with the white, wooly creatures out at night.

"I love you, man," Wes gasped, laughing to regain his composure. Dave sprang back into the Jeep, his deep brown eyes shining in the dark like a deer's.

"You should've seen the look on your face, mate!" Dave joined in laughing. "You've just added years to my life."

CHAPTER THREE

As the news broke on the American's second morning in Auckland, Wes deboarded the bus from Dave's suburban cottage. With uncertain steps, Wes slipped into a throng of foot commuters clutching newspapers, treading with heads slung low across the intersection of Queen and Wellesley. Dave had suggested that Wes scope out the nearby Sky Tower, to *just look for the giant needle,* but it was too cloudy to see much of anything. Besides, nearly every pedestrian looked too sullen for Wes to dare stop and ask for directions. One look at the front-page story in *The New Zealand Herald* allowed Wes to understand their reasons.

John Robert Tyrrell was overseeing a roadway construction in oil-rich Kirkuk, a battleground north of Baghdad. The bold-type headline commemorated New Zealand's first casualty of Iraq, a fifty-three-year-old father of three: DEAD MAN IGNORED FAMILY PLEAS. Wes caught some early reactions from pedestrians waiting behind a chirping crosswalk signal for the light to turn green.

"The bloke was under contract," said a middle-aged man in a khaki trench coat.

"Right," agreed someone else on the sidewalk. "With the Yanks in Washington."

"Yanks are in it for oil. It's a bloody shame our bloke didn't listen."

"This one's on the Yanks."

Wes didn't ever recall hearing "Yank" in the States. The word grated on his ears like a schoolyard taunt, a cacophony spoken never in admiration, seldom with affection, and usually to inflict shame. Now on his own at the bottom of the Earth, Wes could barely see through the mist to make sense of this new and uncharted city. The weight of the war burned in the pit of his stomach. As he strained his eyes on the devastating newspaper headline, a throaty heave of acid nearly provoked him to vomit.

Settling under a vacant bus shelter, Wes reached into his wallet and extracted the business card Bill Sterling had passed him at the restaurant. He trembled, fingers twitching, as he thumbed Stanley's phone number on the Nokia keypad, double checking each digit before placing the call. Stanley hadn't picked up when Wes tried reaching him the night before. But now? Wes's heartbeat thumped faster with each ring. On the fourth chime, Wes sighed before stuffing the cell phone back into his pocket and, with his mind still preoccupied, braved the cloudy murk to cross yet another downtown intersection.

The fog cleared, and soon Wes found the street of a fire brick synagogue he'd looked up on the Internet. He entered through a massive wooden door. Clutching a gold-embossed siddur, an elderly man emerged from the chapel to greet Wes in the foyer.

"Good morning," Wes opened, clearing his throat. "I'm here to inquire about a job opening."

Scratching the wisps of his beard, the older man looked perplexed. "A job opening?"

"Wh-What's the word I'm l-looking for?" Wes stuttered, looking at the man he'd found on the Internet. A *rebbe*, he recalled, briefly thinking back to his search. "Are there any vacancies here?"

"Are you Jewish?" asked Rebbe in a melodic, English lilt.

"Yes, I am," replied Wes Levine, the grandson of Holocaust escapees. Wes had left all his head coverings in Baltimore. He'd slept in his faded denim blue jeans, unchanged for the third straight day.

Rebbe couldn't take his eyes off Wes's black leather jacket, undoubtedly torn from the skin of a *treif* animal. Before Wes could further engage him in conversation, Rebbe turned his back and suggested Wes look for a progressive synagogue, hesitantly admitting that one or two such places existed in Auckland. When asked for an exact location, Rebbe stated flatly that he was unable to advise any further, dismissing himself with an early wish for a "good Shabbos."

Later in the afternoon, Wes creaked through the cottage door. Cold rain had drenched him at a downtown bus stop while he waited for a ride back to the burbs. The Nokia vibrated in his back pocket, and when Wes reached for the phone, he saw an incoming call from his mom, Kathy McKenna, her information flashing onscreen like a telegram from another world. At times, her last name still struck Wes as odd. But when Stanley left, she returned to her maiden name on the grounds that carrying the surname of an estranged Jewish ex-husband felt like a target stamped on her back.

"So, is this your new number?" Kathy asked, a hint of disappointment in her voice.

27

"For now," Wes replied, hastily towel-drying his rain-soaked hair.

"I can't believe you're in New Zealand. Are you any closer to finding your dad?"

"You might say that," Wes started, hesitation stifling his voice. "I've got some news. Are you ready?"

"Sure. What's going on?"

"He lived at Dave's for a while, and then took off just a couple weeks ago."

"What?" His mother's voice sounded incredulous. "Are you sure about that?"

"Your wedding *mezuzah* still hangs in the door."

"Unbelievable. And where is he now?"

"I got his cell phone number from Dave's dad, but no answer yet."

"Hopefully you'll hear something soon," she said. "Let me know how it works out." Then the receiver clicked into silence. Nothing burned up cell phone data like an awkward international call.

Wes had nothing to do but head back to his search. On the city's outskirts, dressed in a starched white shirt and a solid red tie, he hailed a taxi and stopped for lunch at a kosher deli. The cashier who rang Wes up for a pastrami and Swiss on rye wore a Hebrew-English tee-shirt that spelled "Etz Chaim," the Tree of Life. Wes figured it was one of those progressive shuls that Rebbe didn't want to talk about. As Wes scurried to jot Etz Chaim's address on a sketchbook page, the hippie cashier simply passed him a business card.

Upon arrival, the synagogue appeared to be a juxtaposition of old and new, a mishmash of stone and steel from different centuries. Wes approached the towering double oak doors in a shirt and tie he hadn't worn since teaching in his Bangkok classroom. As he turned around, an older woman in a flowery tunic and peace sign necklace smiled his way.

"Hello there!" she called from the other side of a courtyard. "How can I help you today?"

Wes shrugged meekly. "I'm new in town."

"Wonderful! I'm Rabbi Linda Sorenson." She reached out for a handshake, giving Wes and his buttoned-up attire a reticent once-over. "I take it you might not be too keen on joining this afternoon's yoga class."

Wes smiled politely. "Maybe another time. I'd actually like to talk to someone about scribing a Torah."

Rabbi Linda looked at him, dumbfounded. "A *Sefer Torah*?" she asked. "You're a scribe?"

"I've been out of practice for a few years. Dropped out of the scribal arts and went on to major in art and design."

"And to what end did you choose this more creative course of study?" she asked.

"I guess for a time, I thought I could make it as a starving artist. But years passed and circumstances changed, and so now, I'm looking to scribe and dedicate a sacred Torah scroll to my grandparents, who both escaped the Shoah."

"It would be a great honor to keep it in our sanctuary." Then, Rabbi Linda hesitated. "And while I wish I could tell you more, Leah calls the shots here. I'm just a washed-up bohemian who sometimes gives sermons."

"Is Leah in today?"

"Down the hall, last door on the left. I must make a quick run to the nursing home. With our seniors, we can only expect the unexpected," the rabbi said frankly, and she was off.

Dressed in what he thought to be his slickest duds, Wes felt as out of place in the synagogue as a soul-saving bible salesman. He stopped outside of the door to Leah's office. From her door-facing seat, he watched as she looked up from a scattering of papers on the desktop.

"You're a bit overdressed," she pleasantly commented, pulling back sun-kissed strands of her hair into an elastic band. "It's Shabbat. You know, casual Friday?"

"Oh, yes. The thing is, I'm looking for work."

Leah locked eyes with Wes, summing him up with a glance. "Yank?" she asked.

Wes bit down on his lip, nodding apologetically. "Yeah."

"It's okay. You know, not many scribes live in Auckland. How did you hear about Etz Chaim?"

"The deli down the road," Wes began. "One of the guys behind the counter was wearing a tee shirt."

"I see. Do you have any samples of your work?"

"I've been living out of a suitcase for the past year, so all I have is this sketchbook."

Leah nodded as though she understood. "This might be a big ask, but for us to truly see your work, would you be willing to leave your sketchbook for Rabbi Linda and me to review?"

"Of course," Wes replied eagerly. "Consider it yours."

Leah accepted the book, and then returned it to him with a smile he couldn't decipher. "Look, I don't need to review your work. There's no metrics for scribing. Either you've got it or you don't. And I know you've got it."

"How would you know that I've got what it takes?" Wes asked, a little stunned at the praise.

"I feel like I can trust you," Leah went on. "You willingly handed over something that holds great meaning in order to prove yourself. That takes trust. Besides, I was also an art major."

"What I really did at university was design my own major," Wes spoke, truthful and self-effacing. "That book's mostly my drawings. Just some of it's in Hebrew."

"Listen, Wes," Leah began. "You don't have to try so hard. We're a progressive shul. Many congregants don't speak or read a word of Hebrew. We'd be lucky to have a scribe on hand. All we need is a sponsor. Someone to pay for the scroll, the materials, and of course, your stipend."

"Sounds great," Wes replied. "When do I start?"

"Before I can offer anything, Rabbi Linda must first meet with the board of trustees. They handle all that financial mumbo jumbo."

Wes grinned, his eyes brimming with hope. "Hope this is it."

"Seeing as you majored in art and design," Leah began, and then was interrupted when the phone on her desk rang. "Anyhow, I may have a special assignment, something a little more relaxed. You could earn a little travel money to pay your way in the meantime."

"Sure. What is the assignment?" Wes asked.

"Sorry," Leah replied, reaching for the phone as it continued to ring. She slipped him a business card. "I must take this call. Ring me later, and we'll talk."

Back at the cottage, a bewildering light shone through a crack in the door. In the room where Wes had been sleeping, he walked in on Dave wearing boxer shorts, a sleeveless camo green top, and a combat helmet fastened crookedly around his chin. With unflagging focus, Dave flexed in front of the mirror as though challenging his own reflection to a fight. Wes stood between the doorposts, holding his breath, waiting for Dave to say something.

"I'm joining the army." The announcement came like a lightning bolt to Wes's ears.

"Really?" Wes answered in shock. "What if they ship you to Iraq?"

31

"The territorial forces are part-time, only on weekends. I'll serve without ever leaving the North Island."

"Will you have to fire a gun?"

"Yeah," Dave spoke into the mirror. "I've never even touched one before. During training, I'll be given plenty of time to get my bearings."

Wes looked Dave over. "I'm sure you can hack it."

"Did you hear about the first New Zealander to die in Iraq?" Dave returned.

"I did," Wes answered firmly. "That's kind of why I question your timing."

Dave patted Wes on the shoulder and walked out, leaving Wes to peruse the daily *Herald* and process the news. Soon, the body of John Robert Tyrrell would arrive for cremation in Thailand, his wife's home country.

Though born in England, Tyrrell had spent much of his life on New Zealand's North Island as a construction engineer, and a beloved local figure. As a contractor, he had envisioned roads that enabled Iraqi desert dwellers their first-ever access to paved thoroughfares. Tyrrell's sudden death was being grieved on virtually all continents, and Wes couldn't even name one American servicemember who'd died in Iraq.

"Hey, Dave," Wes called out to the living room. "In the paper, I read that Tyrrell was Buddhist. Reincarnation makes sense to me but doesn't."

"Ah, already you're picking up on Kiwi doublespeak," Dave pointed out, strolling back to the room with a rolled yoga mat under an arm.

"Yeah, nah," Wes joked back. "But in all seriousness, I hope Tyrrell comes back in the next life with better luck. Where do you think he'll end up starting life all over again?"

"Perhaps nowhere on Earth if he's gone on to reach Enlightenment," Dave responded in a mellower voice.

He'd just switched from camo green to a tie-dye tee, wearing a Hachimaki red-dotted karate headband in place of the helmet.

"I've always thought that if someone made a lot of sacrifices in this life," Wes pondered. "Somehow they'd get to come back as a pampered, jet-setting socialite in the next."

"You've missed the whole point of Enlightenment," Dave said, now sitting crisscrossed with his palms pressed together. "It's not about sacrificing anything. And it sure as hell ain't about coming back as one of the Hilton brats."

"Then what is it about?" Wes asked, genuinely curious.

In his meditation posture, Dave cracked a knowing, archaic smile. "It's about not coming back at all."

CHAPTER FOUR

The waltzing Nokia ringtone resounded as the phone rattled on the wooden nightstand. Wes sprang from his sleep. He sat up in bed—four-fifteen a.m. on the screen—and looked through the windowpane at a world cloaked in the still of night. On a deep breath of cool, dewy air, Wes reluctantly answered the wee-hours phone call from NUMBER UNKNOWN.

"Good morning, Wesley." When Mom used his full name, he knew it was serious.

During high school, Wes came to prefer his shorter name, because at home it was always, "Wesley, I found another bag of grass in your sock drawer!" or, "Wesley, why does the basement smell like Woodstock?" She'd last called him Wesley on the day they found out Zayde had died.

"Is everything okay? Where are you?" Wes asked. "Sounds like you're in a tunnel."

"I'm at 7-11, across the street from the firm. Sorry to alarm you by calling from an unknown number. I'm using a payphone because I don't want to get caught."

"Caught for what?"

"For a minor lapse in judgment. Wes, I hadn't touched pot since college. But if I take this upcoming test, I'll lose my job."

"Wait," Wes said in disbelief, adjusting the phone against his ear. "You smoked pot?"

"Look, don't judge. Some friends came over last night. I took a few drags. Someone in the office must've smelled the reefer on my hair and said something."

"How long do you have until the test?"

"Human Resources needs a result before the close of business today," his mom sighed.

"Mom, listen. There's a little shop called the Other Side on Alleghany Avenue. It's not far from your office. Just ask the clerk for a bottle of Ready Clean. Drink one now, and your system's clear for the next four hours."

"Wes, thank you. I'm sorry if I was uncool about this sort of thing when you were growing up."

"Don't mention it." But Wes still couldn't believe it. His mom, the strait-laced stockbroker of all people, hitting the joint and covering her tracks on a public phone.

"Your dad was always the fun one. Hope you find him," she said, her voice brimming with acceptance.

"You're going to be fine, Mom. Let me know how the drug test goes."

"Please," she whispered in shame. "Don't call it that."

Some hours later, Wes opened his eyes and lingered in bed. Not having a job felt strange and freeing. Strange, because he'd always held down steady work; freeing, for in the middle of his twenties he saw what good fortune it was to not have to.

A pixelated message popped on the Nokia screen. Mom texted that she came up clean, thanking her son in all caps for coming through in the dead of night. Wes fired off a response, typing the words faster than he could think them:

Stick it to the man! This corporate invasion of your privacy and bodily autonomy reeks of the same foul odor as Nazi human experiments.

He texted it as a dig. Mom, a Catholic who identified more generally with Christianity, had not set foot in a synagogue since her wedding day. She skipped Wes's Bar Mitzvah celebration, didn't think it was that big a deal. During college, Wes stopped talking to his mom for months after they had a heated discussion on the phone about Holocaust education mandates, which she had opposed on the grounds that people should decide for themselves.

Well, that's a bit of a stretch.

Mom's text almost ruined Wes's day, until five minutes later, a follow-up message popped into the inbox:

Human life is more important than any job or title.

With determination, Wes waited in front of Etz Chaim's locked doors, dressed down in blue-checkered flannel and holding the Hebrew sketchbook in the crook of his arm. From across the sidewalk, Leah and Rabbi Linda walked closely. As the women sauntered his way, Wes twisted out a smile to mask any desperation the early arrival might have implied.

"Wes, I have some news," Rabbi Linda greeted him with a smile. "I met with the Board of Trustees. Though they're still fussing over our budget, the Chair has agreed to hire a scribe who will begin a scroll after Rosh Hashanah."

"Amazing," Wes responded, trying to contain the excitement. "This was my grandfather's dream."

"I've never met someone so young with such a strong interest in scribing," the rabbi said. "How did you first develop an aptitude for it?"

"It's a long story," Wes answered. "How much time do we have?"

Barely out of high school, Wes began studying with a *Sofer S'tam* named Hillel. Upon meeting the Master Scribe, who'd been a friend of Bubbie and Zayde, Wes began an apprenticeship with a stipend nearly triple minimum wage. After a blurry Senior Week at the ocean, Wes sobered up and dedicated his eighteenth year to mastering an ancient craft, poring over hundreds of commandments with Hillel stooped behind him on a short stool.

With his wife and seven children, Hillel had moved from Brooklyn to West Baltimore County, relocating on account of New York's saturation of scribes without nearly enough work to go around. Surly, sadness-prone Hillel almost never smiled and usually spoke with a short-tempered disappointment in his voice.

Rarely did a week pass without at least one tense moment when young Wes nearly snapped and quit. In the scribing room, they engaged in no small talk, nothing outside of scripture or that afternoon's Mincha prayers. Hillel's eyes turned wide and fiery whenever Wes referred to the *Sofrut* as the scribal arts. On one occasion, Wes overheard the master scribe kvetching in the living room to an Orthodox rabbi about the horrors of raising a family in New York. Speaking under his breath, Hillel rambled about single mothers pushing baby carriages on the city sidewalks, homosexuals holding hands in the streets, and trannies fixing their wigs on the subway.

A year into the apprenticeship and still without Hillel's permission to proceed with Torah, Wes abandoned the quill to start college. His scribing hand was now steady enough for the buzzing electric needle in Boone's garage. While his cheffing gigs were slow, Boone's dad Lek had moonlighted as a backdoor tattooist. Lek knew all about *yak sant*, having learned to translate ancient blessings from a heavily inked Brahman master in Thailand. While Lek outlined the sacred geometry on stenciled paper, Wes earned an hourly cut for helping him to push black pigment into the white skin of trend-chasing Gentiles.

At university, Wes indeed had designed his own major, splitting enough courses between several faculties—the visual arts, music performance, and environmental science—to convert three minors and the usual mix of liberal arts credits into a bachelor's degree in art and design. After a long silence, Wes once again reached out to Hillel as Zayde's eyesight dimmed more and more each year. Wes wanted to retrain as a scribe, to do whatever it would take to finish a Torah scroll while his grandfather might still have the honor of reading from it.

But by his fourth year on a university campus, Wes no longer envisioned himself as a scribe in the Internet age. He took to the guitar. He took Ecstasy at Lollapalooza. He took showers on Yom Kippur, when his attempts to fast the whole day usually fell apart by noon. He took a World Religions class and realized they were all full of shit. As a Jewish atheist, Wes no longer said prayers; those rhythms and formulas had fallen out of his routine. With Mom, Wes had taken a succession of trips to big cities to see her childhood friends in Boston, a business partner on a real estate deal in Atlanta, a hippie aunt in Seattle, and their cousins living up and down the California coast.

Wes had already seen so much of the country. Now, he was ready to see the world, and that simply wasn't happening within the cloistered walls of Hillel's suburban Baltimore scribing room.

Hillel kissed Wes on the cheek, sending him off with one final remark. *Never rely on tomorrow. For all we know, there is only today.*

"I disagreed with Hillel all the time," Wes admitted to Linda and Leah. "But what he said stuck. There really is no tomorrow quite like today."

"What do you mean by that?" Leah asked.

"I've got to get this Torah scribed," Wes said. "It's for my grandparents."

"I appreciate your work ethic," Rabbi Linda reminded him as they walked to the lobby. "But today, let's have some fun."

Older congregants meandered into the sanctuary with their grandchildren, schmoozing with Rabbi Linda, who led them outside to a bus brightly painted with flower power emblems and cartoonish peace signs. That ride to the outskirts ended on the jagged borders of an alcove. Everyone grabbed a folding easel out of an overhead compartment and headed for the grass.

They gathered on a rocky hill overlooking snow-capped mountains. Standing in the middle of her loosely circled congregation, Rabbi Linda brought three words: *am, eretz, medina.* People, land, state. Wes, still making inroads in the community, wished not to show off with a killer landscape or a finely detailed rendering of the U.S. Capitol Building. He decided on a simple human figure. But with little more than an outline on paper, a sudden gust of wind blew the drawing Leah's way. Wes watched as Leah studied the outline, and wondered what she was thinking about as he noticed a small smile raise a corner of her mouth.

The chill persisted, prompting the group to wrap up early. They shuffled across the grass to board the bus. As Wes climbed through the door, Leah tapped his shoulder.

"You draw bodies so well," Leah said, returning the drawing.

Wes looked down at the unfinished anatomical art he'd just penciled. "It's nothing really," he replied. "But if you like, you're more than welcome to keep it for the exhibit."

"I had something else in mind," Leah proposed. "Rabbi Linda mentioned you're looking for extra work?"

"Yes," Wes said. "Maybe I could teach the next art class with you?"

Leah's playful grin indicated something else. "Will you draw something for me?"

"Okay," he replied dutifully. "You name it."

Her terms were bold and stark as letters of the Alefbet. Wes thought Leah's offer of three hundred dollars to draw a simple portrait of her standing in a waterfall was too generous, but three hundred dollars didn't seem like a lot of money to the highest-paid employee at Etz Chaim Congregation. When Wes asked for a time and place, Leah suggested waiting a few days for the temperature to warm up. She touched him on the shoulder, cracking a reserved smile as the shul director slipped one more provision into the verbal agreement.

"And Wes? I want to be completely naked when you draw me." Leah replied in an almost-whisper.

Wes's jaw dropped, and he stood there, holding a hand over his mouth as if scared to speak. "Are you sure you're comfortable with that?"

"Why, yes," Leah answered playfully, underscoring the obvious. "But if you'd rather think it over, that's fine, too."

"It's a cool idea," Wes said quickly, nervous that she'd change her mind on his hesitation. "You can count me in."

"Rabbi Linda's cool, too. But we best not let her find out. Some of our congregants might piss their pants if they knew."

Wes snickered. "Okay."

"I mean it, Wes. This stays between us."

"Of course. Total privacy," Wes agreed. "I won't even sign my initials on the portrait."

"Every artist should get to do that." Leah winked at Wes. "But only if you're comfortable with it."

"Sounds good to me."

"Great," Leah replied, stepping aside to guide the bubbies, zaydes, and little ones into the bus. "Then it's a date. I'll ring you."

The Nokia buzzed around eight-thirty on Thursday morning. Wes was still in bed, his body not yet on board with a clock six hours ahead of Thailand time. As Leah read her address to a groggy Wes, he simply agreed and plugged her information into his phone before falling back into a restless sleep.

Later, revitalized and a bit more than excited, Wes stepped outside. A passing taxi stopped along the street, the driver offering a ride to the downtown address Leah had given him that morning. After an anxious ride, Wes got out, having arrived in front of a Circle K. Leah promptly stepped through the sliding doors of the convenience store, dropping a paper bag into her hemp-made satchel.

"Thanks for meeting me here," Leah said, landing her fingers on Wes's arm. "Lovely to see you."

"Great to see you, too," Wes said as the casual touch slipped into a hug.

"You'll be seeing a lot of more of me before the day's through," Leah replied.

She handed Wes a money clip and pointed across the street to a high-rise. "I've got the other half over there in my flat," Leah told him as they crossed the street and hopped into her sleek green Lexus. The ride didn't take long. From the fire escape stairwells of Auckland proper, they'd arrived at a stony roadside in five minutes flat. Leah led the way to a grassy hill, setting out for a steep, upward hike. From a distance, crystal blue waterfall curtains shimmered into an unseen basin below.

Leah clutched Wes's hand as she pointed across a gorge at natural springs gushing from open caves through which power flowed eternally. Once they reached the top, Wes turned around to face the downward slope. Shades of green flashed before his wide eyes as Wes watched and then tumbled behind Leah on the rugged hill. It was her daily health routine, she told him after the roll: a hill every day as preventative medicine. As they walked to the waterfall, Leah went on about a local legend who rolled religiously and lived to see her hundredth year.

Wes followed Leah to a dirt trail that opened into a forest of leafy crowns weeping over a sparkling cascade. And then there was Leah, dancing out of her flounced skirt as Wes forced a straight face to conceal his sheer wonderment. With a bashful but mischievous smile, Leah nibbled on her fingertip. Her pink lace panties slipped to her ankles. As Leah bared everything to him in paradisical surroundings, Wes quietly thanked God for his eyesight and immediately got to work.

"Just so you know, I haven't done anything like this before," Leah revealed to Wes, striking an arched pose against a boulder.

"Why not?" Wes asked. "I mean, why me?"

"I've had the idea for years. But until now, I'd never met an artist I trusted enough."

"That means a lot to me," Wes said in a measured, professional voice, struggling to keep both eyes on the sketch. "It's a first for me, too. Hope you'll be satisfied with my work."

Wes looked up from the half-drawn portrait to greet his subject, a smiling goddess who took him by the hand and pointed to the glistening falls. From rocks at the shallow basin's edge, water splashed all around as their bodies came together in slow motion. Soon after their lips touched, Leah delicately captured Wes by his tongue, taking it deep into her mouth. Losing himself in the kiss, Wes rolled out of his denim jeans and howled on the plunge into icy waters.

Their body heat made the cold temperature more bearable for Wes, blanketed as he was in Leah's smooth, freckled, sun-kissed arms. Wes held his breath to go under the water, finding his way to her navel, and lower still. When he finally forced himself to come up for air, Leah begged him to never stop.

"You're going to turn me into a waterfall if you keep doing that," Leah whispered, breathy and sensual, tickling Wes's ear. "Come here and give it to me. Please."

"Protection?" Wes asked.

"My satchel," Leah replied quickly. "Some condoms are in the little brown shopping bag inside."

"Okay." Wes dashed out of the water and hurriedly dipped back into it with a box of Trojans in hand.

When their bodies touched, the water falling over them no longer felt cold as together they turned the basin into a heated, passionate paradise. Leah's fingernails etched marks into Wes's back as she rocked her hips against his, in and out in perfect rhythm until both moaned a symphony of release. Their chests heaved and trembled with excitement as Wes wrapped himself around her, limb to limb.

As soon as they finished and caught their breaths, Leah smiled quickly, almost politely, and turned to one side as Wes leaned closer for a kiss that landed on her cheek. Out of the water, Wes tiptoed on rocks, going across the trickling waterfall to dress himself quickly and finish the drawing she'd commissioned him to produce. He could sense Leah watching him from behind as she guided his hand, touching up spots with a block eraser. Her dreamy, faraway tone spoke volumes as she declared her love for the drawing.

Back in town, Leah turned into a parking garage connected to her apartment building. She invited him into the kitchen, bringing Wes a glass of water. In stone cold silence, she counted out tens and twenties on a spare place mat. Leah puckered her lips for a quick peck on the cheek, backing away straight after. Wes leaned closer to return a kiss, but she edged away and began raving about how much she loved the finished portrait. How, she said, only someone who'd experienced her body firsthand could ever truly replicate it in art. Her transactional tone left Wes disoriented, the room around him spinning like a dreidel.

"I feel like three hundred dollars is too generous," Wes suggested, reluctantly holding a colorful stream of New Zealand currency between his fingers. "Would you be willing to consider the drawing a gift?"

"Please," Leah dismissed the idea, waving away Wes's hand. "You deserve to be paid for your work."

"I just feel ..." Wes staggered his words as though unsure exactly what he felt. "Getting that much money for so little work would be like taking advantage of someone."

"Oh, Wes," Leah said. "If anything, I feel like I might be taking advantage of you."

Wes rubbed his forehead as he gazed into Leah's crystal blue eyes. "What? Why do you say that?"

"I'm getting married next week," she answered gleefully.

"You're about to get married?" Wes knew he asked a question, but his words sounded almost like a statement. "You're with someone?"

"Yes," Leah exhaled. "This was just supposed to be my one final fling."

Perplexed, Wes took a step back. "But what if I really like you?"

"Please don't be sad," she responded in a honeyed voice. "You were wonderful. Today was exactly what I needed."

Wes puffed his cheeks, trying his best to force a smile. "Well, then, mazel tov. For whatever it's worth, I enjoyed your company."

"Okay, great," Leah said, relieved. "See you at shul?"

"Maybe." Wes pocketed the money, feeling like a thief as he turned around at the door with a tightened face to conceal how let down he felt. "Thanks for today, I guess."

A taxi picked him up in front of the Circle K. On the ride back, his pocket full of money and his chest sinking with unspoken defeat, Wes wondered if coming to New Zealand might have been nothing more than a short-sighted mistake.

When he finally reached the cottage porch, Wes felt a vibration in his pocket. Stanley's phone number flashed on the Nokia screen. Wes jumped and pressed the wrong button, fumbling the call. He dialed back, and a rough *hello* came through the line in a thick English accent Wes didn't expect. According to the gruff-sounding Kiwi, who now possessed Stanley's cell phone, new sellers came into the store every day to trade unwanted belongings for cash.

"The other day, I tried reaching someone on this number," Wes stated. "Is there a chance that someone named Stanley Levine works with you?"

"No one here by that name."

"Who called me a minute ago?"

"I rang you by accident while clearing out an old SIM card."

"Can you help me find the person who sold it to you?" Wes asked, desperation seeping into his voice.

"Can't help you there, mate. We're pawnbrokers, not detectives."

"The phone belonged to my dad. I'm asking you to please help me contact him."

"We don't keep records of our sellers."

The pawnbroker hung up on him. Wes scratched off another prepaid card, doggedly redialing again, and again, and again. Each time, a different voice answered the phone, putting Wes on hold until the call timed out. Finally, Wes dialed into a generic, anonymous voicemail greeting. At the tone, he made a final plea to no one who could hear him.

"It's been years. Ten. Long. Years," Wes emphasized as an expiration beep signaled the last bit of credit on his calling card. "Please. I'm looking for Stanley Levine."

CHAPTER FIVE

By the time he'd hit the three-week mark in Auckland, Wes had settled into a routine of boozy afternoons in the sports pubs of Herne Bay. The hilltop cottage felt chilly and abandoned, with Dave was reporting for training with the New Zealand Defence Force. On most weekday afternoons, Wes lost himself in the company of strangers who'd gathered around the telly for rugby. Without knowing how to follow the fast-paced matches, Wes pretended to watch while sipping heavily hopped pints of ale with local pensioners and their much younger girlfriends.

For that idle stretch, he lived on fish and chips and went on long walks alone on dirt trails winding into beach forests. Leah had left him a voicemail message about joining Etz Chaim as an employee. Out in the wild, Wes tried returning the call, but his Nokia didn't hold a signal for more than two rings.

He trekked back to the pub, where drunken louts hollered at the TV as Wes once again returned the phone call. The conversation began on a double apology: Wes, for anything he might have said to dampen the experience she'd paid him for; Leah, for not sooner disclosing her relationship status.

"Wishing you the best," Wes accepted. "I guess I didn't see the wedding announcement coming."

"Would you've gone with me if you knew I was about to marry?" she asked.

"I don't know."

"I only have a moment," Leah spoke, putting on a tense, professional voice. "I'll discuss those accounts with the financial department first thing next week."

"I'm sorry? What accounts?" Wes wondered if Leah changed her voice in case her new husband had walked into the room. Then the call ended abruptly, and Wes texted her back just as fast.

Looks like we got disconnected. Please ask the rabbi to keep me posted on the scribing vacancy. Looking forward to working with you.

That last bit was a lie, and Wes knew it from the moment he clicked send. In truth, he dreaded the prospect of working with Leah. He couldn't regret their fling at the falls and the full-body high that came with it. But Wes now second-guessed the decision to come to New Zealand, a far-flung country where he had no known ancestral ties. When Dave joined the army, it felt to Wes like losing his best friend.

Dave's boots creaked on the floor as Wes tucked a handwritten letter back into a desk drawer. Wes had just finished reading what Stanley Levine had written into fine paper as smooth as parchment, and he felt like an empty shell, sick to his stomach. At that moment, Wes wondered if he'd ever be able to fully trust anyone again.

In his army green uniform, Dave marched locked steps to the bedroom door, swinging a bulky duffel bag on his shoulder. Wes looked him up and down, shaking his head in disappointment.

"Why didn't you tell me about the note?" Wes asked.

Dave looked at him dumbfounded. "What note? What were you doing in there, anyway?"

"I was looking for a pencil sharpener." Wes pointed to the drawer.

"Oh, boy," Dave sighed, turning away to look out the window as Wes, in a scathing and sarcastic voice, read the letter aloud:

Dear Bill, Nancy, and Dave,

Thank you for having me as a guest in your home. Over the last year, it's been a pleasure to stay in this beautiful country. I'll be leaving New Zealand in a few days. Please forward my mail to the Baltimore address on the letterhead. Years ago, some mistakes were made and I had to leave my family behind. I'm not ready to face them yet. But now that my financial house is a little more in order, I'd like to see what Southeast Asia might have in store for me.

Best,
Stanley Levine

"Don't get me wrong," Wes began on the defensive. "I'm glad he's doing well. But how could you and your parents not share this with me?"

Dave picked up his duffel bag by the strap. "I barely knew him," he said with his back turned.

Wes lumped some of his clothes into a ball, stuffing them into his suitcase. "It's not you, dude. Stanley said it himself. He's not ready."

"Just try not to take what he wrote too personally," Dave suggested, his voice imbued with a genuine concern. "I'm sure he'd be happy to see you."

"Bullocks, mate." Wes echoed the British bar talk from the rowdy sports pubs. "It's like I'm wasting my time here, in the world's most beautiful country with nothing at all for me to do."

"Come on now," Dave said, resting a hand on Wes's shoulder. "Your father ..."

"I don't have a father," Wes snapped, firming his large suitcase upright on its little wheels. "See you around, buddy."

A taxi dropped Wes downtown. On the fringes of Queen Street, Wes dragged the luggage through the arched cathedral door of a limestone façade with long rows of sash windows. With a bulky suitcase at his side, Wes searched for the guesthouse address. On either side of the road, the Victorian-style buildings looked older than electricity.

After finally locating and entering the correct building, a slouching twenty-something behind the front desk counter scanned Wes's passport for the ID page, returning it with a room key. Wes found his own way down a long hall to open the door to new living quarters, which smelled faintly like sweat. He retired his suitcase next to the bunk beds, abandoning the gray industrial carpet for warmer, fresher air in the commons.

The shared living space in the front of the house was homier than Dave's cold English cottage out in the burbs. A fireplace crackled as guests sipped cocoa over their board games on long, wooden tables. In a flash, Wes came to the idea that he might find love in a place where people from around the world were huddling together, there in Auckland, on the brink of winter in the last world city before the South Pole. Everyone who lounged in the commons went out of their way to bring good vibes. Paolo, a smiley blond from Brazil, threw down for pizza. Soon a stack of pies came upon the long, communal dining table. In a matter of minutes, Wes shook hands with at least one new person from each continent: an Aussie, a Californian, a German, a Korean, a Peruvian, and a South African.

Wes and Paolo liked a lot of the same music, particularly rock and metal from the Headbangers Ball era. Everyone swooned and some even slow danced when Paolo, acoustic guitar in hand, brushed back his golden hair and belted out "More Than Words." Halfway into the song, he stopped, and it was like all the lights went out. Paolo shrugged, smiled, and then handed Wes the guitar as he dug in for more pizza.

Just as he started to strum, Wes felt his pocket vibrate. He quickly stopped playing and took the incoming call. It was Linda Sorensen ringing him for a second time within the hour.

"Hi, Rabbi Linda," Wes spoke into the tiny Nokia speaker. "I think I missed a call from you. I was just setting up camp downtown. Not far at all from Etz Chaim."

"Just let me know if you need anything. We're here for you," Linda said warmly.

"I appreciate that," Wes said. "I'm just taking it one day a time for now."

"Well, just in case you're still looking for work, my nephew, Harry, has a kiwifruit farm in the Bay of Plenty. He's looking for some staff to finish picking for the season."

"Does that sort of work pay well?" Wes asked, reluctant to accept the rabbi's offer.

"Harry can meet you to talk more about it," Linda added. "How about at your place?"

"Sure, that's fine," Wes replied.

"As a Kiwi, I may be a little biased," Linda said. "But our countryside will take your breath away."

The battery in his Nokia gave out before Wes could finish saying, "That's what I've heard."

"Hey," a pleasant voice greeted Wes. "You're from Baltimore? Sorry. Lotta names today."

"It's okay," Wes replied, his heart beating faster as he located the speaker, who smiled at him from across the room. "I'm Wes."

"Hi, Wes. I'm Kayla."

"I remember you from lunch. You're the other American, from California?"

"Born and raised," she answered, cool and reverent. "Enjoying New Zealand?"

"Sure. How about you?"

"I love it here. Reminds me of home. It wouldn't surprise me if millions of years ago, the North and South Islands had broken off from California in a tectonic shift."

"I could see that," Wes responded, playing it cool as Kayla twirled long strands of her silken, black hair around a manicured finger. There was something about her casual demeanor that attracted Wes more and more as every second passed.

"Tell me something special about yourself?" Kayla asked.

"I've been living, um, in Bangkok for a year," Wes hesitated, bashfully aware of the city's reputation for wild sex.

"Bangkok?" Kayla's eyes brightened, which Wes did not expect. "I got offered a job there!"

"Why didn't you take it?"

"Thailand was too much of pay cut after Shanghai. I taught English to local businessmen with more money than God."

"My rent in Bangkok was never more than a hundred dollars a month," Wes said. "It was so easy to live on less."

"So," Kayla said, her tone curious and playful. "What brought you to all the way to New Zealand, then?"

"At the moment, I'm waiting on a job offer here in Auckland."

"That's cool. But sadly, I won't be here much longer," Kayla said. "I'm heading back to Amsterdam next week."

"Amsterdam?" Wes asked in bewilderment. He almost couldn't believe the coincidence.

Bubbie and Zayde had never talked much about their lives in the Dutch capital, a transitional residence where nearly all their time was spent sheltering in place. Other than that, everything Wes knew about Amsterdam was from college classmates who had returned from Spring Break raving about so many decriminalized vices being flaunted out in the open: tourists could legally purchase pot and hashish at coffeeshops, while across the street, women in lingerie fulfilled fantasies from behind their red-lighted doorways. Wes struggled to balance those rose-colored snapshots of easy sex and carefree cannabis smoking with what happened to his grandparents who, just fifty or sixty years before, had escaped that city on a secret ship in the middle of the night.

"I'm still not entirely sure I'll stay here," Wes finally said. "By chance, have you ever had to apply for a work permit in New Zealand?"

"I don't work here," Kayla said quickly. "Came here to see some Kiwi girlfriends of mine. They know the country from top to bottom. We took a tour on a double decker, went skydiving over a mountain range, and crossed into the South Island by ferry."

Wes cracked a hopeful smile. "Maybe you can show me around."

"After all that running around, it's time to rein in my lavish spending. When I go back to Amsterdam in a couple weeks, I need to find a roommate to help meet all my expenses."

"I understand. For now, I might be headed to the countryside for a temp job somewhere in the Bay of Plenty."

Kayla's eyes softened. "You're leaving so soon?"

"Just for a few days. But if I ever go to Amsterdam, I'll look you up, if that's okay. Here's my number." Wes pulled up his digits on the Nokia screen.

As Kayla sent him a missed call, a new text message flashed into Wes's inbox:

My nephew Harry will meet you tomorrow at the guesthouse. The kiwifruit job is yours for the asking.

"I got the gig," Wes announced, slipping the Nokia back into his pocket as Kayla stifled a yawn. "Guess I'll see you in a few days?"

"Sure," she replied, looking him over before casually shrugging her tanned shoulders. "Have fun picking fruit."

CHAPTER SIX

Harry Jarsdel arrived at the stately, economical lodge with the top of his tobacco sunburst Cabriolet rolled back. When Wes came out to meet him, Harry stood over the trunk, tire iron in hand, firming the lugs on a big, spare wheel mounted over the bumper like an ornament. Earlier on the phone, Rabbi Linda gave Wes the lowdown on her nephew's disposition. Harry got married to a woman in Thailand after his great-grandfather, a British steel magnate, had left his heirs a fortune. Barely a week had passed since Harry and his bride, Wan, had exchanged vows in her rural hometown.

By Harry's account, he'd been facing impossible stipulations for the dispensing of his inheritance. Wan, thirty-one and with no previous proposals, had wanted to give her drought-stricken family a better life. Her father, a buffalo herder, worked in one of the most scorching pockets of Thailand. But Harry had supposedly jumped in financially to "help Wan."

Wes wondered if he really wanted to spend a week working with Harry, a preppy-looking white savior Englishman in a flat top cap who'd basically paid a woman from a developing country to pose as his wife. He pondered the new situation. Harry wore Brooks Brothers and a bowtie, and had a Gatsby-like air and attitude. Would this really suffice? But then Harry whipped out a thick billfold lined with a rainbow of currency notes, and it only took Wes a moment longer to warm up to Harry's offer: a thousand dollars with room and board for a week, a much sweeter deal than braving the journey alone and pounding the pavement on the other side of no man's land.

"That seems like a lot of money," Wes said.

"Picking is not easy work," Harry declared. "I'll pay in cash. To hell with the tax man."

Wes felt obligated to laugh, and did so just to keep it on an even keel. "By the way," he said, looking for further connection. "I'm sorry to hear about your great-grandfather. May his memory always be for a—"

"Come on," Harry interrupted. "Spare me all that nonsense. Mum's Jewish, Dad isn't. Gramp was on Dad's side of the family. Besides, I wouldn't piss on him alive or dead."

"Sorry if you had a difficult relationship with him."

"Don't apologize to me," Harry returned. "He was the bloody homophobe. I didn't need his inheritance hush money to show me that."

"I'm always an ally if ever you need one," Wes told him. "Is this something you feel like talking about?"

Harry didn't answer right away, but after a minute, Wes heard him sigh. "Might as well," Harry finally said.

His great-grandfather, Alfred Jarsdel, was a Robber Baron who made his fortune shipping pig iron around the world. Soon after the funeral, copies of the old man's will had been dispersed into the expectant mailboxes of surviving family members seeking their shares of the massive estate. For Harry, one of just two great-grandsons to carry on the family name, a handsome sum of twenty million British Pounds Sterling was to be paid out on the day after his entry into lawful matrimony.

After Gramp died, twenty-five-year-old Harry came out to his parents. His mom, Judith, Rabbi Linda's sister, broke down in tears. She was crying for herself, mostly, having realized her failure to express unconditional love well enough to spare her only son from the torment of living in the closet for as long as he had. His dad, Keith, a high-powered London attorney, tapped into personal connections to help Harry secure his birthright.

Apparently, Gramp had spent his final years in a maelstrom of pious whispers from family elders who'd speculated that Harry seemed queer, notwithstanding that dear old Gramp's money might steer him in the right direction.

As his cousins staked claims to their millions, Harry didn't see a single pound. Even younger relatives still in Secondary were out crawling the pubs before Gramp went into the ground. Someone had spent enough time in the old man's ear to convince him that one of his two great-grandsons was gay while the other, a jocular bachelor cousin of Harry's named Oliver, caroused around London in a brand-new Aston Martin. The parties were everywhere, but no one was inviting Harry out on the town.

With no other options at his disposal, Harry boarded a Thai Airways flight to search for a wife. At a hotel in Bangkok, he took a liking to Wan, the maid who cleaned his room. While she worked, Harry told Wan about the predicament he faced: his great-grandfather had just died and left everyone in the family huge sums of money. But without the paper to prove a legal marriage, Harry would see none of it. Wan's family lived upcountry in Buriram, a desert province closer to Cambodia than Bangkok. She feared for their ability to thrive, and in that moment, Harry knew what to do. When he proposed to her in the hotel suite, Harry popped a proper diamond ring in a tiny box. That was Wan's suggestion. She wished to experience the thrill of a real proposal, to feel like it was more than just an act, even if she knew that was all they'd ever be. They signed some documents and taxied together with their passports to the British Embassy, knowing that the money would soon come rolling in.

On the day after the legally binding ceremony, Harry flew back to London to claim the jackpot in one lump sum. For the wedding day shindig, marching elephants carried the couple and a gold-plated dowry, and Harry transformed the bride's parents into millionaires. Harry's financial planner found the kiwi orchard as an investment, assured that within a few years, he could sell it to the New Zealand government for a nice profit.

"What's the big draw here?" Wes asked, genuinely curious. "Aren't there any orchards for sale in the UK?"

Harry cracked a knowing smirk. "Let's just say some of my family members who live there are not so tolerant of, well, fruit."

As Harry pulled a latch to fold back the leather top, Wes chucked a duffel bag into the backseat. In the last of daylight, Harry steered with both hands, cutting through blinding fog encountered somewhere between Auckland and the Bay of Plenty. Traffic stopped for a flock of sheep staggering across the road to graze on the other side. By midnight, they reached the cabin on the farm, where inside, Harry poured a warm pint of ale into a chilled flute glass. Wes was still feeling thirsty the next morning, perching under a trellis with gooseberries that bobbed from above.

Rays of sunlight pierced through tiny interstices. Wes stared up at the clustered, leafy canopy, his only buffer from the disorienting glare of a ripe tangerine sky. He sprang to his feet as a tractor roared across the open field. Harry shifted in reverse to maneuver the growling engine into a spot between trellises. A small, old man with a goatish white beard rode in the back, sitting between stacks of empty bushels and glass water jugs. Robert Winter hopped down from the tractor bed to greet Wes, first reminding him to stay hydrated while picking. The old man cleared his throat three times before getting out his full name. They didn't shake hands. Wes balked at Winter's twisted, veiny fingers. On the drive that previous night, Harry had mentioned that the old man had arthritis and no longer worked.

Most fruit pickers who ventured to Winter's farm, Harry mentioned, were either young Kiwis and Aussies with backpacks paying their way through a holiday, or Samoan Islanders traversing the South Pacific for seasonal work. Winter had never met an American before, and didn't own a cell phone, a computer, or a television. Before picking up Wes at the guesthouse, Harry had burned an hour at an Internet café, printing out contract pages that could have more easily been e-mailed.

While Harry and Wes took turns picking and hauling, Winter retreated to the kitchen table to review the papers before signing away his land. It was his life's work, his family's legacy, his whole world. He could've asked for more than one-point-five mil, but Winter was eager to cash out, especially since no one besides Harry was bidding.

Wes plucked from the vines over his head, dropping each kiwifruit into a basket strapped to his shoulders. He wasn't used to having all that open space to himself. From the sparse field where he stood, the sky looked wide enough to swallow everything whole. He separated the kiwifruits into trays: firm, fully ripe, and squishy. Beside the tractor, Harry stood across the canopy with his back turned and trousers rolled to his knees. He pissed a faint yellow stream that sizzled on the grass in front of him. Harry looked over his shoulder, quickly covering his bare ass as Wes stepped into his personal space.

"The closest loo is in the cabin." Harry said, casually pulling himself together on the notches of his belt. "Five minutes on foot."

When the tractor bed was brimming with fruit, Harry steered it back to the farmhouse with Wes holding himself between the crates. That evening in the rustic, wood-slatted kitchen, Old Man Winter sharpened one blade against another, turning the cubed lamb loins and home-grown vegetables into a feast.

"Your kitchen skills are remarkable," Harry told Winter.

"Been on my own for twenty years," Winter replied without turning from the cooktop, slowly stirring the stock pot with a long, wooden spoon. "When my wife died, it was a matter of survival.

"Hey," Wes whispered to Harry. "Do you know if the lamb is kosher?"

"Quiet, mate!" Harry shot back, suddenly stern. "Man's worked all day to feed us."

Winter poured a bottle of white wine into the pot. Wes had been breathing in citrus all day, and the warm, fruity whiff of evaporating alcohol went straight to his brain. They served themselves, taking the meal in silence until out of the blue, Winter flipped a joint out of his flannel shirt pocket.

"It's for the arthritis," Winter admitted, blowing out a perfect smoke ring.

After supper, Wes and Harry returned to the cabin. Harry unzipped his travel bag, revealing a stash of his own. The fireplace log crackled as they passed a pipe and talked about their families, setting aside an uneventful card game of Uno to focus on a more significant conversation. Keith Jarsdel, according to Harry, ranked high in his profession, having assembled an army of legal eagles from Britain to Bangkok who'd been planning out his son's wedding before Harry even set foot in Thailand. Harry already knew the whole story about absent Stanley because his aunt had let slip out what Wes had shared with her in confidence.

"It's no big deal," Wes dismissed. "I would've rather told you myself, but I don't fault your aunt for making conversation."

"She's prone to gossip," Harry warned as he reached for the lighter. "Linda is a rabbi and a yenta at the same time."

"Did you come out to her?" Wes asked.

"I was outed," Harry said, emotionless. "Big difference."

"Not that it's the same thing, but I should confide something, too. This whole trip to New Zealand is starting to feel like it's one big bust," Wes finally confessed, staring at the flickering embers in the fireplace. "I came here looking for my long-lost father, who, for all I know, might be back in Thailand."

"Maybe I can help," Harry said. "My family's got contacts in the House of Windsor, Interpol, you name it. At the very least, when I get back to the UK, I can ask to track your dad's most recent international passages."

"Look," Wes said. "I appreciate the offer. But in case he's been involved in something unsavory, I don't want to risk putting him on any radars."

"What do you mean by that?" Harry asked, inching closer to Wes on the sofa.

"It's complicated. I know you're trying to help." Wes turned to face Harry. "But ..."

Harry leaned in to kiss Wes on the cheek. "I like you, Wes."

"Dude," Wes spoke tenderly, locking eyes with Harry. "You're married."

"Right," Harry replied, suddenly stiff and solemn. "Look, I know it must be difficult without your dad. I don't know what I'd ever do without mine. If you change your mind, I can help you."

Harry stood as upright as a peacock, slowly making his way to the cabin's only bedroom. "Sleep well, Wes."

Alone on the sofa, Wes drifted off and he was five years old again. With bare knees covered in sand, he impressed a plastic pail of moist sand into a sandcastle. Little Wes called out for his dad, who was up to his waist in rough Atlantic waters. Waves crashed to the sound of thunder. When Little Wes darted across the beach and into the water, his dad scooped him up and dashed back into deeper territory. The next wave rolled over their heads, splashing them all over. Stanley teetered in the furious ocean as Wes clutched his dad's neck, begging him not to let go. Echoes rang of a promise Stanley made two decades ago with a final wave toppling father and son in one roaring wallop that snapped Wes out of his sleep.

"I won't ever let you go, son," Wes could still hear Stanley say.

After the dream, Wes couldn't keep his eyes closed. He bundled himself in a coat and scarf to start the day before it began.

The blue-black night cracked into dawn as Wes worked. With the smaller trellises now picked bare, Wes rushed with the shears, pruning the shrubs so that by afternoon he'd still have a few good hours to draw the landscape.

By noon, after a few skipped water breaks, his arms felt heavy and weak as though he'd been toiling for an age. He laid on his stomach and started a new page in the sketchbook, scratching what he saw into life. New

Zealand's Fruit Bowl was a spectrum of green. A partially dull No. 2 would have to be good enough.

Out of nowhere, Harry popped up, and Wes cradled his sketchbook like he never meant to crack it open in the first place.

"Hey, no worries," Harry said to Wes forgivingly.

"I was just taking a break."

"Your letters are really choice."

Wes squinted for a moment, processing Harry's compliment. "Thanks."

"Aunt Linda told me you're looking to write Torah."

"That's the plan." Wes followed Harry to the parked tractor. "Guess getting a work permit here takes a while."

"May I offer a suggestion?" Harry asked as they walked to the tractor.

"Sure."

"You may find it easier to pursue that kind of work in the Netherlands."

"What?" Wes stopped in his tracks. "Why do you say that?"

"While on holiday in Amsterdam, I went shul for Shabbat. The scrolls were in such bad shape that they didn't even bother taking them out during services. They need a scribe. And I recall you mentioning that you had some family there, no?"

"Not since 1940. I'd never heard either of my grandparents say a word about going back to the Netherlands. But I've always been curious. Amsterdam's this mystical city no one in my family ever liked to talk about, and it's come up a lot in my life lately."

"When I was there, I got to know Rav Cohen, the senior rabbi. Rav used to be a scribe until he lost an eye protesting the war last year."

"But I thought your aunt was going to offer me a job at her shul in Auckland."

"She might not have the clout to follow through with whatever she's promised you."

"She hasn't promised me anything yet."

"Exactly," Harry quipped. "You practically fell into her lap. But there's a shul in Amsterdam with a half-blind rabbi that needs help to complete a Torah."

Wes drew a deep breath into his nose. "I think I'd rather see what plays out at Etz Chaim."

"You might be in for a wait. Work permits in New Zealand are scarce. But since your grandparents were displaced by the Holocaust, you're legally entitled to European citizenship. While the application is getting started, you could take a job without any hassle."

"I'll keep that in mind," Wes said.

Standing behind the tractor, Wes unzipped his pants, turning to look over his shoulder as he took a leak. Peeing outdoors, he'd decided, was less awkward than invading the old man's domain every time nature called. First day on the job, Wes had dragged a muddy trail into the tidy farmhouse while desperately searching for a toilet. The old man never mentioned the dirtied floor, but Harry told Wes to start pissing outside after that.

Harry parked the tractor beside the storage room, pointing Wes to the open garage door. Wes turned open the hatch to haul off brimming crates and empty water jugs. On the way off, he stumbled into Harry, who slouched on the rails with pants rolled to his ankles. Wes stepped sideways and slipped on the wet grass, where Harry was still doing his business. The crate in his arms tipped upside down, spilling out kiwifruits across the grass. Knee-deep in his pickings, Wes bent down to gather up pieces from the fallen batch. That was when he noticed the strange expression on Harry's face.

Something had shocked Harry as he was dribbling out the last of his bladder. Swiftly, Harry swiped the trousers from his ankles, awkwardly covering himself as a stunned look crept into his eyes. Wes swiveled on his knees, turning around to glimpse at what stood behind his shoulders.

Neither Wes nor Harry knew how long they'd been being watched. Old Man Winter shrunk back into the shadows, looking on like a terrified, half-dead man eyeing his own grave.

CHAPTER SEVEN

Mister Winter dangled a kiwifruit under a flickering lantern, closely inspecting it. His hairy eye loomed large on a magnifier held between twitchy, arthritic fingers. Winter tossed the lens at the rails of the tractor bed and dumped the crate of fuzzy, brown fruit into a cardboard bin. Then the old man looked to the sky, kicked the ground, and spit.

"The whole day is wasted," Winter grumbled. "One tainted kiwifruit is all it would take to ruin my farm. Do you understand this is more than a hundred and fifty years of my family's work?"

Harry nodded. "I understand."

"This land," the old man started, waving a finger in the air. "It was settled long ago by serious, God-fearing people. I'm not one to judge a man for what he does in private. But what I saw today is not acceptable."

Wes looked bewildered. "What exactly did you find unacceptable?"

"Is Jarsdel a Christian name?" Winter asked, sidestepping Wes's question.

At that, Wes Levine, the lone grandson of Holocaust refugees who'd snuck aboard an ocean liner while roundups swept the canals of their Amsterdam neighborhood, held his breath.

"I'm not sure what you're asking," Harry answered.

"I am asking if you, your mum, and your dad are Christians."

"Like many Brits in his generation, my father was raised in the Church of England. My mum's a Jew, and that makes me one, too. If that's a problem, we should talk about it."

"I'm also Jewish." Wes spoke a notch above usual as he stepped in. "And I don't understand what that has to do with anything at all. Harry was taking a piss, and it startled me. When I lost my balance and slipped, a crate of fruit tipped over. That's it."

"Don't tell me what my eyes have seen, you cock jockey!" Winter shouted, waving a bent, bony finger in Wes's face. "You were both carrying on like a couple of poofs."

"Wes was gathering some fruit that spilled on the grass," Harry explained to the old man in a child-friendly drawl. "What do you think we were doing?"

Winter gritted his rotting, brownish teeth. "He was on his knees!"

"So, what's the problem there, Christian man?" Wes came in. "You would know a thing or two about kneeling, wouldn't you?"

As Wes puffed his chest, Winter backed off, turning over a plastic bucket for a makeshift stool. The old man's knees creaked as he sat down, face buried between his folded arms. Each night at the dinner table, Wes and Harry had learned a little more about Robert Winter. That he hadn't set foot in a school since he was twelve, but instead spent those younger years tending

67

to his family's crops. That he'd been growing pot for personal consumption since the sixties. By the second night, Winter trusted Wes and Harry enough to show off a few homegrown plants, those pointy green leaves nestled in a small bamboo forest behind the cottage. Perhaps most telling of all, Winter had not seen any of his grown children or grandchildren in years, and none of them wanted to be bothered with the hassle of taking over the farm.

"I'm a Christian man," Winter insisted, waving a crooked finger in Harry's face. "He's coming for all of us. He's coming whether you believe in Him or not!"

"Get your bags," Harry said in a calm tone, countering the old man's spiteful outburst. "We're leaving."

Harry left the Cabriolet running, hauling ass in and out of the cabin to pack up. "Can you grab those papers on the coffee table?" he asked Wes as they hurled their bags into the backseats. "Just one more order of business to take care of."

Together, they returned to the garage, Harry with clenched fists and Wes cradling an accordion folder under his arm. The old man blocked the entrance, standing in the door with a hateful glare in his faded, sky blue eyes. A few pages at a time, Harry ripped through the documents that Winter had spent days reviewing with a magnifying glass. The old man and Harry exchanged some words. None were pretty. With a too-perfect flick of his wrist, Harry haughtily sent the torn documents scattering into the air. Winter forced a cough to loosen the gunk in his throat, spitting in their direction. Unfazed, Wes and Harry slowly walked away. Winter trailed them outside to the car.

"How nice of you," Wes said sarcastically to the old man, who'd come out of the garage with a tire iron in hand. "All the tires look fine."

"You'd better leave now," Winter muttered under his breath, clutching the blunt instrument as he cocked it back, poised to swing.

Wes knocked the tire iron from Winter's feeble hands. "You don't have any idea who you're fucking with," Wes said calmly, flashing the Star of David pendant around his neck. "I trained Masada tactical. Now go back into the garage and stay there until we leave."

With a snakelike twist, Winter dropped to his knees and crawled to the fallen tire iron.

"Uh, no," Wes said, securing the long, blunt tool under his foot. "That comes with us."

Wes jumped over the passenger-side door of the convertible, landing into the seat. To Wes's right, Harry floored the gas pedal on the dirt driveway, leaving Robert Winter in a trail of dust. Passing Winter's wide front yard fence, Wes chucked the tire iron into the grass, he and Harry laughing all the way out to the countryside highway.

"You think he'll soon forget what just happened?" Wes asked.

"Not likely," Harry replied, pushing back the Ray Bans on the bridge of his nose. "I reckon we gave him the shock of his life."

"Hope I didn't make things worse," Wes said.

"Not at all. What you said in the garage was spot on. You helped me realize what a piece of shit I was dealing with."

"So, what's next for you, then?"

"Anything but this. From here on out, I'll no longer be doing business with bigots. I'd been jumping through hoops because of the homophobes in my own family who didn't want me to see any money at all."

"Never thought Winter would flip out like that," Wes added. "His loss."

69

"The nerve of that old coot to ask me if my family are Christians. That sort of talk makes me wonder if it might happen again."

"If what might happen again?" Wes asked.

Harry lowered his head. "The Holocaust."

Wes couldn't think about that. He looked at Harry's serious expression before shifting the subject. "So, will your aunt be able to get me a work permit?"

"She hasn't mentioned much about it to me. But yesterday when I rang my dad in London, I asked him a few questions about your rights to European citizenship."

"Yeah? What did he say?"

"He told me you'd have a much easier time finding work as a scribe in Europe. The partners at his firm are more than willing to help you out on the legal side."

"Your dad seems like a great guy. But I can't imagine that the services of a London lawyer would come cheaply."

"You just saved me a cool mil and a half. You're like family now." Wes watched as Harry briefly looked over at him and smiled, and Wes knew that what his friend had said was true. "So, family should help family out. My dad will work with you pro bono. He just needs to know if your grandparents were married in the Netherlands?"

"They had a small wedding in a Venice ghetto," Wes said. "My grandmother was trying to get away from Mussolini when he started stripping Italy's Jews of their citizenship."

"How did they end up in the Netherlands?"

"Zayde was Dutch, from Utrecht originally. He used to say that the canals in Amsterdam reminded him of Venice. They came to the city because it had a strong and thriving Jewish community. For centuries, Amsterdam had been a haven. And then, just like that, it wasn't."

70

The married life of Isaac and Malca (née Bassano) Levine began in the upstairs of a teetering canal house. After they were forced from their professional capacities as a university treasurer and a legal clerk, they went into hiding in a loft furnished to them by a Dutch Gentile, a language professor who'd faced frequent taunts in the streets from German informants in plainclothes. The righteous professor pointed Wes's grandparents to a secret ship commissioned by an English businessman under the guise of an ice shipment. By the spring of 1940, when the Occupation of Amsterdam began, the ice trade was past its heyday. Gestapo agents patrolling the Central Station inspected everyone coming in and out of the trains, while the strange, massive glacier on a liner docked in the Damrak canal was an eyesore that raised the brows of some Nazi henchmen on lookout. Once sequestered into the bottom cabin, Isaac and Malca Levine could still hear sirens bundling closer.

"By chance, do you know the financier's name?" Harry asked.

"What do you mean, the financier?" Wes replied, still thinking about his grandparents.

"The ship. Who paid for it?"

"They never mentioned anyone by name. All I know is that the ship was owned by someone from England."

On the arrow-straight rural road, Harry balanced the steering wheel with his legs. He turned to Wes with a wink and smile. "You're a European soul."

"Please," Wes scoffed. "I've never even been to Europe."

"Doesn't matter. You can obtain citizenship because of what your grandparents endured in the Holocaust," Harry said. "That's your birthright. It's who you are, mate."

Wes looked at Harry skeptically. "Your dad will do all that legal work for free?"

"I owe you that much," Harry answered.

Wes smiled back as the sun warmed his shoulders. "For what it's worth, you don't owe me anything."

Harry laughed. "Mate, had you not come with me to the Bay of Plenty, I would've handed over a nice piece of my fortune to that old sheep fucker. Like I said, I'm not here to make bigots rich."

"Glad I could help," Wes said. "It was good, honest work."

"Tell you what." Harry glimpsed his Blackberry screen as he steered through the crystal blue country sky. "If you're willing to relocate again, I'll sponsor you to scribe a Torah at *B'Nai Havurah Kehillah.*"

With curious anticipation, Wes turned to Harry. "Where is that, exactly?"

"Amsterdam."

Before Wes had a chance to think it over—the prospect of flying halfway around the world to scribe—his phone buzzed. For the first time since leaving Auckland, the network signal bars on his Nokia blinked back on the corner of the screen. "Talk about timing," Wes said. "Looks like I just missed a call from your aunt."

Back in his room at the guesthouse, Wes dialed the rabbi at her office extension. When the call connected, Rabbi Linda's voice sounded upbeat. The receiver went fuzzy. Wes could make out every other word and thought he heard her say that one of the trustees had secured him a working permit.

Wes walked down the street to Etz Chaim. Linda met him in the lobby with a clipboard in her hand that listed the perks of the job, which included free room and board close to downtown. In the pictures that Linda spread out on the wooden tabletop, the standalone abode looked quaint and colorful, quite like a little gingerbread house from a fairy tale. With the scribing room and a mikveh bath drawn into the floorplan, Wes could work from home and enjoy the best of both worlds: green, comfortable solitude and a ten-minute bus ride from the vibrant city's pulse. The offer sounded more than enticing.

But Linda pitched one major caveat when she asked Wes to endow the scroll to local congregants who'd always wanted their own Torah.

"I've got to think about this," Wes replied. "My grandparents, more than anything in the world, wanted the same. Harry can help me find my footing in Amsterdam."

"I suppose Harry might have an easier time to support you in this endeavor," Linda said. "I understand your dilemma. Wes, you should follow what your grandparents wanted. In the back of my mind, I worried about whether our sponsor would follow through, anyhow. I do wish you well."

"Thank you, Rabbi Linda."

"Glad you and Harry got on so well. In his honor, and because it is the right thing to do, I will always support the freedom to marry. We're a very liberal congregation."

"Mazel tov," Wes said, drifting into a moment of thought. "New Zealand leads the way once again. Women's suffrage. A woman president. And now, same-sex marriage."

"The Civil Union Act is on the chopping block here," Linda added. "We Kiwis are still trying to get civil unions passed."

On that note, they hugged and said goodbye. Wes walked home, excited, and was more than amped when Harry finally rang him.

"I'm ready for Amsterdam," Wes said. "The sheep here are really starting to freak me out."

Harry laughed heartily. "Consider me your sponsor. I'll set up a ledger to pay out your monthly salary. Do you need me to ask the rabbi about setting up your living accommodations?"

"Actually, I know someone," Wes precociously replied.

Hey Kayla! Wes texted from the guesthouse commons. *When do you go back to Amsterdam?*

Kayla quickly responded. *The day after tomorrow.*

Could you meet me by the fireplace? Just wanted to know if you're still looking for a roommate, Wes typed, and Kayla turned up just as he clicked send.

"Definitely." She smiled confidently. "When would you like to move in?"

"Soon as I can get a plane ticket out of here."

Kayla cracked a knowing smile. "I can help you with that. I've been doing a little work for a travel agent down the street, Mister Lee. He gets cut-rate air tickets and won't charge anything."

"Really?" Wes asked, astonished. "That's gotta come out of someone's pocket. Are you saying he'll fly me to Europe for free?"

"He's getting me a ticket, too," Kayla added, her tone cool and dismissive as she waved a hand in the air. "It's all fine. But money's tight, so I really do need a roommate. Are you sure you can get a job?"

"I've been offered something with a decent stipend," Wes said. "Can I pay you a month at time?"

Kayla smiled. "That's exactly how I roll."

From the guesthouse, Wes walked beside Kayla under a faint blue neon glare along an alley off Queen Street. Kayla led the way through a dead-end path narrowing into an office with a shopfront lantern light that hummed off and on. Mister Lee sat behind an otherwise vacant front desk counter in an unmarked window. Going back and forth in a British-sounding dialect of Chinese, both Kayla and Lee laughed as Lee checked his computer screen for the latest fares.

"The best deal in the entire world right now," Lee said, looking at Wes as he slipped off his microphone headset. "Can you leave in a few hours?"

"Sure, I'll take it." Wes turned to Kayla. "But I'll be arriving a few days before you get back."

"Lars will give you a house key," she clarified. "Do you have a ride to Auckland International?"

"Yeah," Wes said, checking the Nokia screen for an incoming message. "My friend Dave in Herne Bay just texted me. How about you?"

"I'm staying here tonight," Kayla told him. "To do some work for Mister Lee."

"Guess I'll be on my way in just a few hours."

Kayla flashed Wes a beaming smile. "Safe travels. See you in a few days."

As Wes ducked in the low-standing doorway with a ticket in hand, his eyes scanned on the plexiglass a faint reflection of Mister Lee, a skinny man with a skinny mustache, powering off his computer. With Amsterdam on his mind, Wes wondered about the sort of work Kayla and Lee would be doing, after-hours and with all the lights out. The flight to Amsterdam would take off in six hours, leaving little time for Wes to get lost in his thoughts. He gathered his belongings and turned in the key, checking out of the guesthouse with the duffel bag and suitcase he'd brought into New Zealand.

On the taxi ride to the cottage, Wes pictured Dave in a thick camo suit, his face painted green like a boy playing war in the backyard. But instead, in the doorway stood Yoga Dave, barefoot in tie-dye shorts and a tank top.

"How you been?" Dave asked, breaking the silence.

"Good. I'm glad you called. Just wanted to see you before I leave," Wes answered. "And I'm sorry if I overreacted to Stanley's note."

"It's fine. Don't give up. I know you'll find him," Dave spoke, candid and somber.

"Is everything okay on your end?" Wes asked, concerned that Dave wasn't his usual upbeat self.

Dave patted Wes on the shoulder. "Come on in, buddy. Have you heard anything from Arthur lately?"

"I haven't."

Dave puffed his cheeks, blowing out the air slowly. "I hate to burden you with bad news. But the body of an English teacher has been found in Bangkok. It was Colin."

"Oh, no," Wes gasped, raising a hand to his mouth in horror. "What happened to him?"

"After he didn't show up to work, Arthur sent someone to Colin's practice space. They found him suffocated with a plastic bag tied around his neck. I think the Germans were behind it."

"You mean Heinrich's buddies?"

Dave nodded. "I know I could've done a better job as head teacher at the branch. The big shots at Head Office would always say *mai pen rai* every time I rang them."

"Colin was a good guy," Wes exhaled into his palm. "I can't believe he's gone."

"If it's any consolation, Heinrich is now rotting in a Bangkok prison."

"It's something, at least. Why don't we have a drink in Colin's memory?"

"I've got a better idea." Dave pulled a joint from the pocket of his shorts. "Let's toke and scope out some stars."

Wes's jaw dropped as Dave lit up. "You can get high in the military?"

"I'm in the reserves." He slowly exhaled a pungent stream of smoke. "And now I'm on my own time."

"Speaking of time, I'm flying out to Amsterdam for a new job in a few hours," Wes said as Dave passed him the joint. "Thanks for offering me a ride to the airport earlier."

76

"Sure. And Amsterdam? That's where your Bubbie and Zayde were from, no?"

Wes returned the joint to Dave, his eyes burning with smoke and tears. "They hid there for a couple years."

Dave rested an arm on Wes's shoulder. "I didn't mean to ..."

"No, it's not that. I'm just remembering Colin. He beat Heinrich with a chair, which sent the Nazi prick to the hospital."

"No doubt he was seeing stars," Dave mused, pointing Wes to a wide bay window beyond the kitchen. "Come have a look."

They stumbled past the kitchen, huddling around the long telescope by the wide bay window. Dave rotated the tripod for an angle. Wes took his turn and tweaked the knob on the eyepiece until a constellation slid into focus. The lens became a kaleidoscope. One star expanded like a supernova about to implode. From the living room, Dave clicked a radio to life and fiddled with a remote control until landing on an acoustic Green Day song Wes hadn't heard in years.

"Hope you had a good time in the Big Zed, buddy."

"I only wish we had more time. These days, you're probably busy with the army."

"Before we go to the airport," Dave began, setting his clunky keychain on the coffee table. "Is there time for a quick game of truth or dare?"

"Um, sure," Wes replied slowly. "You first."

"You're the guest," Dave said, grinning. "Go ahead."

"Okay, then," Wes slowly replied. "Truth. Do you remember what you were doing on the morning of September eleventh?"

Dave wiped the lens of his telescope, turning his back on the galaxy behind him as he pondered an answer. "I didn't hear about it until the next morning. Remember, we're twelve hours ahead of you. When the planes hit the towers, it was already late into the evening of the eleventh. I woke up and saw Mum sitting in front of the telly with tears in her eyes."

"Oh, man," Wes muttered.

"Dad was holding her hand. They looked so serious. At first, I thought someone in our family died. After I asked Dad if that was the case, he said yes, that three thousand Americans had just died. At that moment, we were all Americans. Even all the way over here in the Big Zed."

"I'm speechless," Wes said.

"Alright, then, Speechless," Dave chuckled. "Hit me with a truth."

"I had a rough flight from Bangkok. And for a few minutes, I thought it would crash. Sometimes I think about what it was like for the people aboard those flights on 9/11," Wes shakily admitted. "They never had a chance to tell their families and friends 'I love you' one last time."

"Here's another truth, then. I love you, buddy." Dave leaned closer to Wes, pressing a kiss upon his cheek.

Without hesitating, as he did when Harry tried to kiss him, Wes returned the gesture.

"I love you, too, Dave."

They tiptoed into the guestroom around stacked boxes of an incoming boarder's belongings. Nowhere in the doorway was the gold *mezuzah* that Stanley had affixed to the doorpost while living there. Without saying a word, Dave carefully placed the parchment case into Wes's hands.

Wes stared in awe at the tiny Hebrew inscriptions inside the encased scroll that had been gifted to his parents on their wedding day. As Wes clenched the *mezuzah* in his palm, Dave slipped him a ziplocked bag of tiny bolts and a precision screwdriver with a star-shaped head. Wes wrapped an arm around Dave's shoulders as they prayed the words of their ancestors.

"She'ma Yisrael, Adonai Eloheinu, Adonai Echad.
Hear O' Israel, the Lord is our God, the Lord is One."

CHAPTER EIGHT

Wes passed through the turnstile gate at *Centraal*, dragging his suitcase and duffel bag through a stretch of bike racks long enough to enclose the train station from city proper. Amsterdam's deepest-seated borough, Centrum, was three things: water, cobblestone, and brick. Wes drifted into the passing mix of tall, well-dressed pedestrians speaking in low, conversational tones. In front of the station, a long bicycle rack bloomed with chained bikes. There, Wes passed a blond man in a battle with a stubborn wheel lock.

"Kun je me met mijn fiets helpen?" the cyclist asked Wes. "Help me with my bike?"

"Sure, *natuurlijk*," Wes said, the first language of his grandfather coming back to him like a gentle wave lapping ashore. Slowly counting it off in Dutch, Wes braced to separate the skinny bike wheel from the aluminum slot. *"Één, twee, drie."*

"Dank je wel," the cyclist thanked him, peddling into a wide lane to cruise along the cobbled sidewalk.

Beside the train station, Wes approached a massive ship docked against the quay wall. A horn blared, signaling an imminent departure for shipping cubes stacked like baby building blocks. Hypnotic bicycle bells dinged as a tram glided into the street on an overhanging cable. Wes turned his head for a moment, and the ship was gone.

Though his grandparents never called the river by name, Wes knew this had to be it. No other Dutch port was big enough for a boat that size, not in 1940 when Nazi bombers had leveled neighboring Rotterdam—the largest seaport in all of Europe—into heaps of bodies and rubble. From the train station, Wes crossed into the slow, casual foot traffic along the bustling Damrak waterfront. In these new and unfamiliar surroundings, Wes set out to look for his new home among rows of brick townhouses built into the waterway like gabled islands.

The three-story canal house belonged to Lars's uncle, a virologist forever traveling around the world on research. The doctor gave his nephew the freedom to dedicate two levels of the house to an art gallery, while renting the third-level loft to ensure the bills were paid.

In an earlier voicemail message to Wes, Kayla had offered full disclosure. She and Lars had been an item, but his obsession with another lover eventually turned Kayla off. They reached an agreement: Lars would keep his street-level quarters while Kayla moved upstairs. Kayla also admitted to Wes that occasionally she shared with Lars the rental income from the loft, whenever his paintings didn't sell, and money became tight.

When Wes reached the house, the front window was vacant but for a wooden easel propped over a pristine tarp spread across the floor. He tapped on the window until the front door cracked open. Lars appeared in paint-stained denim overalls and a black beret, a rustic yet revolutionary aesthetic.

At first, they spoke Dutch, going back and forth about the weather until Wes could no longer keep up with the longer words.

"I paint in the window," Lars shifted to English. "Are you comfortable with that?"

Wes looked to Lars and shrugged. "Yeah, why wouldn't I be?"

Lars sneered, taking a moment to respond. "Kayla said you were a scribe."

"So what? Your window is your business, not mine."

"Then welcome to Amsterdam," Lars stated, his voice and posture stiff like a bellhop.

As Wes lifted his trunk suitcase into the narrow stairwell, Lars creaked ahead of him. When they both reached the top, Lars passed him a tiny wooden clog keychain. Wes picked up the suitcase by the handle, squeezing it through the slim doorway as Lars plunked backward steps up another steep, narrow path.

The foyer of the brick townhouse split into two directions, an art studio on one side and a doorway to stairs on the other. On the middle story, a series of dreamy canvases covered the walls with lucid colors.

"Your work's really fabulous," Wes stated, stopping to admire what struck him as a particularly blissful piece.

"Hou je mond," Lars shot him a cross look. "Shut up."

Wes crinkled his brows, confused. "I'm just paying you a compliment."

"Never mind," Lars growled back, turning to open the doorway to another flight of stairs.

Treading cautiously on the creaking floors, Wes dragged his suitcase, following Lars up the steps. "Hope I didn't come at a bad time."

"It's fine," Lars said. "I didn't sleep much last night. Times are tough, and we need all the help we can get with the rent."

"When do you need the first month?" Wes asked.

"That's between you and Kayla," Lars answered. "She returns from New Zealand tomorrow. Sorry to be bitchy with you. I didn't sleep much last night."

"No worries," Wes said as the stairs opened into a kitchen. A wooden table from the old world contradicted the steely, sparkling cabinets from the new.

Pointing to Wes's new quarters, Lars led the way to a secluded loft under an arched ceiling. From the bedside, Wes took in a bird's eye view of pedestrians strolling along the Prinsengracht. He'd agreed to pay Kayla eight hundred euro monthly. Because what Kayla was asking for in rent had equated to a full month of expenses in Bangkok, Wes felt like he was getting away with something in a high-cost city like Amsterdam.

Soon after settling in, Wes left the building to explore the heart of town, taking in alley after alley of bright lights and brick tenements. The tight space opened into an expansive passage along a canal crossable by footbridge. Ogling passers lingered around the windowfronts of undressed women standing under warm pink rays illuminating the footpath. A topless blonde, all legs in tattered short shorts, looked straight at Wes. She waved him over while mouthing the words "come on," and on the glass door Wes could see his own clueless-looking reflection.

Beyond the paved bricks of the central canal front, Wes spotted a string of Hebrew letters engraved behind a twenty-foot fence. *B'nai Havurah Kehillah* translated into Children of the Fellowship Congregation, and Wes tapped a call button on an intercom box. The steel gate clicked open when Wes said his name into the speaker to a receptionist who thanked him in Hebrew.

As Wes entered the temple grounds, he passed a bronze sculpted Lion of Judah perched regally upon a marble pedestal. A bald white man in black leather combat boots sneered from across the street. Wes didn't know what to make of the man, just as he hadn't known what to think about the seductive blonde standing in a city window.

The kinder looking man who greeted Wes at the door had two eye colors, one a natural-looking hazel and the other a frozen shade of blue. As Wes first addressed him by his clerical title, the rabbi quickly expressed that he preferred *just Rav.*

"Harry called me from London earlier today," Rav said. "He mentioned his father is working on your application for citizenship based on Jewish ancestry."

"I haven't decided whether or not I want to become a European citizen," Wes stated defensively. "I just need enough time for a Torah."

"That's thirteen months if you follow each *parashah* on the Hebrew calendar."

"But I've only got ninety days on my visa," Wes said. "Can I scribe at a faster pace?"

"As long as the work doesn't endanger your health, there's no reason Jewish law wouldn't permit it. Is there an urgency?"

"My grandfather, Isaac Levine. His second *yahrzeit* just passed. He was supposed to scribe a Torah, but couldn't, because of his cataracts."

"May his memory always be for a blessing," Rav began, pointing to his paler-looking eye bouncing lifeless in the socket. "I protested the Iraq War in Israel. Cops fired baton rounds into the crowd."

Wes scanned the portraitures lining the synagogue's walls. He recognized a gleeful Jerry Garcia holding his signature red Gibson guitar and a mindful Malcolm X with a finger on his temple. The building was mostly hardwood on the inside, with the chapel, the mikveh bath, and the sofer room all under one roof like an ancient synagogue.

A scribe in a blue striped tallis stood over a blank parchment. In place of a traditional kippah, she wore a sunburst head covering that reminded Wes of the stunning turban on Vermeer's *Girl with a Pearl Earring*. They shook hands. Aviva, the scribe, stroked a thumb across his palm. In response, Wes grinned uncertainly. Her hand felt calloused and scratchy, which didn't match the youthful glow of her diamond-shaped face and the freely flowing strawberry curls sweeping the fringes of her silken shawl.

"Tell me, Wes," Aviva inquired as she unfolded an aluminum chair, presenting it carefully to Wes like a proposition of real estate. "This is nothing personal. But, when we shook hands, yours felt quite soft. What exactly do you do for a living?"

Wes cleared his throat. "I've been a classroom teacher for most of the last year," he said humbly.

Aviva parted her lips as though waiting for more, but Wes offered nothing further. "Have you ever been involved in the scribal arts?" Aviva finally asked.

"After high school, I spent a year training with a master scribe. How long have you been a sofer?" Wes returned the question.

"On and off since my service in the IDF," Aviva replied, her voice cold and brisk. "When I wasn't flying fighter planes, I spent most of my time in *Ye-ru-sha-la-yim,* where I learned to scribe from the masters."

"May I ask how many Torahs you've written?"

Aviva rolled her eyes, looking to the heavens for a number. "I've lost count. Since last year I've been writing two or three Torahs at a time."

"That's incredible. So, now, when do I start?" Wes asked.

Aviva smiled suggestively. "You already have. Do you have any other concerns?"

85

"Yes, I do. Early this morning, I saw someone hanging around the gate who was carrying a crowbar and a spray can. Leather boots, sailor hat, completely bald. Possibly a Skinhead."

"There are provocateurs all over Amsterdam," Rav chimed in, his voice unconcerned. "Mostly they just like to get a rise out of people. After the Shoah, this gate was built to keep us safe. Don't worry about intruders, as it's always locked."

"I've never seen a fence around a synagogue before," Wes said sympathetically. "Is it that unsafe in Amsterdam?"

Rav winced. "Time and time again, history has shown us that nowhere is truly safe."

The room turned somber. Rav dismissed himself, leaving Wes to get his bearings with the master scribe who had been tasked with preparing him for the new role. Aviva passed Wes an empty crystal inkwell and asked him to fill it. Within minutes, Wes had relearned a process that, since his apprenticeship with Hillel, had become alien to him: mixing Arabic gum and gall nut juice to make kosher ink, and whittling at the quill tip with a pen knife. Aviva spoke passionately about combining those ingredients with a precision that struck Wes as innate.

She was nothing like Hillel. Aviva told jokes in three languages and exuded sheer joy over her work. Most days, Hillel had tottered between tears and rage. He was prone to depressive episodes and unwilling to seek therapy, as he didn't believe in that sort of thing. While spending his eighteenth year as Hillel's understudy, Wes had a few brushes with despair and sometimes went numb in bed after long days copying block script from right to left and back again.

Rav and Aviva walked with Wes through the fenced courtyard, sending him off with hugs, air kisses, and mazel tovs. Aviva abruptly released her arms the instant that the locked door buzzed and clicked open. Outside of the gate, they said *erev tov* for the evening and parted in three different directions.

An autumn sunset sank softly into the afternoon sky. On the new walk to his new home, Wes strolled through the heart of town, where tourists flocked. A throng of passers dispersed from the canal front into red hot alleys to check out girls beckoning from behind glass windows to the drunk or stoned men on the sidewalk. A warm medley of spices floated from the open door to a walkup. At one of the tables, Wes spotted a young couple in hoodies huddling closely around a meal wrapped in aluminum.

"I'll take what they're having," Wes called across the counter to a white-capped chef tending to the slow turning rotisserie, a hollowed-out animal carcass perspiring oil on a giant steel spit.

"Sure thing, brother," the chef replied, dropping chickpea patties into sizzling oil. "I'm Zayin. Visiting Amsterdam?"

"Hi, Zayin, I'm Wes," he said, instantly connecting the kabob chef's name to the seventh Hebrew letter. "Cool name. I moved here for a job."

"How long you plan to stay?"

"Not sure yet." Wes looked through the open entrance at people passing by. "I guess it's still a work in progress."

Zayin returned to the counter, making Wes a plate of falafel patties in a pita, with minced cucumbers and tomatoes, and a tangy white sauce that stole the show.

"This might be the best I've ever had," Wes said as a touch of sauce dribbled on his chin. "No lies, man. I'm a falafel connoisseur. Yours takes top prize."

Zayin placed a hand upon his chest. "Thank you, brother." His voice resonated over the din of customers shuffling into a queue. "Come back anytime."

Wes followed the distant sound of a tram chiming around the ground track. From not far away, a church bell tolled its solemn, hourly gong. The mechanical ding of public transport led Wes to a string of crooked houses with moored houseboats floating in the canal. As Wes located the house and opened the door, he crossed paths with Lars, who concealed a sly, shit-eating grin. Wes walked inside as Lars carried out a SOLD bubble-wrapped canvas under his arm. Having the entire place to himself, Wes retreated to a washroom—a water closet, really—and took his first-ever bath on the old continent.

A creaking sound from somewhere down below had spurred Wes from the water. He raced against the approaching footsteps to towel dry himself, throwing on a pair of plaid pajama bottoms. At the top stair, Kayla turned up in a black raincoat, her dark hair soaking from a storm of wind and rain. She dragged her dripping wet luggage into the kitchen and hugged shirtless Wes. With tired, bloodshot eyes, Kayla plopped her brimming leather satchel on the kitchen table before heading to her bedroom, beckoning Wes to accompany her.

"So, you met Lars?" she asked.

"I did," Wes said. "When I told him that I liked his paintings, he kind of snapped."

"Don't take it personally," Kayla said, touching Wes's bare arm. "Lars has been stressing over some haters in City Hall. They don't want him painting in his window."

"Oh, that's a bummer."

"Anyway," Kayla said with a sigh, taking Wes's towel to strands of her drenched hair, "I have to work tonight."

Wes checked his Nokia screen for the time. "This late?"

"One thing you should know about Amsterdam," Kayla announced, changing quickly into black nylon stockings and a lace bustier. "This city never sleeps."

"Yes. Right. Well, Lars said I should talk to you about the rent." Wes slowly got the words out, trying hard not to stare. "When do you need it by?"

"The first of the month is two weeks away," Kayla replied, puckering her mouth as she popped a lipstick case into her lambskin Balenciaga handbag. "Don't worry about it 'til then."

Wes reluctantly saw Kayla off at the staircase, lingering by the door as the thin heels of her boots clicked rhythmically down the hardwood steps. He couldn't help but wonder what line of work she was in, though he took a few educated guesses. With all the pubs in central Amsterdam, Wes figured that Kayla might be working at one. Bartender was the only job that made sense.

"Do you need an escort home?" Wes called out.

"Thanks, but I'm okay," Kayla replied, tapping a zippered compartment on her silver-studded black purse. "I always carry a knife."

CHAPTER NINE

Harry sounded breathless on the phone, rambling a mile a minute about something Wes couldn't grasp. From bed, Wes put the call on speaker and let Harry do all the talking as stock market bells clanged in the background. Weary and jetlagged, Wes could hardly raise his head from the pillow until Harry finally made it clear that he had important news to share.

"What is it?" Wes asked groggily, oblivious to time. "Did you win the lottery?"

"Ha, no," Harry returned. "Dad's contacts at Interpol have located Stanley Levine. He's in Bangkok."

"Okay. Thanks. I mean, I'm glad to know, but it's just a lot for me to digest right now," Wes said, frustrated and weary. "As soon as I land in a country, he always turns up in another one I was just in."

"Do you still want to apply for European citizenship?" Harry asked.

"Maybe," Wes said, his tone noncommittal. "Can we at least meet in Amsterdam to start the process?"

"I'm too tied up to come see you right now. But my cousin Oliver makes monthly trips to Amsterdam. He'll bring you the paperwork."

"Okay. When do I get paid from the synagogue?"

"As your sponsor, I'll be paying you directly. Your monthly stipend will hit your local bank account at the end of the month."

"Yeah?" Wes said, irritation seeping into his voice. "And what am I supposed to do until then? Eat at the soup kitchen?"

"Look, mate, I'll make a deposit for you today. Two, three thousand euro," Harry offered. "Whatever you need."

"I'd appreciate it," Wes replied. "Thanks. And look, I'm sorry for being an ass right now. This is my third time zone in three months. I'm still adjusting to, well, everything."

"Thank God for Red Bull, right?" Harry said in a hurried voice. "And speaking of bulls, I gotta run."

Wes crossed through town dressed in a black suit and velvet kippah, earning his stipend by practicing letters with Aviva. Every block of handwritten Hebrew turned into a planet of ink; the script comprised the land, and the untouched white parchment, the water. On his last line, Wes passed Aviva the scribed letters. Almost playfully, she held the sheep skin sheet between her hands like putty, the carbon pigments blurring as ink particles dispersed.

"Your strokes are good," Aviva said, and then stopped for a thoughtful moment before continuing. "But Wes, do you see all that smearing? It's because you gave me the *klaf* too soon. Your ink never had a chance."

Wes backed away from the desk. "My bad."

"Don't worry," Aviva said soothingly as she unfurled another blank sheaf. "Touch the *klaf.* Feel every part of it. Get intimate with your canvas. Try to understand what she is made of. I like to run my fingers across the blank lines before attempting to apply any ink."

"Why is that?"

"A sofer is commanded to touch the parchment. Otherwise, the scroll is meaningless. Before you pick up a quill, embrace your parchment entirely. Ideally, Wes, you'll become comfortable with the textures before you try to create a new world out of it."

"I feel ready," Wes asserted. "What do you think?"

"If you're going to go all the way with a *Sefer* Torah," Aviva said as she returned the quill to its holder. "You should know that the masters teach us to keep two quotes in mind. What are yours?"

"I really don't have a mantra or anything," Wes answered. "Sometimes I zone out on the yin and yang symbol."

"That's a good start. Now put that into words. Show me you're balanced enough to scribe a *Sefer* Torah on your own."

"Okay," Wes said. "Give me a question, and I'll give you an answer."

She smiled, responding favorably to his confidence. "How will you be remembered in a hundred years?"

"Sorry if this sounds played out," Wes paused. "Think globally, act locally."

Aviva nodded in approval. "Good. But what does that mean to you?"

"My grandparents came from this city to take a ship to America during the Shoah. That's global. And now here I am in Amsterdam, ready to scribe a Torah in their names. That's local."

Aviva tilted her head closer to him. "Beautiful. Now give me one more."

Wes thought about Iraq, that war which was occurring synchronously with his journey around the world. "Good relations with all nations."

Aviva stared through him. "And what do you mean by that?"

"I mean, it's just an ideal," Wes replied, feeling ridiculous and quixotic for sharing a canned line he'd remembered from an old college textbook. "I hope I live to see a day when countries around the world treat each other in a more dignified way."

"Try telling that to Palestine," Aviva put in, turning her back to him.

"Doesn't everyone have a right to live in peace?" Wes asked.

"Yes," she answered, now looking him squarely in the eyes. "But if liberals take over the Israeli government, there goes our security. We will be doomed."

At first, Aviva's politics irked him. She loved Netanyahu, whose war hype grossed Wes out whenever the four-letter word *Iraq* passed his lips or hers. But as the summer breezed into fall, Wes and Aviva broke bread together more and more often. Wes had never been around anyone who prayed so much. Her chanting and swaying somehow blessed him with the focus he'd need to scribe a Torah for his grandparents.

Sometimes Aviva rolled back her eyes and slipped into a half-conscious trance while uttering words of the Amidah under her breath, bowing unlike any prayer gesture Wes had ever seen in secular Baltimore. Aviva had a mystical presence that led Wes to feel something deep in his bones for her. Despite their cultural differences, or perhaps *because* he was a liberal American and she a Hasidic Israeli, Wes started thinking of Aviva as the yin to his yang.

Wes spent the High Holidays with Aviva's host family, the Rubensteins, and together they sat for Yom Kippur services in the historic Esnoga, a synagogue and a safe haven for Portuguese Jews since the Inquisition.

Wes stayed for a few nights in the humid attic loft, sleeping in a tiny bed with his feet stretching beyond the end of a child-sized mattress. He joined the family of nine on Yom Kippur. Instead of covering the top of his head with a kippah, Wes wore the sudra that Aviva had gifted him a month ago, on Tisha B'av. The ancient Judean garment curtained his face like a scarf, while Aviva wrapped hers into a ball like a turban. While the Rubenstein family broke the fast at home, Wes and Aviva went out on their own that night. From behind the counter of the kabob shack, Zayin greeted them like royalty. Zayin went on with his usual *brother this* and *brother that,* slipping into a sweeping verse of Arabic. Wes handed him some cash, and Zayin intervened.

"I'll take care of it today, my brother and sister," Zayin insisted, pressing the twenty euro against Wes's outstretched palm.

"Peace, brother," Wes said, smiling back at Zayin.

When the High Holidays passed, Wes returned to the Prinsengracht. Neither Kayla nor Lars were home. Wes hadn't seen them very much and missed their company. The last thing he wanted was for his cool, cosmopolitan roommates to think he'd gone holy roller. The house was like a resting place for the rootless. Lars painted whenever he felt like it, and Kayla usually woke up late in the afternoon before dashing off to work in a hurry. On most days, the three housemates lived like ships passing in the night.

The sour, sulfuric smell of ink somehow stimulated his appetite. Wes crossed Jodenbreestraat, in the Jewish Quarter, and followed a trail of cannabis smoke into the Red Light District, the heart of it all. A paradisical aroma of deep spices swept throughout the alley, and Wes smiled, knowing the scent quite well. As he approached a rotating grill, a lamb carcass swayed like a giant punching bag, and Wes breathed in the intoxicating aroma of natural oils dripping inside a rotisserie machine as vertical as a skyscraper. From behind the counter, Zayin waved Wes over, tossing his balled-up apron into a bin as another chef swooped over to the register.

"I was thinking about going to a pub tonight," Wes said to Zayin. "You game?"

"I'd love to join you, brother. But I don't drink," Zayin replied, fingering the crescent moon on his necklace.

"Would you like to hit up a coffeeshop instead?"

"Yeah," Zayin answered. "I'd like that."

They settled on a basement-level smoking room with a vibe too bleary for a rotating disco ball to fix. Zayin pointed to the seats farthest back, a quieter respite from the loud, pulsating throb of house music blaring out of clunky floor speakers on either side of the door. Zayin sparked up the spliff and puffed first, blowing out perfect smoke rings that caught the attention of a few young women nearby.

"Mijn vriend is nieuw in Amsterdam," Zayin chirped in Dutch. *"Hij leert nu Nederlands."*

"It's okay. We speak English," one of the young women answered in a posh British accent. "Do you like Lenny Kravitz?"

Wes hit the joint, exhaling in a hurry as he passed Zayin the joint. "Do you mean *the* Lenny Kravitz?"

"We're going to his concert tonight," added a blonde in the shortest skirt Wes had ever seen.

"Well, you're very lucky," Wes commented. "Any chance that you might have a couple extra tickets?"

"There may still be some tickets available at the door. You're welcome to follow us by tram to the Ziggodome if you fancy," the British woman said.

Tense lines creased between Zayin's eyes. "Kra-vitz?" His voice dripped with bewilderment and scorn. "I'm not going."

"If I'd known Lenny Kravitz was in town tonight, I would've gotten a ticket myself," Wes countered.

Zayin waved them away. "Have fun, ladies."

"Why did you do that?" Wes asked, shaking his head in dismay as the young women walked off. "We could've had a good time. They seemed nice."

Zayin coughed out a mouthful of smoke. "Save your money, brother."

Wes led the way outside the coffeeshop, bummed to be missing the Lenny Kravitz concert and a little vexed with Zayin for snarling at the friendly, pretty women. They ambled through the Canal Ring, navigating the rose fluorescent lamplight into the city's incandescent core. Those blurry red lights cast a weblike spiral into luminous little alleys with a scantily dressed woman in every window. Zayin stopped at one of the cabins, where a blue-eyed cowgirl stood in her doorway. She wore an Amarillo sky hat, knee-high tassel boots, and not much more. Mesmerized, Wes watched as Zayin stared into the blazing portal with the eyes of a lost child. Wes backed away from the window. The thought of having sex for money repulsed Wes, who parted ways with Zayin as the lady in lingerie whisked the oil-stained kabob chef inside, swiftly drawing her red curtains shut.

Wes passed a darkened dance room with a disco ball chandelier as the only light. He poked his head in the door of the lively night club, unable to recognize the house music blaring from a sound system too massive for the small space. Everyone who was getting down on the dance floor looked either younger or older than Wes. He sighed, wishing he'd gone with those girls to the Lenny Kravitz concert. Instead, he went home alone.

The joint he'd sucked down for dinner kept him sleepless until another morning sun seeped between the drapes. Wes nearly left for synagogue still wearing his pajamas, which probably would have been fine with everyone. There, the code of dress was lax. Sometimes the rabbi showed up for the afternoon Mincha prayers in yoga pants and a tie dye spiral tee.

On this morning, Aviva wore a black beret tipped to the side like Che Guevara. A Star of David pendant, like the one Wes sometimes wore around his neck, was pinned to the brim. The cap, Aviva told Wes, was a remnant of her service years in the Israeli Air Force.

At the desk, Wes scribed verses as Aviva recited them. She watched him closely as he dipped the quill tip into the inkwell.

"If it's okay, I'd like to touch your shoulders," Aviva said, shadowing Wes from behind.

"Is something wrong with my shoulders?" Wes asked skeptically.

"Your posture is too rigid," she answered, her thumbs kneading into his back. Aviva leaned close enough for her lips to brush his ear. "Don't be afraid to look hunched like an old rebbe. Relax and get close to the scroll. Remember, a human touch is what validates the Torah."

"So, what else are we doing today?"

"Today, I will read from the first book of Genesis," Aviva said, and backed off quickly. "Now, before scratching a drop of ink into the *klaf*, you'll repeat each line of scripture after me. Then with your quill, you'll recreate everything on these scrolls."

"How much time will I have?"

Aviva plucked a sand timer and raised an eyebrow. "Starting in three, two, one."

As Wes trained his eyes on the faint *sirtut* lines, Aviva stood close enough that he could feel her breathing on the back of his neck. She told him not to get cocky when he scribed the *taggin* first, thus giving crowns to letters that had not yet manifested. As Wes turned in his seat to face her, Aviva stood nearly close enough to kiss him.

"You move very fast with the quill," she noted softly. "Did I make any mistakes that would ruin a Torah?"

"Most mistakes can be scraped and erased after the ink is dry enough. But I noticed a lack of consistency after the letter structure was already set into ink. Start here first." Aviva paused briefly, studying Wes's face, and then continued. "That tiny tip in the corner of some letters is a starting point, not an afterthought."

Wes nodded. "Thanks for being so patient with me. Guess I've been out of practice for a while now."

"Of course. Let's break for lunch. Where do you want to go?"

"Do you like falafels?" Wes asked.

"I'm Israeli," she replied with a playful smile. "So, I love falafels."

"I do, too," Wes added, unpinning the black velvet yarmulke from his shaggy brown hair. "I'll text Zayin and let him know we're coming."

On the walk to the Kabob Shack, Wes tapped his Nokia for a response from Zayin, nodding as if to assure Aviva that everything was fine. Business was dead, with the dining tables empty and the uncut giant rotisserie slowly browning in a revolving cage. Behind the front counter, Zayin sat on a milk crate, idly bobbing his head at a soccer match on a tiny color TV. Wes sat across from Aviva, following her sporadic, mistrusting glances across the room. When Zayin came to their table, he gruffly tipped up his chin to greet Wes, a customer who he'd so quickly dubbed a brother earlier in the week.

"Hey, brother," Wes greeted Zayin. "Could we get two falafels for lunch?"

"Is she your girlfriend?" Zayin asked, his voice low and scathing.

"She's my teacher," Wes responded, turning instead to Aviva for approval. "We were just in here the other day. Don't you remember?"

"Whatever. Two falafels coming up."

Wes sighed, trying to decipher Zayin's tone. "Aviva," he finally said. "Could you tell me more about the *cholol?*"

"What do you want to know?" Aviva answered with muted tension in her voice.

"You mentioned a technique for improving my symmetry. You know that little space you were talking about between certain letters?"

"Treat every blank space in a beis or khaf like a letter in its own right," she whispered across the small table. "Before even a drop of ink goes on the *klaf,* the *cholol* is already on the parchment."

"What should I do with that space?"

Aviva cast Wes a serious look, then smiled politely. "Honor it."

Zayin crossed the counter with wrapped falafels on porcelain plates that wobbled on the palms of his hands. The dishes clinked as he carried them to the table before slamming both plates upon the table at once. Balled, fried chickpea patties rattled out of the pita pockets.

From across the rotisserie counter, Wes watched Zayin grind a long chef's knife against a honing rod. Zayin stared admiringly at the blade, laughing to himself as though marveling at the menacing sound of steel sharpening. With a mixture of concern and irritation, Wes turned to face him.

"What's going on, Zayin?" Wes asked.

"Who are you with, Wes?"

"Look, man. I already told you who she is. We work together. Is there an issue?"

"You tell me." Zayin curled his lower lip as he ignored Wes and turned to Aviva, his eyes blazing with scorn.

"Let's leave," Wes said to Aviva just as she confronted Zayin at the counter, trading barbs with the kabob chef in guttural Arabic. Wes couldn't make out

99

the words until Zayin switched to English, holding up a finger to make a point.

"Tell me something, *sharmuta,*" Zayin called across the counter, flickering his teeth in Aviva's direction. "Did you enjoy dropping bombs on my village in the West Bank, or were you just following orders?"

"What did you just call me?" Aviva asked, standing with her arms akimbo.

"Do you know who you're talking to, brother?" Wes stepped to the counter. "Her name's Aviva, and she's a master scribe. Why don't you show a little respect?"

Zayin trained his eyes on Aviva and spit hard on the floor. "Respect? They killed my father and destroyed our home. I lost my family when I was nine years old and had to stay with my cousins in Turkey. And you want to tell me about respect?"

"Brother," Wes said, resting a hand upon Zayin's clenched fist. "I am sorry for what happened. But Aviva didn't kill your father."

At once Zayin abandoned his stoicism, seemingly accepting the apology with a placid expression. Then and there, Wes realized Aviva no longer stood at the counter, her departure the only explanation for Zayin's swift change in demeanor.

"It's not you, brother," Zayin returned, calmer. "Never was."

Wes swiped his raincoat from the chair, stopping back at the front counter as he and Zayin stood close enough to shake hands, but they did not.

"I've got to get back to my job," Wes told Zayin, who nodded understandingly.

"Wat voor werk doe je?" Zayin switched to Dutch, his voice playful and curious.

"It's okay," Wes answered, smiling his understanding. "You know, I speak English. To answer your question, I'm a scribe."

"Good for you, brother," Zayin replied in yet another accent, a carefree California valley boy. "My dream is to go to Hollywood and try my hand as an actor."

"You've got the personality for it." Wes spoke in a neutral tone, trying to be supportive while edging his way through the open door, as dueling, dissonant-sounding sitars seeped through an unseen speaker. "Hope you make it, brother. Take care of yourself."

An afternoon drizzle dampened the cobblestone alley. Wes dashed down the streets in search of Aviva, passing pot shops, pubs, and nearly-naked prostitutes standing in windows. At the corner of a canal bridge, Wes caught up with Aviva in the hazy red ambience of a bustling alley.

"I don't know what to say," Wes approached Aviva, his breathing heavy.

"You sure had a lot to say to your buddy in his terrorist cell," Aviva fired back, walking blankly ahead.

"Come on, Aviva. That's an ugly statement to make."

"Here's something ugly," Aviva said, finally stopping at the other end of the bridge. "He called me a whore in two languages. And what did you do about it?"

"I told him to show you respect," Wes replied. "I've eaten there a lot, and he's not usually so loud or confrontational."

"You trust him to make your food?" Aviva asked in disbelief. "If he knows that you're Jewish, you should see a doctor to make sure he hasn't been poisoning you."

Wes froze in place, waiting for her to say something more. "What?"

"I'm going to give you the rest of the day off." Aviva announced, her voice strained. "A trip to the health clinic could save your life."

With that, Aviva went one way and Wes, feeling more misunderstood than poisoned, dragged himself on a long walk through the mist. Back at the canal house, Lars handed off a bubble-wrapped canvas to an overdressed couple pushing a covered, antiquated baby carriage. As they sauntered with their bundle over the footbridge, Lars, on the front stoop, flipped open a red pack of Marlboros.

Lars held a cigarette between his lips. "I usually don't do this," he mumbled while lighting up. "Only after one of my paintings sells."

"Today sucked, and that's putting it mildly," Wes said. "I just want to smoke a joint and forget the whole thing."

"Then check this out." Lars reached into his pocket and produced a colorful, plastic tin with a fire-breathing dragon logo emblazoned on the lid.

"Wow." Wes stared at the image, certain that he knew what Lars was about to offer.

"These are strong," Lars added. With two hands, he slowly passed Wes the packaged mushroom truffles like a precious object. "I prefer not to take them alone."

Lars turned the lid open, and Wes held the dose under his nose, picking up on a faint earthy whiff through the plastic hermetic seal. With so much still unsettled at work and home, Wes figured he needed to improve his headspace before dabbling in anything hallucinogenic. At college, he'd sampled MDMA a few times, swearing it off after witnessing a dramatic overdose. A girl in the dorm flipped out and had a seizure. She wriggled on her bed like a fish out of water, desperate for air as her roommate cried too frantically to dial for an ambulance. Paramedics eventually rolled through the corridor with oxygenating machines and a stretcher, flanked by the scornful faces of pudgy campus cops following their drug-sniffing German Shepherds.

Wes had seen the product before, but had never tried magic mushrooms. He was leery of ingesting a new and unfamiliar substance that, for all he knew, might send him into outer space without a return ticket. With Aviva and Zayin on his mind, Wes texted wellness checks to them both. *Hope you are okay*, Wes sent the messages in tandem. A reply from Zayin came back in under a minute: *I'm okay, brother. Thanks for asking.* Wes checked his phone on the hour, receiving nothing from Aviva, his teacher, or from Harry, his friend and Torah sponsor. When he woke up the next morning from a fitful sleep, he reached for his Nokia once again, finding no new messages in the inbox and feeling like he had nothing left to lose.

Before leaving the house for the day, Wes posted a note on the gallery door.

Count me in, Lars, if you'd still like to do 'shrooms together, Wes had scribbled on the Post-it note. *Tomorrow is never guaranteed. Then again, what is?*

CHAPTER TEN

"I'm sorry about what happened yesterday," Wes greeted Aviva in the hallway. *"Boker tov."*

"Yeah, good morning," Aviva grudgingly replied as she jiggled a big, antique key into the door, entering the sofer room ahead of her student.

Wes stepped forward, slow and unsure. "Is everything okay?" he asked.

"You called him brother," Aviva answered in disgust, focusing on the tassels that dangled from her head covering.

Wes shrugged. "That's what he called me."

Aviva swayed closer, flashing Wes a small smile. "Fine. But next time we go out to eat, I'll pick the restaurant."

"I'd like that," Wes said, grinning affably.

Aviva's tallis slipped from her shoulders. Wes swooped up the tasseled garment, awkwardly cradling it in a wrinkled ball. She swiped the prayer shawl from his arms, taking it away. When Aviva returned with an identical garment, she draped it over Wes's arm like a tailor at a custom fitting.

"Should I wear this today?" Wes asked, unsure but willing.

"It's for me to wear," Aviva established. "But I won't be scribing today. I want you to touch me."

Wes felt the stress lines rising like an ocean wave on his forehead. "I'm sorry?"

"Put the tallis around my shoulders, Wes. And please don't be timid with your hands."

Gingerly, he slipped his fingers across the shawl, trying to read Aviva expression. "Is that okay?" Wes looked up and asked.

"If you're hesitant to touch a woman, how do you expect to handle a Torah?" Aviva asked impatiently.

Wes backed off. "I think I can manage."

Aviva sighed. "In that case, would you meet me at the mikveh bath tomorrow morning?"

"Are we allowed to be there together?"

"Listen to yourself, Wes. If I followed all the rules, I'd still be in Israel, where no one will let a woman scribe Torah."

"I know. So," Wes struggled to get the words out. "We'll both be naked in the mikveh?"

"Yes," Aviva said. "Just like the Garden of Eden."

"I'll look forward to seeing you tomorrow," Wes responded in his most polite voice.

"Try to get comfortable with me," Aviva appealed, massaging Wes on the back of his shoulders. "In the morning, you're going to see every part of my body. And I will see yours. All these sacred clothes will come off. That's when I'll know for sure that you're ready for this huge undertaking."

"I'm ready," Wes said, trying not to moan as Aviva dug her thumbs into his back, turning his senses around.

"Good," Aviva finished, reaching for a piece of frayed white rope. "Now, for today, let's see how you assemble your own scroll."

Aviva aligned a blank parchment page on a wooden Torah roller. Feeling the master scribe breathing on his shoulder, Wes threaded a needle, running the string through a tiny opening. While taking turns with a thick sewing needle and tiny scissors, they wove pages into a scroll. Aviva's face glowed with delight as she pierced the pieces of parchment, stitching them into a finished *klaf.*

"Scribing a Torah in Israel must be quite an experience," Wes said, breaking the silence. "Isn't it?"

Aviva turned aside, stirring a quill tip in a shot glass holder of black ink. "Sure, as long as you're a man and they allow you to do it."

"Those rules seem so backwards."

"It's not backwards. It has always been that way. I trained with the most accomplished quill slingers in Jerusalem, but no one will let me scribe a Torah there. Meanwhile, every halfway liberal shul in Europe has me in their Rolodex."

"Amsterdam's pretty liberal overall," Wes went on. "I enjoy being here."

Aviva frowned. "I'm tired of teaching the Rubenstein boys to scribe in exchange for my room and board."

"What exactly do you teach them?" Wes asked. "Is it anything like what we've been doing?"

"There are secrets I'll share with you," she said quietly, edging closer to Wes. "If you're willing to set aside the Hebrew calendar and work on your own time, a Torah can be scribed a lot sooner than a whole year."

"Well, I'm here on a ninety-day landing visa," Wes pointed out. "And already, one month has passed."

Aviva turned the cracked door all the way open, and Wes could hear Rabbi Cohen reciting Mincha prayers from across the hallway. "We'll talk about that in the morning," Aviva said.

"About what happened at the falafel shop—" Wes started to apologize.

"Not to worry. I did some research on your friend. Your *brother.*" Aviva exaggerated the word "brother," drawing it out almost like the word itself was cursed. "He's got no criminal history, and no known ties to any radical groups. It was wrong for me say that he would've poisoned you."

"No harm, no foul. Zayin is a good Muslim man who lost his home in Palestine. Despite everything he's been through, I don't believe he'd wish harm on anyone."

"Believe whatever makes you happy," Aviva spoke softly, resting a hand on Wes's chest. "See you after the sunrise."

Wes cut a cobbled path into the Red Light District. On the way home, his usual commute took him through ambient fluorescent bulbs spotlighting oglers lurking outside doorways where temporary companions beckoned in leather and lace. In the heart of town, Wes soaked up the nervous energy of men scurrying around the canals like rats searching for a drainpipe. From behind half-curtained plexiglass doorways, beautiful girls beckoned to Wes—with one noticeable, startling exception.

He'd never seen her like this: the smoky winged eyeliner and ruby red lip gloss, the scorpion tattoo crawling up her thigh, the high ponytail that transformed her from college hippie to schoolgirl. How had he not pieced it together, considering the bustiers and stockings, the fancy designer handbags, and all the late-night comings and goings?

Kayla slowly cracked open her door, inviting Wes into her cabin. Hesitant, Wes stepped forward as she whisked him inside, firming the door and drawing the curtains shut.

"Well, now you know," Kayla broke the silence. "What are you doing here?"

"I don't know," Wes replied honestly. "But I didn't plan to find you. I thought you were a bartender." As Kayla rolled her eyes, Wes added, "I know, I know. Willful ignorance. But I'm not dismissing you or your work, okay?"

"Okay," Kayla said. "But have you ever done anything like this before, Wes?"

Wes scanned the little cabin, furnished with no more than a cot, a small nightstand, and a pedestal sink. "Anything like what, exactly?"

"Come on," Kayla laughed, nudging him. "You lived in Bangkok. You've paid for it before, haven't you?"

"No, I haven't."

"Well, sorry for assuming. Just so you know, I only do this when enrollment drops in my language classes." Kayla sighed, looking wearily at Wes as she waved her arms around. "You do what it takes to survive," she added. "This is sometimes what it takes."

"No judgment on my end," Wes responded, his voice calm and firm. "I'm just not sure if I'm in the right frame of mind to do this."

Kayla stared him down, her eyes playful and seductive as she raised an eyebrow and reached into her bra for a slightly dented skinny cigarette. "What, exactly, do you think 'this' is?"

"I mean, can I at least take you to dinner first?"

Kayla exhaled a stream of smoke. "You don't have to do that. Just pay me fifty euro for a quick roll in the hay, and then we'll both be on our way."

"Like I said," Wes began, parsing the words in his head. "This doesn't feel like the time or the place. But if we do at some point, I just want the chance to connect a little more with you first."

Kayla smiled warmly, stubbing out her smoke in an open skull ashtray. "You're a gentleman, Wes. I knew I made the right decision when I asked you to be my roommate. So, yes. Dinner. Do you feel like having Thai?"

"Sure," Wes agreed. "I know a place."

Kayla shut off the lights, locking arms with Wes as they exited her brothel cabin. They walked across the footbridge as casually as any other couple out on the town. At a quiet Thai restaurant facing the main drag, Wes ordered off the menu and spoke to the waiters in their native language. In the dining room with orchid petaled placemats and silk tablecloths, Wes looked across the table at his gorgeous roommate from California who, still to his surprise, was employed as an Amsterdam sex worker.

"Lars has some magic mushrooms," Wes whispered, glancing around him. "Would you like to join us tonight?"

"We can talk about it openly," Kayla spoke a notch over her usual voice. "It's legal here.

"So, do you want to go for it?"

Kayla cracked a half-smile. "That wasn't what I'd planned to spend my night doing."

"And what was that?" Wes asked, clearing his throat. "Your other plans?"

"Just need to make sure the landlord gets his cut," Kayla responded decisively. "Another fifty euro should put me over the top for the evening."

After the meal, Wes and Kayla strolled across the canal, slipping back into the dim doorway of her cabin. She turned on a lamp at the bedside, asking him for the cash payment. Upon receiving it, Kayla held the bill in the light, sniffing it for authenticity.

"We live together," Wes said. "You know I'm good for it."

Kayla wiggled out of her overcoat. "Sorry, babe. It's just protocol."

"You look amazing," Wes said, standing at the bedside. "But I thought that when we first met."

Kayla smirked, kissing him on the cheek on her way to the door of a tiny washroom beside the exposed sink. "You're too cute, Wes."

Five minutes on the bed felt to Wes like forever. Waiting for Kayla, he rested his head on the pillow and stared through the drawn window at rosy lamplight warming the brick and cobblestone street. Another five minutes ticked away, and Wes began to grow concerned.

Just as he was about to knock on the door to check on Kayla, she emerged from the washroom, clutching her stomach. With a firm nudge, she shut the door as the toilet flushed.

"I owe you a raincheck," Kayla said. "I'm sorry. I'm not feeling so well."

"It's okay," Wes responded. "You don't owe me anything."

Kayla's eyes dimmed. "Do you want to try this again another time?"

"Sure," Wes answered. "Why not?"

"Go have fun with Lars tonight." Kayla paused. "Hope that you find whatever answers you're looking for in those magic mushrooms."

"Wait," Wes said. "Since you said you're not feeling well, are you coming back to the house?"

"Not for another hour. The collector comes to the cabins on his little bike. I've got to give him the red envelope."

Wes nodded, reaching for his raincoat on the rack. When Kayla kissed him quickly on the lips and unlatched the door, Wes slipped outside into the hazy mist. Heading home, Wes spotted a scrappy young man making the rounds on a motorbike. Some of the working girls kissed both his cheeks as he stopped at their cabins to collect his due. From a walkup espresso bar across the street, Wes trailed the collector, who'd plundered at least five cabins in as many minutes. He didn't know what to text Kayla, or how to not sound like a social worker when he did: *I'm here if you need anything. Let's continue our conversation soon. Be safe out there. Let me know if you'd like an escort home.*

Good times tonight were his chosen words. Wes finally hit the green button on his Nokia after deleting those previous attempts.

Back at the house, Lars answered the door with a mushroom truffle tin in hand. Wes held the plastic canister to his nose as Lars dipped into the kitchen. He returned with a plate of apple wedges and biscuits: comfort food, as Lars called it, in case the trip turned more intense than what they'd bargained for. Standing beside the couch, Lars knocked back the first handful of truffles. Reluctantly, Wes followed suit and plugged his nose as bitter morsels crunched between his teeth. He waited a moment, listening to nothing more than the sound of their own breathing.

At first, not much had changed but for a technicolor tint that transformed the living room into the set of a sitcom. Though surprised at how quickly the trip had taken effect, Wes waved off the plate of munchies.

Over the warm crackling of the record player needle, the album spun a country western electric guitar which played into a loose shuffle groove. Then came the familiar "Venus" hook, and Lars passed Wes the cover. Under a psychedelic blue light, the band members looked tailor-made for the Summer of Love. Lars raved about Shocking Blue, one of the first pop bands in the Netherlands ever to reach a worldwide audience while the British Invasion waned.

"Hey, speaking of things, is everything cool between you and Kayla?" Lars asked, quickly changing the subject.

"Sure," Wes replied. "Why do you ask?"

"She texted to tell me that you found out about her work."

"It's really not a big deal." Wes tried to sound casual as his voice cracked.

Never had Wes considered paying for sex. Something about money changing hands cheapened the act, which was why his paid encounter with Leah in the Auckland waterfall still felt odd to him. He wasn't naïve, however. He'd seen *Pretty Woman* in high school. He'd read several novels in which a character had received money in exchange for sex. And throughout his college years, he'd been friends with plenty of middle-class coeds who drove luxury cars that their sugar daddies paid for.

But his first impressions of the world's oldest profession had been formed while driving through the gritty city limits of East Baltimore. In his hometown, the only picture of prostitution he'd cultivated had been courtesy of half-dead crack moms staggering like zombies around bus stops on Old Harford Road. Those impressions still lingered strongly in his mind.

"I guess she's still waiting for her teaching schedule to fill out," Wes added. "Kayla says the Red Light District is temporary."

Lars cracked a conceited grin. "That's what most sex workers say."

"So, why didn't things work out between you and Kayla?"

Lars shrugged. "I tried to roll with it, but after she went to work in the District, things between us got weird. It was better to end it. At least we've stayed close as friends."

Wes nodded. "It was so normal in Thailand to see that sort of thing going on. When I lived in Bangkok, I'd go out and chat with working girls in bars and clubs. Maybe we'd drink or dance, but without going to bed."

"Why not?"

"When I was growing up, I only knew one person who had ever done that. My best friend back home, Boone. He's from California. On his thirteenth birthday, his dad bought him a night at the Sheraton in downtown L.A. The kid got to spend the night with a gold card escort as sexy as Jennifer Lopez."

"And what did you get for your thirteenth birthday?"

The question gave Wes a moment of pause. "A Bar Mitzvah. My dad catered it with subs and pizzas from his shop."

"Still, there must have been temptations for you in Thailand, no?"

"On my first week in Bangkok, one of the other English teachers tested positive for HIV after having sex with a hooker. The guy was a crying mess, swearing up and down it was the only time he'd ever done that."

"Working girls in Amsterdam are clean," Lars spoke with conviction. "Condoms and routine health checks are required. Things are different here."

Wes shot him a skeptical look. "How do you know this for sure?"

"My uncle is a virologist. He's written peer-reviewed studies published on the subject. And the transmission rate of sexually transmitted infections in Amsterdam's Red Light District is practically nil."

Wes checked his cell phone, taking a break from the conversation. Scrolling through the missed calls, Wes found three attempts from Rav within the past hour. Before Wes could even dial back, Rav rang him again. Sensing the reserved urgency in the rabbi's voice, Wes stood up to take the call into the quiet foyer by the stairwell.

Something had shifted in the universe, and Wes could physically feel it. Aviva was going home to the south of Israel, Rav reported over the phone. As the rabbi choked up, Wes immediately thought the worst had happened: that Aviva went down with the plane in some horrific crash. Instead, her family's house had been hit by a missile. According to Rav, Aviva's sisters were travelling back from the city and found their home reduced to a gaping brick hole. And with Aviva rushing to the airport for the very next flight to Ben Gurion, Wes would be on his own.

"A-Are you telling m-me that I can scribe a Torah?" Wes stammered.

"Yes," Rav said. "I wish I was saying this in better circumstances. Mazel tov, Wes."

"My grandparents were refugees here in Amsterdam. They hurried in and hurried out. If the Nazis had their way, Bubbie and Zayde would've never started their family in America. Now I'll get to finish what Zayde dreamed to start."

"I know you will, Wes, because it's who you are."

"See you tomorrow, Rabbi Cohen."

"Have a good night, Wes."

Wes powered off his phone as the room swirled like a kaleidoscope. "Tell me something, Lars," he said, stumbling back into the room. "When will this wear off?"

"Maybe in a couple hours," Lars answered.

"Do you think I'll be okay to work in the morning?"

"Ja," Lars answered in Dutch. "Wat voor werk ga je morgen doen?"

Wes shrugged. "I think you just asked what I'm doing for work tomorrow morning?"

"Ja."

"Ik, ik," Wes tried to say in Dutch. "I'm going to scribe a pretty important book."

"First time?"

"Yeah. The Master Scribe had to leave town on emergency. So that means I'm the second choice."

Lars rested an arm on Wes's shoulder. "Tripping like this can bring all your doubts to the surface.

114

Wrestling with your thoughts is one of the most Jewish things you can do."

"Are you Jewish?" Wes asked.

"Atheist," Lars replied. "I've never been much for fairy tales. But I know my history."

"I'm not that observant," Wes said. "But before my grandfather died, he was losing his eyesight. He wanted me to write a Torah for him, and so that's what I'm about to do."

"Mazel tov!"

"Who taught you to say that?"

"My family is of Ashkenazic descent."

"Mine, too!" Wes exclaimed without trying to sound too clever.

At that, Lars laughed hysterically, which triggered a signal in Wes's brain to indicate the truffles had taken effect as intended. On the couch with Lars, Wes fell apart laughing. But back upstairs in the loft, he'd soon forget what exactly had made him lose it.

Without remembering how he made it up the stairs to his bed, Wes awakened to his full capacities. Through the arched bedroom window, Wes looked at the last warm rays of summer fading from Amsterdam like disillusioned tourists on a fast train to the airport.

On the walk across town, Wes stopped on a footbridge to dig into the pocket of his black trousers for a halfway-smoked joint from the day before. Feeling around for a lighter that wasn't there, he scanned the nearly vacant canal walkway for someone with an available flame. A man walking his pup approached, holding out a plastic lighter. As Wes lit up and the buzz quickly kicked in, the droopy-eared Dachshund stared up at him with big, brown marble eyes. In a daze, Wes returned the lighter to its owner, catching a lick on his hand from the pooch. As he walked on and took a couple drags, Wes thought it wiser to deposit what remained of the joint into a plastic cone holder. Under pressure to recreate the Bible out of an animal feather, Wes needed something to calm his nerves. A puff or two would do, but anything more than that and he'd be stoned silly.

At the front gate, Wes buzzed himself into the courtyard, feeling the weight of history in those heavy wooden doors. The Lion of Judah statue seemed to stare from behind as Wes Levine entered the synagogue as the only known Hebrew scribe in the Netherlands.

CHAPTER ELEVEN

Wes hoisted himself out of the mikveh, a soothing tonic awakening body and soul at once. At the edge of the bath, he wrapped a towel around himself and then suited up in black and white. Across the hall in the sofer room, Wes draped his shoulders with Aviva's old prayer shawl. The rolled-out parchment looked pristine as a wedding dress, with the onus now on Wes alone to produce the perfect bride.

Without a master scribe chanting from behind, Wes sang the lines to himself, reciting scripture from dog-eared pages yellowed by the passage of time. Dipping the quill in a glass inkwell, Wes held a finger on the scroll to feel the block reserved for the initial marking. Scribing the Hebrew letter bet, Wes expressed the inaugural stroke of black ink on ivory-white parchment. By the second line, he botched the first lamed, a letter that pointed like a stick outside of its designated space. Wes picked out ink specs with a thin blade, using a pumice stone to smooth over the error. As he returned

117

the rock to a drawer full of others like it, Wes found a little note atop the pile.

"Don't worry about mistakes. I make plenty." Wes mumbled the words Aviva wrote for him. Then and there, a pendant slipped out of the folded paper: two Hebrew letters, chet and yud, which combined to make the symbol of life and hope, the chai.

To Wes, you've got a steadier hand than anyone I've ever taught. I wanted to give you this after the Torah was finished. Anyway, it's yours now. Here's to life. L'chaim! Wear it well. Always, Aviva.

As Wes scratched ink into the *klaf* for the last time that day, Rav lifted a wooden board to set it over the verses in ink still drying into parchment. Standing over the covered scroll, they came together for a hug, and a quick mazel tov. Rav reached into his wallet pocket.

"Um, thanks," Wes said, reluctant as Rav passed fifty euro into his hand. "What's this for?"

"Just have a little fun tonight," the rabbi permissively told the scribe. "You've certainly earned it."

"Well," Wes returned. "I pass through the Red Light District every day."

"Whatever you want to do. Spend it on something that brings you joy."

Wes swallowed. "Are you suggesting that I go get laid?"

That made the rabbi blush. "It's a gift," Rav responded, leaving the question unresolved. "But not if I tell you how to spend it."

"Not saying that's what I'd do," Wes contemplated. "But what else in this town costs exactly fifty euro?"

"I was planning to give you thirty-six," Rav explained. "You know, in Jewish tradition, multiples of eighteen carry greater significance. But I didn't have anything smaller than a fifty."

Wes smiled. "Understood."

"What happens in the District is its own ancient tradition," Rav spoke, eloquent and sermonic. "Centuries of sailors have passed through this port after spending months at sea. When their ships came in, they'd follow the lights of sex workers who carried red lanterns out to the docks. They'd pair off and take shelter in warm little rooms where an intimate human connection could be made. Throughout our difficult history, Amsterdam has given us a haven more than anywhere else in the western world. With that, I say that our Judean traditions can most certainly coexist with the local, liberal traditions."

"Thanks again for the gift," Wes said, taking comfort in the ease and honesty of the rabbi's words. "I'll try not to spend it all in one place."

"Enjoy the rest of your day," Rav replied as they locked up the Torah-to-be in the sanctuary of the sofer room.

At three o'clock, the old church bell tolled, near enough to be heard from the Jewish Quarter. Lars turned up on Jodenbreestraat to meet Wes, as they'd previously planned, to have a joint together in the afterglow of their mushroom trip.

"This is the girl I'm looking for." Lars flashed a photo on his cell phone as they walked. "Her name is Roos. I just want to see if a spark might still be there."

"Do you know what kind of spark I'm looking for?" Wes asked, placing a hand inside of the pocket with Rav's monetary gift. "The kind that lights up a big, fat joint."

They stumbled into a coffeeshop with a reggae tune seeping through the door. Inside, a spacy guitar echoed to an island beat. Behind the counter, a scrawny white kid with dreadlocks held a small flashlight over a laminated menu of indica, sativa, and hashish. The cannabis strain names sounded either silly or mysterious: Bubble Gum and Durban Poison, Granddaddy Grape and Acapulco Gold. Under an open jar of buds smelling like heaven on Earth, Cannabis Kid hovered over an open jar of Laughing Buddha, his steel tongs trained carefully on a light green nugget. The quiet budtender's tee-shirt did most of the talking, with the words "Smoke America Out of Afghanistan" blazing in a red and white Coca-Cola font.

With craft joints in hand, Wes and Lars settled at a quiet corner table to dig in. A burning, pine-smelling sensation filled the room as Wes exhaled on a hacking cough. Lars calmly breathed out, clear-eyed and impervious, as though enjoying THC solely for the taste.

"So, how long were you and Roos together?" Wes asked.

Lars flipped open his cell phone again, flashing the same blurred image. "On and off for about a year."

From across the table, Wes squinted at the tiny screen Lars held in his palm. "If you have a clearer pic, that might make it easier to find her."

"I'm also a photographer," Lars said nonchalantly. "But I only have one image of Roos. She'd put up her guard every time I used a camera."

"Someone who works in the District might be guarded when it comes to their privacy," Wes reasoned.

Lars took another puff on his joint. "She's the great mystery of my life."

"How does she feel about that?"

Lars looked out the window. "I just miss her is all."

Wes rolled his eyes. "All right, man. Can I take another look at that image on your phone?"

After polishing off their joints, Wes and Lars stumbled out of the coffeehouse to merge with a river of humans shuffling across a canal bridge. Beyond the waterfront bustle, the alley doorways brimmed with young women under red lamplight, none of them bearing any resemblance to the shadowy image of pixelated Roos on her ex-lover's phone screen. Wes stopped to talk to a few of the Asian girls: a cute Japanese nurse in a skimpy lab coat, a tall Indonesian knockout with big breasts and braces, and a petite Filipina who looked too young for her profession. None who opened their doors to Wes and Lars knew of anyone named Roos.

"You'll never get any information out of them," Lars insisted. "I don't entirely trust the working girls of De Wallen."

"But you trust Kayla, don't you?" Wes asked.

At first, Lars let the question go unaddressed. But after a minute, he spoke, his affect flat. "I wouldn't live with someone I didn't trust. Kayla's window is her business, and my window, mine."

"There's no window where I work," Wes shared. "The scribing room is always stuffy with the smell of ink. You're lucky to have windows."

"I'd say you're lucky that you don't have one," Lars shot back. "A window makes you an easy target."

Wes checked his watch, untangling the gold timepiece from threaded *tzitzit* flowing from his pockets like spaghetti strands. "What makes me more of a target than anyone else?"

"Look at yourself," Lars said plainly, stopping to give Wes a once-over. "Amsterdam isn't what it used to be."

"I wear these clothes because they're appropriate for the occasion," Wes stated. "I'm scribing a Torah in a country that lost more Jews to the Holocaust than anywhere else in Western Europe."

"Some in my family were among them," Lars revealed. "Not everyone belongs in an Amsterdam window."

"Ain't that the truth," Wes concluded as they parted ways at the canal bridge. "See you back at the house."

It was a quarter past seven, the night still young as Wes itched with the hole burning in his pocket from Rabbi Cohen's fifty euro gift. Beyond the bridge, a string of red electric lights over doorways formed an illuminating filament on the rain-streaked sidewalk. Almost instantly, the rosy reflection guided Wes to Kayla's cabin windowfront.

"Now are you ready for me?" Kayla asked Wes, pouting through the plexiglass.

"I think I've been ready for you since the moment we met," Wes declared with calm confidence, hoping she could hear him from the other side of the doorway. "But if you're okay with it, could we do this back at the house?"

Kayla pulled the door open, leading Wes to the edge of her small cot. She took a seat at the bedside, daintily patting the spot beside her.

"Come on over, honey." Kayla put on an enticing voice. "I promise there's no bedbugs."

Wes winced, laying his hand on hers. "Just want to be sure you get to keep all the money."

With soft eyes, Kayla melted before him, staring as though interfacing with the Taj Mahal. "That's very kind of you. No one's ever looked out for me like that."

"This room feels a lot warmer than it looks from outside," Wes said, standing tensely beside the mattress as Kayla uncrossed her legs. "But maybe we can make it more special at home, up in the loft. You deserve flowers and candlelight. Something romantic. Something for you."

"Have you ever thought about taking me to bed, Wes?"

"Naturally." Wes swallowed, eyeing the sink and mirror next to the bed. "But I guess I never thought it would happen in a cramped little hole in the wall."

"With all the back rent I owe for this room," Kayla counted on her lace-gloved fingers. "Fifty euro's a drop in the bucket."

Slowly, Wes sat on the bed next to Kayla. With an arm around her waist, Wes looked at her with alert eyes. "I'll do whatever I can to help you."

Kayla sighed as she leaned against his shoulder. "It's a lot. I'd have to turn ten tricks a night just to put a dent in my debt."

"Okay, then," Wes replied. "How about if I pay you five hundred to spend the night with me. Your bed or mine, or a hotel room if you like. Anywhere but here."

"Let's say my bedroom in about an hour," Kayla proposed, flicking off the lights to her cabin. "I've got to go have a word with Roos."

"What?" Wes's jaw dropped. "I just heard that name for the first time today. Lars couldn't stop talking about her. You've seen her?"

"Look, don't say anything to Lars."

"But he's looking for Roos."

"And that's why I need to talk to her. Roos used to be the biggest draw in the entire Red Light District. She had a prime spot in the most picturesque windowfront overlooking the main canal. Now she's switched to a cabin in the silo, where there's less foot traffic."

"Do you mean that little indoor section of the District?"

"Yep. It's so drab and dreary, kind of like a haunted house. The silo is where sex workers go when they don't want to be so exposed."

"Lars and I did more than just talk about Roos," Wes confessed. "He asked me to help him find her. But I had no idea he was stalking her."

"And because of that, Roos is planning to sue him," Kayla said. "Her income has evaporated. In her old spot, there was always a line outside the door. Now she's barely making rent."

"Would you like me to come with you?" Wes offered.

Kayla smiled back as they dipped out the cabin door. "Yeah. Sounds good."

Wes and Kayla strolled into an alley gleaming with tightly-packed windows. Wes brushed his hand against Kayla's as they entered the District's most secluded section. Walking closely through the cobblestone alley, they passed the walls of women in their underwear. The long train of rose-colored tube lights dropped into a confined cave where the cabins looked more like cattle pens. A small mob of men barreled through the darkened space—a fishbowl, really, of pose-striking hookers—skimming radiant windows as though unraveling Matryoshka layers for a perfect little doll.

Kayla led Wes to the corner room where Roos stood sulking under red-hot lamplight. Seeing Kayla's wave and smile didn't brighten the disappointment on Roos's face. Instead, she sullenly swung open the door. The room was even smaller than Kayla's: a floor mattress and coat rack with a busted out washroom door exposing a toilet bowl.

"Hey, Roos. I know you're in a tough spot," Kayla sympathized. "But please don't press charges against Lars. We're trying our best just to keep the lights on in that house."

Roos fired up a skinny cigarette. "Do you have any idea what it's like to go from having all the clients to almost none?" As Roos complained, an angry glimmer sparked in her otherwise exhausted eyes.

"Go take back your old window in the heart of the District," Kayla encouraged Roos. "If anyone approaches your cabin, then just press your security button."

"I've already made a request for my old window on the main canal," Roos replied firmly. "If you don't make Lars disappear, then I will."

"Who's the guy with the shoulder bag hanging around the door?" Wes asked, glimpsing the sunglasses and bandana lurking between cabin brothels across the dim hallway.

"That's Hektor. He's coming for today's rent," Roos answered with urgency. "And I haven't seen a trick since this morning."

"Maybe we should be going," Kayla suggested, her fingers gracing the back of Wes's neck.

"Give me something," Roos demanded, holding out her hand toward them. "If Hektor sees that you were in here, he'll expect that we had sex for money."

"I'll give her something," Wes said to Kayla as he reached into his pocket.

"No." Kayla gripped Wes on the arm, shielding him from Roos's advances. "Don't give anything to this lying skank. She's trying to scam us."

"Whore!" Roos shouted, waving a white bone knife handle. "Get the fuck out of here!"

"Try not to hurt yourself," Kayla shot back as Roos nervously fumbled with the flipper.

Roos concealed the blade under her mattress, pulling herself together for a client lingering outside her door. Wes and Kayla went out, as an Italian man in a slick leather jacket came in. Romeo wore way too much cologne, but Roos didn't seem to mind.

"*Buena sera,*" he greeted her with a kiss on both cheeks.

"*Mi amor,*" Roos softly whispered into his ear.

Wes could hear them negotiate the terms of their arrangement.

"Five hundred euro," Roos offered the Italian. "You can have me the whole night."

"Wes, you need to have a talk with Lars," Kayla urged as they quickly returned to the bustling alley. "Make sure he gets the message."

Wes tapped his pants pocket for his cell phone. "I'll call him right now."

"No," Kayla cautioned him. "Never air out dirty laundry in the District."

"Lars is giving me an art lesson tomorrow afternoon. I can bring it up with him then."

"I'm counting on you," Kayla said expectantly to Wes, her pink-painted nails lingering softly on the underside of his wrist. "Because if Lars goes anywhere near Roos again, I just might have to kill him myself."

Young London millionaire Oliver Jarsdel stumbled through the front door of Vinnie's, a breakfast joint facing Centrum traffic. A boarding pass poked out from the pocket of his snug shirt, an awkward tell that he was fresh from Schiphol's international arrivals gate. At first, Wes couldn't believe it was him. Oliver looked a little shorter and a lot heavier than Harry, whom he resembled only in the glimmer of his icy blue eyes, a mirror to the ocean.

Oliver came to Amsterdam for his monthly fix of weed and women, or so Harry had briefed Wes over e-mail, along with a disclaimer: *a sexist remark or two is par for course,* Harry wrote of his cousin. As Wes and Oliver shook hands, Oliver nodded before unlatching his shoulder bag to pluck from it a file folder of official-looking immigration documents with twelve-starred circle letterheads. As a favor to Harry, Oliver had agreed to deliver the papers to Wes and later collect the signed documents after a long weekend in town.

Between mouthfuls of Eggs Benedict, Oliver raved about the latest strains to make waves in Amsterdam's perennially booming cannabis industry. When the server came with the check, Oliver flipped out a twenty to cover both their breakfasts. On the way out, Oliver suggested meeting up over the weekend and passed Wes a hotel business card.

126

"You can leave a message if I'm not around," Oliver said with a cold, distant grin. "Just so you know, when I'm in Amsterdam, it can get quite unpredictable."

"Sure." Wes reluctantly took the card. "I'll have the papers ready for you Monday morning before your flight."

Those papers would grant Wes Levine permission to make permanent his residence in Amsterdam, or anywhere else in the EU, notwithstanding how volatile his living situation had become. Back upstairs in the loft, Wes eagerly wanted to thumb through the documentation. He cracked open the file folder and got to work. But just as he began, he watched Kayla come out of her bedroom with a girl Wes recalled seeing under pink lamplight in the Red Light District.

"Hi, Wes. This is Toy." Kayla introduced her stunning counterpart.

"I, um, might have seen you somewhere," Wes stumbled on his words, instantly turned on by Toy's blonde-streaked, freeform locs and shimmering brown complexion.

"Toy used to work on the main drag," Kayla pointed out. "She's one of the most beautiful girls in all of Amsterdam, and now her window is in an alley with a lot less foot traffic."

"Oh, right," Wes uttered. "I may have passed your window last night with Lars."

"Yes," Toy said decisively. "You were with him, all right. And you'd better tell Lars that if he keeps stalking Roos, she'll get all her sisters in the union to kick down his door and teach him a lesson."

"Look," Wes returned defensively, pulling together his papers from the tabletop. "I'll have a talk with him, okay?"

"This morning, we met with the sex workers union," Kayla added. "Toy has agreed to give Roos back her old cabin."

"I'm making a sacrifice here," Toy spoke with a finger pointing to a long, stiletto heel on her boot. "It's to keep peace in Red Light District. Have a word with Lars, and do it soon, because this is the final warning."

"In a bit, I'll be heading downstairs for an art lesson with him," Wes assured Toy. "I won't leave without discussing this with Lars first."

"How can we be sure you'll do this?" Toy asked, inching closer to him. "I just want this to be over, Wes."

"I know, but all of this seems very passive aggressive," Wes replied. "Why can't you just approach him?"

"We've tried that already," Kayla responded. "You're a guy. We're thinking that maybe he'll listen to you."

"All right," Wes said swiftly, prepared to leave and get to it. "I'll do what I can."

Toy swayed closer, gently resting a finger across Wes's lips. "Are you sure you wanna do that right now?" she asked, her smirk as playful as her name.

"You see, Toy and I have a little idea," Kayla said as she inched closer to Wes, who was already feeling Toy's slender finger glide between his lips. "Would you like to fool around with us in bed first?"

Wes puffed his cheeks, blowing the air on Toy's finger. "As much as I'd love to do that, I just want to be sure we're all on the same page."

"I find you incredibly sexy," Toy stated. "We're good. You ever been with a Black girl before?"

"Yes. And you and Kayla are both goddesses," Wes declared as his blood ran hot. Smiling shyly, he dipped a hand into his pocket. "It's only fair if I pay you fifty each."

"Well, all right then," Kayla replied, her voice bouncing with satisfied sass. "It's not every day a client wants to pay more."

Kayla's dimly lit bedroom was a hippie shrine with its lava lamps on the dresser, a tie-dyed peace sign hanging over a small vanity, and a flower mandala tapestry blanketing the wall beside the bed. Wes settled on the queen mattress, a vast improvement from the slender cot in the brothel cabin. Kayla sat beside Wes and reached over to rub her hand against his already-hard crotch, and he grew further erect as she caressed him with smooth strokes. As they kissed on the lips, Toy climbed out of her knee-high boots. In a flash, she stripped naked at the footboard and crawled slowly to the center of the mattress. When she reached Wes, she bit him gently on the nape of his neck. Toy joined in, and Wes shuddered at the lips and the fingernails trailing down his sides.

The sex was so good—relaxing instead of exhilarating, the focus solely on pleasure and not possession—that Wes tumbled out the door without paying, his head spinning as he replayed the erotic encounter with Kayla and Toy in a nonstop loop of ecstasy.

Resting her head on a pillow, Toy plucked a plastic lighter from under the mattress to fire up a cigarette. "Forgetting something, baby?" she asked, her tone smooth and coy.

"Sorry. Yes. Of course." Wes turned around in the doorway and reached into his pocket. "And now that I'm feeling more chilled out, I'll try to talk some sense into Lars. He won't bother Roos again."

"And if he does," Toy mumbled, lighting up a cigarette, "The Amsterdam Sex Workers Union knows where he makes those pretty paintings."

Wes hopped back to his loft to change into a tie dye shirt and hemp pants before settling into a stool by the front window. Lars turned up with an Abstract Techniques textbook. Crouching on the hardwood floor, Lars stirred three gooey acrylics into a little tin can, swirling the colors with a popsicle stick to make an electric rainbow.

"How many colors does a scribe work with?" Lars asked.

"One," Wes answered. "Black."

Lars peeled open the drapes. "Try looking through the window. Look at the canal, the houseboats, the windows in brick homes on the other side of the water. Keep looking. Now, close your eyes."

"Okay. For how long?"

"As much time as you need to process it."

"I don't know," Wes said, still clenching his eyes. "I see that same canal every day."

"Keep them closed," Lars directed Wes from behind. A few minutes passed before he spoke again. "Okay, now open them. Tell me the first color that comes into your mind."

"Red?" Wes answered.

"Just that one color," Lars ordered, handing over a red palette. "Now make the canvas wet with a river."

While Wes wasn't looking, Lars had rearranged the gallery, clearing chairs and stools to make a more open, creative space. A blank canvas awaited Wes and his paintbrush. Lars dropped to his knees, and with an inviting glance, leaned on his side to paint a canvas of his own.

"Not sure if I can make a painting lying down," Wes doubted.

"Don't just make a painting," Lars suggested, a little too arrogantly. "Make an explosion."

Wes crouched beside the canvas, timidly touching the surface. "What if I make mistakes?"

Lars raised a finger in the air. "Look for the beauty in those imperfections. Celebrate them."

Wes, having never painted while in a yoga position, held the dry brush over the panel and prepared to read the blank canvas like Braille. With Lars watching from over his shoulder, Wes glided his fingers over the soft texture until he could feel it in his bones. Then, he dipped the brush and traced a blood red horizon with timid strokes. Eventually, the foundation would be uneven, and that seemed like the whole point of the exercise. With everything so freethinking and *laissez-faire* about abstract art and all its non-rules, Wes felt a culture shock without all the ancient laws to direct his every stroke on sacred parchment. Stretching on the hardwood floor like a child at play, Wes lit up with surprise when Lars praised his blotchy creation.

"Let this layer dry and come back to it later," Lars advised.

"Are you kidding me?" Wes said, genuinely shocked. "This is a piece of shit. I'm not coming back to it."

Lars didn't respond right away. "Try something different."

"This has been a welcome break from the precision of scribing a Torah. I appreciate that. But there's something more important that we need to talk about."

"What is it?"

"It's over between you and Roos," Wes declared. "You need to stop looking for her in the Red Light District. She doesn't want to be found."

"And how do you know that?" Lars popped off his stool, raising his voice as he spoke. "Did you see her?"

"She moved to a more hidden location." Wes paused to sift through his thoughts for what to say next. "And from what I understand, it's all because she's trying to avoid you."

Lars froze, the ghostly pallor of his face looking sicklier by the second. "I'm done now."

Wes shot him a perplexed look, unsure if Lars could even process anything in his near-catatonic state. "What do you mean by that?"

"Lesson's over," Lars responded coldly. "You can leave now."

"This is serious business, Lars. Roos has been missing out on a lot of clients, and if she doesn't sue you, she might send someone to hurt you."

Lars stared, listless and indifferent, through the window overlooking the Prinsengracht. "What did you just say to me?"

"Consider it a warning," Wes said, standing close enough to feel droplets of spittle when Lars turned toward him.

"You really should go now, Wes."

Wes raised a hand and backed off, but stood in the doorway, staring Lars down. "Seriously. Don't look for her again."

"Get out!" Lars shouted, tipping over his paint tin. Blood red paint smoothly seeped into the hardwood floor as Wes, stepping sideways, left the room.

On the morning of departure, Oliver waited for Wes at a table in the back at Vinnie's. He looked like a mug shot, dry and wrinkled beyond recognition with his prickled face weatherworn like an old tombstone. After living it up for a few days in the District, Wes figured that Oliver's brain had spent up all its happy chemicals.

"I think I'm done coming to Amsterdam, mate," Oliver wearily opened the conversation.

Wes set the folder on the breakfast table. "Rough weekend?"

"Bloody hell," Oliver griped, picking a fork at his half-eaten Dutch pancake. "The girls here will barely let you touch them. I might just take a cue from my cousin Harry and fly to Thailand. I've heard that's where the real whores are."

"I lived in Thailand," Wes responded defensively, waving off the server's offer of a menu. "What exactly do you mean by that?"

Oliver looked Wes up and down. "You know what the score is, mate. They'll let you do anything if you pay them."

"So, are you married, or do you just not wear your ring in Amsterdam?" Wes asked.

Oliver curled his lip. "No, mate."

"Then answer a question for me. Why would the old man make it so hard on Harry? You're both equals as far as I can see. I mean, you're not even married, and your dear great-granddad left you a big slice of his fortune, free and clear."

Oliver clenched a fist. "This ordeal has cost me some serious quid. Harry staged his so-called marriage to that random Thai bird just to conceal what everyone already knew."

"So, you're saying Harry should inherit nothing?"

"That stunt he pulled shaved a few million off my share. Now give me back those papers, mate, or I'll miss my train to the airport."

"Never mind." Wes snatched the folder from Oliver's reach. "I'll mail them myself."

On the way to the central post office, Wes considered tossing the application for European citizenship into at least three different bins. At the last moment, he sent it off anyway. Nothing was ever set in stone.

The tensions at the house prompted Wes to consult with Rabbi Rav Cohen, who agreed to keep an eye out for a fallback rental in the Jewish Quarter in case Lars lashed out again. Wes and Kayla began to deal with those tensions in the same bed, clinging tightly to one another as Lars wailed the nights away. The resident painter had turned the ground floor studio into a dark, demonic pit of aimless painting and hideous screaming. Wes and Kayla plotted various escapes over candlelight dinners and mindless strolls through Vondelpark at night. The prospect of moving into a refugee shelter in historic Haarlem was not taken off the table until Roos returned to her prime location on the city's busiest canal and was once again entertaining boisterous crowds in a cowgirl hat and short shorts. With that reclamation, peace seemed to swiftly return to the house on the Prinsengracht.

Meanwhile, Wes struggled to make peace with his grueling routine. Scribing the Torah far into every night except Friday, Wes worked himself sick and more than once nearly fell asleep in the Mikveh bath. And on most mornings, Wes crossed paths with a leather-clad faux mohawk in combat boots and a bomber jacket. On the street corner, between a synagogue and a senior residential building, Mohawk rattled something under his coat. A muscular powerhouse in pilot goggles waved a black leather gloved hand to greet Mohawk from across the street. Wes stared in disbelief at Muscles and Mohawk snickering as a metal pea clinked at the bottom of the spray paint can. Passing through the fence, Wes picked up on the grating slur of "kike," a word that gripped the air in his lungs. Inside, when he addressed it with Rav, the rabbi assured him that the Dutch word *kijk* had probably been an invitation to look at something.

"So, what was he telling his buddy to look at exactly?" Wes asked. "A synagogue fence that needs a swastika painted on it?"

"The epithet you're thinking of doesn't translate into Dutch. At least not directly," Rav explained. "I appreciate your sensibilities. But please don't worry too much. Our gate is secure."

Mohawk and Muscles stopped coming around the synagogue until later that week. Wes saw them spraying their cans on a nearby brick housing complex already tagged with scrawled graffiti. He sighed, afraid of what image would appear upon the building.

But their painting was an image of someone, a picture full of light and depth. First, Wes saw the wispy black hair, and then the innocent, inquisitive smile they'd replicated in color from a black and white photograph. From across the alley, Wes stared through the eyes of Anne Frank on the finished mural as Muscles pulled the goggles over his head.

"*Dat is heel mooi,*" Wes said, fighting back tears to witness the most famous Holocaust victim painted larger than life. "So beautiful."

"*Heel erg bedankt!*" Mohawk thanked Wes. "Fuck the Nazis."

The District kept red lights off until well into the afternoon, when bikini-clad girls started cropping up in doorways. In a dank smelling, smoked out alley, Wes happened upon Toy's cabin. Under the warm glow of her window lamplight, Toy tapped gently on the plexiglass to invite Wes inside. As Toy twirled a beachy blonde strand of her hair, she pressed her breasts against the window. Wes felt beads of sweat foaming on his brow. He wanted to proceed, but didn't. Toy's face sank in disappointment as Wes politely smiled and walked on. Things had been getting serious with Kayla, who, after five years in overcast Amsterdam, was now yearning to reconnect with some California sun.

On the other side of the old church tower, Wes cut a path away from all the brouhaha around the bars and brothels in favor of a calm, all-cobblestone street. The Nokia buzzed in his palm over a missed a call from the United Kingdom. Wes played the voicemail message twice to hear Harry ask in a muffled voice for the exact dates when Isaac and Malca Levine had departed Amsterdam in that secret ocean liner to Ellis Island.

"Hello, Harry?" Wes returned the call from the quiet street. "Your message sounded important, but I couldn't quite make out what you were saying."

"Are you sitting down right now?" Harry asked, slow and sobering enough to stop Wes in place.

"No, I'm not. Just strolling around town. What's going on?"

"This is a revelation, Wes. What I'm about to tell you may be quite moving."

"Tell me," Wes pressed on. "I can take it."

"Okay, here goes. Your grandparents, Isaac and Malca Levine, came to America on my Gramp's ocean liner."

"Get the fuck out of here," Wes replied in disbelief. "Don't even joke like that."

"This is no laughing matter, Wes."

"Does it sound like I'm laughing? I told you about my grandparents in confidence. But I never expected you to use it against me like a conniving prick."

"What? What are you going on about? Are you high?"

"Earlier I smoked a joint. Sometimes it makes me read into things."

"Look, I'm sorry. I warned you that it was important, but I didn't mean to ruin your day."

"Ruin my day? Harry, please tell me this is just a sick joke."

"When my dad told me that their names and birthdays matched the records in books Gramp kept on his old liner, I felt a connection to you. You have a right to know."

Wes felt his heart sink into his chest. "I don't know what to say. You're sure?"

"Malca and Isaac appeared to have registered for the voyage under the name Lewis, probably because it sounded more Christian than Levine. Dad found them in the travel book. It was the same liner, the only one Gramp had chartered in 1940."

"Sorry for being such an asshole," Wes said through a teary chuckle, as Harry's choking up on the phone confirmed the veracity of his story. "How did your gramp pull it off?"

"The old man apparently staged the whole journey as a dry shipment of iron ore."

"My Bubbie and Zayde used to say there was also a big glacier of manufactured ice on the ship," Wes recalled. "Once they were at sea, everyone grabbed shovels to haul what they could into the ocean before it melted in the sun."

"Wow," Harry responded. "That's amazing."

"Do you know if your gramp had helped anyone else escape?"

"Wish I could tell you, Wes. Many of those he intended to help ended up in the camps anyway."

"It just doesn't make sense," Wes stated unequivocally. "How could someone who saved people from the Nazis disown a member of his own family for being gay?"

"Apparently," Harry disclosed, sighing in regret. "Someone persuaded him shortly before he passed."

"Do you think Oliver had something to do with it?"

"My cousin is fine. Why would you say something like that?"

"Because he's playing you, Harry. Just so you know, I personally mailed the application to your dad's firm because of Oliver. When he was in Amsterdam, he said some vile things about you. Oliver complained to me that your inheritance somehow took something away from his share."

"What else did he say about me?" Harry asked in a soft undertone.

"Look, I cut him off as soon as he started talking shit," Wes said defensively. "I took the papers and left. Mailed 'em to your dad myself."

"Stop pussyfooting around," Harry raised his voice. "Tell me what Oliver said to you!"

137

"Okay," Wes returned, reluctant. "Oliver knows that your marriage to Wan is a sham."

"How lovely of you to phrase it in such a manner." Through the receiver, Wes could hear Harry grinding his teeth. "Tell me how you really feel about something that doesn't even concern you."

"I didn't mean it like that," Wes backpedaled. "Your marriage is your business, and I've got nothing but respect for what you've had to go through just to claim what's rightfully yours. But believe me, your cousin is not on your side."

"When were you planning to tell me all of this?" Harry asked. "Look, you had no way to know this, but the last couple of bank transfers to Wan's family in Thailand have been stalling. All money from Gramp's estate has been going through the same financial firm. It's likely that Oliver's been in the executor's ear again."

"Harry, I'm sorry for not calling you right away. I really didn't know all the tricks Oliver was potentially pulling. But for what it's worth, he's a snake that you need to watch."

"I've got to go," Harry said, clicking out of the call before Wes could say anything more.

Wes woke the next morning in a race against time to finish the Torah. Taking a bath in the mikveh an hour earlier than usual, Wes carved out a new quill sharpening routine, taking a thin blade to ten feathers per sitting. He scribed without interruption, no longer minding if a quill tip went dull or snapped off. Wes took no breaks except to count forty-two new lines in the *klaf* for every hour in the sofer room. The formula was working. But at the end of that daylong scribing bender, Wes had inhaled so much ink fume he could barely breathe through his nose. His cough rang loudly and uncontrollably through the drizzled, dampened Red Light District. He sneezed into his hands and shivered in the rain as a middle-aged man packed a bong under his oversized tee-shirt.

Wes then overheard the man say in passing to one of his travel buddies, "AIDS. He probably has it. They all do."

Wes was now working himself beyond exhaustion, while on both sides of the North Sea his support system crumbled. Rav had turned mum about consulting a lawyer to get Wes an extension on his stay in the European Union. And Harry had stopped answering his phone. Wes shuffled into the sofer room where Rav sat, hunching over the most recently scribed tract. The night before, Wes had grown delirious and only barely stopped himself from drooling on the parchment. With his eye fixed on a detective magnifying glass, the rabbi examined the Torah scroll, chanting in melodic, biblical Hebrew as he scanned the *klaf* from right to left and back again.

"You didn't lock up last night," Rav announced without looking up, his one functional eye zoomed in on a scripture letter. "Was anyone else here when you finished yesterday?"

"No, just me. Guess I lost track of the time." Wes stifled a yawn. "I've just been a little ambitious lately."

The rabbi lifted his head, resigning the magnifier to a desk drawer. "Well, I still have one good eye, Baruch Hashem."

"Thank God for that," Wes echoed the rabbi, bracing himself for criticism.

"And after spending a few hours this morning checking your recent scripts, I found nothing in need of repair."

"Really?" Wes said, concealing the corrective pumice stone he'd swiped from a drawer. "No mistakes?"

"Not one. You're quite ahead of schedule. I'm proud of you. And more than that, your bubbie and zayde would be, too."

Both men had tears in their eyes—the burned-out scribe who was falling apart and the empath rabbi who felt the pain for him.

"Why don't you take the rest of the week off?" Rav suggested.

"I'll be okay," Wes answered in a low voice, covering a forceful cough with the crook of his elbow.

"It's not even Hanukkah yet, and already you've finished the *parashah* for Passover."

"Thank you for your concern," Wes said. "I mean that sincerely. But I don't have a lot of time before the stamp on my passport expires. And I'm not even sure if I want to stay much longer in a city that my grandparents had to escape."

"I'll find a way to get you that extension for your passport," Rav offered. "My friend, Martin Greenberg, is an international lawyer who just flew into the Hague. He might be able to help."

"My dad's in Thailand," Wes revealed to the rabbi. "I don't know what he's doing over there, but he's there, in the same country where I have a teaching contract to fulfill."

"Okay. But let me know if you need a rest. There might be a contractor coming tomorrow to make some repairs in the main sanctuary, so the gate should be open when you get here."

Wes walked home in a stupor and dropped into bed. While the morning sun played upon the horizon, Wes, deeply fatigued, slept soundly at last.

He didn't hear Kayla or Lars, having likely dosed off when their late-night comings and goings would have rattled the temperamental floorboards. Wes finally woke, alone in the silent house. With the space all to himself, Wes exercised in the nude, humping the floor until his chest muscles burned and his heart rate now pumped for a taste of cardio. After pushups came reps of jumping jacks, and the floorboards creaked so loudly that Wes didn't notice Kayla walking up the stairs. Nearly naked in her work attire from the night before, Kayla beckoned with her eyes to summon Wes to come into her room.

They fooled around in Kayla's bed until she gasped and looked down. Her period had started. Wes looked down as well, his now-bloody appendage still thrusting in and out of her, and for a split second he worried that she was in pain.

"Huh. Well, my period came. Looks like I get a week off work," Kayla said, her tone casual as she pulled Wes deeply inside her. Wes shook with both pleasure and relief as they moaned and clutched one another, while trickles of blood gently stained the sheets beneath them.

Later, Wes arrived at a wide-open gate with an odd trail of red droplets staining the footpath to the big wooden doors of the synagogue. He shook his head, figuring someone had hired a sloppy contractor.

In the corridor, Wes nearly tripped over an open can of paint. He followed big boot tracks across the hall, where thumping and banging turned louder each step of the way. After days and weeks of slogging away, Wes wanted to break out of the stuffy sofer room, unable to fathom why this careless buffoon was urgently hacking at the doorknob with a flat hammer and chisel.

"What's going on?" Wes asked, tucking in the tassels of his sudra. "Do you have permission to be here?"

The large, bald man looked up for a moment and then scowled. He looked like a cold-hearted brawler, with thick, fleshy hands held perpetually as fists. His potbellied paunch bulged from the hem of his olive green tactical garb, cut two sizes too slim.

"Just stop what you're doing for a moment," Wes spoke above his usual voice. *"Wat doe je?"*

Baldy didn't respond to English or Dutch. He turned his back and banged harder and more hastily until the door handle broke off. At that second, Wes charged forward. He swiped the hammer by its barrel-like head, leaving only the chisel in Baldy's grip.

They brandished their wares like weapons in a duel, facing off for combat. But then Wes saw something that distracted him. He narrowed his eyes and took in a string of Dutch words, written in fresh red paint still bleeding into the wall.

The headlock came like a flash from behind, startling Wes back into the reality of his situation. Stuck in a chokehold, Wes resisted the chisel jabbing into the back of his shoulder like a hot poker.

"Hammer!" Baldy yelled, the veins in his neck bulging like tree roots.

Baldy pressed the blade harder upon Wes. Through his shirt, Wes felt the chisel breaking skin on his back. With his sharp fingernails clinging to Baldy's forearm, Wes wrestled his neck from Baldy's clutches, losing the sudra and catching his breath.

At least once a week, Rav had reminded Wes to keep his nails trim so that dirty particles wouldn't fall upon the Torah scroll. But out of habit, Wes decided to keep it raw and real, swearing off any personal grooming services at least until the finished scroll was home in the ark. The masters in Jerusalem probably didn't keep manicurists on speed dial, either. And though Wes enjoyed such frivolities on occasion in Bangkok, he'd resolved to scribe Torah in his most natural condition.

Baldy bitterly scanned the scratches on his own arm, staggering backward and colliding with the open can of red paint. Wes saw a shot and took it, lunging forward with all the might he could muster. As his knees buckled and the chisel slipped from his grasp,

Baldy kicked the paint can over and collapsed to the floor. But before Wes could retrieve his sky blue sudra, that cherished Judean shawl Aviva had gifted him, a red wave washed over the garment, staining it beyond recognition.

Blood-red paint trickled down the staircase, seeping to the front door. Wes stood back and watched in shock as myriad people flooded into the synagogue at once: the rabbi, the cops, the medical staff with a stretcher in tow.

Wes's hands were too caked in paint to touch a Torah any time soon. He handed the paint-stained hammer and chisel to one of the officers, who secured them in a big Ziploc bag.

"He was trying to break into the room where I'm writing a Torah," Wes told the Dutch *politieagenten,* two women and one man, all suited up in the same Velcro strapped emergency vests under buttoned navy jackets. "He had weapons. I hadn't thrown a fist in years."

"Yeah, and it shows," the young male cop snapped, reaching behind his belt to tinker with handcuffs. The women officers stepped between Wes and their fresh-faced male partner as the paramedics tended to Baldy, scooping him off the hardwood floor. Baldy stirred and snatched gauze out of the first responder's hand to pat the gash on his forehead.

"Joden aan het gas?" Wes sounded out Dutch words sprayed in red across the wall. *"Gaskamer?"*

"It says, 'Jews, go to the gas chamber,'" the rabbi emphasized. He shook his head sadly before steeling his expression. "Listen up," he continued, turning his attention to the cops. "I'm very close with the *burgemeester.* Our mayor already knows about the vandals who stalk the Jewish Quarter."

"Interesting that you have no injuries." The young copper confronted Wes directly while a medical squadron whisked Baldy out on a battlefield stretcher.

"He had me around the neck and almost drew blood with that chisel. I felt it pressing into my back. If I had said another word, he could have killed me. What other options did I have?" Wes asked, his voice weary and exasperated.

Young Copper flashed a toothy smile. "That hardly equates to assault. You had a weapon in each hand, and the other party has been seriously injured."

"The other party?" Rav said in disbelief as he surveyed the damage done to the structure of his temple. "Wes was defending himself and protecting our sanctuary. That's more than anything you've ever done for us. If charges are pressed against anyone at this synagogue, I'll see to it that the mayor defunds your department."

At that, Young Copper backed off as one of his partners folded up the police report. The other female officer passed Rav a business card, offering it like an apology for damages to the building. Baldy, gurgling and half-conscious, kicked at the stretcher handles as medics moved him through the courtyard and into the ambulance.

The two women officers followed him out, tracking red footprints to their scanner car. Before entering, they tied plastic bags around the soles of their boots. A blue light flashed and a siren blared as the driving officer accelerated the cruiser into the wind, leaving Wes Levine and Rav Cohen to face the devastation before them.

CHAPTER TWELVE

The rabbi and the scribe left the paint-tarred synagogue, walking their bicycles through the courtyard. In the Red Light District, the typical daily grind felt more like pandemonium. Canals brimmed over with a moody mob of pussy-chasing potheads slouching aimlessly among the suits and yarmulkes dashing through Gomorrah to make the next prayer service. On his Nokia screen, Wes scrolled into the calendar to count off the dates remaining on his tourist visa, and there were twelve: one day for each weekly *parashah* of Deuteronomy. Rav had enlisted the aid and counsel of his friend Martin Greenberg, an American attorney working on a case in the Hague.

"Isn't that where war criminals go to trial?" Wes asked the rabbi as they chained their bikes to a rack.

"Sure, when we're lucky enough to have that happen," Rav quipped.

"It was a close call," Wes said. "Had I come to the sofer room just a minute later, our Torah would've been drenched in paint."

Rav eyed Wes with a seemingly newfound admiration. "You're a Judean warrior," the rabbi dubbed the scribe.

"When I was a kid, some of my friends took Karate. But I trained with Masada at a massive training center back in Baltimore," Wes shared, lowering his head. "I'm not proud of myself for whacking that bozo on the head with a hammer, though."

"But think of what might have happened if you didn't," Rav pointed out.

"He had a crowbar," Wes recalled, clenching his red-stained fists. "It wasn't a fair fight to begin with. Still, that doesn't make me a warrior."

"Well, according to Jewish law," Rav began. "You were protecting a Torah, which has the same value as a human life."

"I hadn't thought of that. But what about Dutch law? That cop said I committed assault. Could they really charge me?"

"The mayor would never let those charges stand," Rav assured him as they entered an Amstel bar on the corner of a canal bridge. "If what happened today were to reach international media outlets, Amsterdam's tourism would take a big hit."

"I've only been living here for a short time." Wes gathered his thoughts. "But I kind of get the feeling that locals don't like the constant traffic."

"How do you feel about the tourists?" Rav asked, his tone warm and heartfelt.

"To be honest, it gets old dealing with the same boorish slobs. They're so predictable and such a pain in the ass. Smoke. Sex. Shroom. Eat. Sleep. Rinse. Repeat. Nonstop, no break. Seems like every week, we get yet another cavalcade of shitheads from Schiphol airport arriving by the trainload. Same in, same out."

Rav smiled, locking his bike around a post. "You're very quickly assimilating with the locals," he commented. "And you speak Dutch quite well. People here will respect you for that."

"What about the cops?" Wes asked.

"I've been living here for twenty years," Rav said. "Amsterdam cops have enough on their plate as it is."

"The young copper's tough talk worried me a little, that's all."

"Don't sweat it. Dutch officers sometimes like to show what they know about criminal proceedings. That doesn't mean their information is accurate, or that they're going to follow through with any threats they might make."

A man sitting at a corner table inside the bar stood to shake Rav's hand, and the handshake quickly turned into a hug. Apparently, they knew each other well.

A little reluctant, the rabbi's lawyer friend reached to shake Wes's paint-stained hand. "I'm Martin Greenberg. Don't worry, Wes. I've been informed about the situation, and I can assure you that frivolous lawsuits are uncommon on this side of the pond."

"Even though I was the one who hit him?" Wes asked. "Are you sure that counts as frivolous?"

"Loosen up a little," Greenberg replied, flicking the buttons on his Polo shirt to unveil a plume of dark chest hair. "Your rabbi is going to talk to some local officials, who will see to it that the neo-Nazi asshole vandal is charged with a hate crime. Why don't we focus instead on adding a few more weeks to your tourist visa?"

With each sip of beer, Greenberg seemed more and more confident that he'd get Wes an extension to stay longer: anywhere from two weeks to two months, depending on the immigration official's mood. Wes kept his plans to himself, perhaps doubting his own delusions of finishing the remaining one fifth of the Hebrew Bible in under two weeks. Wes stopped short of blurting out his intentions when he recalled Aviva's e-mail message cautioning against taking on more than one book per month; apparently, according to her words, trying to scribe Numbers or Deuteronomy in two weeks would be like suicide.

"I don't know if I even want an extension on my visa," Wes flatly told Greenberg. "Having a time limit is what keeps me motivated to do this until my fingers are too sore to hold a quill. But with more time to spare, I tend to procrastinate."

"Wes," Rav began wearily, setting his Amstel bottle on a coaster. "I appreciate your energy more than you'll ever know. But you really need to get a good night's rest. Maybe treat yourself to a manicure."

"Scribing is an ancient art," Wes pointed out. "I don't care what the more conservative *soferim* might say. It's an art. And I tend to create my best art when I'm in my natural state. Nails, hair, beard."

Rav and Greenberg stared in silence across the table at Wes, the haggard-looking scribe picking at his unclipped nails. Wes stared into his palm lines, still caked with red paint. "I've got to finish this Torah before my visa runs out. I have twelve days."

"That's your call," Rav said. "But I'd like to ask something of you."

"Sure, ask away."

"Will you please try doing something joyful tonight? Take a little time for yourself."

"I second what the rabbi is saying," Greenberg put in, wiping a spot of beer froth from his mustache. "Enjoy Amsterdam while you still can. Do something you wouldn't normally do in your hometown."

"I wouldn't normally eat crabs in Baltimore," Wes said sarcastically. "After all, that's what everyone in Baltimore does, including the tourists. So, I don't really feel the need to treat Amsterdam like I'm still a tourist. What do you want me to do, eat crabs here and call that 'enjoying Amsterdam?'"

Rav tapped Wes on the shoulder. "Come on. Are you feeling okay?"

"Just hear me out," Wes said, his voice growing jittery. "I don't want to eat crabs in Amsterdam, either. Not because they're not kosher, per se. But I simply don't want to eat them. What I really want is finish scribing that Torah. That's what no one else in Amsterdam is willing or able to do."

Greenberg raised his drink. "Well, amen. There's no harm in having a little fun. Now go get laid, maybe smoke some hash," he nonchalantly suggested to Wes, the words smoothly rolling off his tongue. "Just don't think too much!"

As Wes mumbled, "Yeah, right," under his breath, he watched as Greenberg checked the time on his cell phone. Then the attorney stood to say his goodbyes, leaving behind a half-full beer as he realized his returning train to Den Haag was now twenty minutes to departure. Wes retained his passport rather than giving it to Greenberg for processing.

"I don't want to bet against myself," Wes told Rav after Greenberg left. "Just entertaining the idea of getting an extension on my visa feels like I've already lost."

"All right," Rav replied acceptingly. "Let me know if you change your mind."

Rav and Wes walked their bikes across crowded canal bridges in the District, returning to a somber Jodenbreestraat where, in the desecrated sanctuary, they put their soiled hands together to rummage up a cleaning solution among cluttered wares in the custodial closet.

"This is something I never imagined doing as a rabbi," Rav said, dropping the bottle of orange

149

degreasing soap into Wes's bicycle basket. "Tell me, what makes you feel so driven to finish this Torah?"

"I don't know," Wes answered honestly. "There's nothing about the Bible that makes me want to put it in writing. It's difficult to believe that any of it is based on actual events."

"More than half the congregation would agree with you on that," Rav put in, calm and certain.

"It's getting late," Wes said. "The sooner I crash out, the sooner I can be back in the sofer room."

"You're the hardest working scribe I've ever seen. And so, in your honor, I'd like to make a significant contribution to a Jewish charity of your choice."

"That's really kind of you. But I must first ask—does the charity have to be Jewish?"

"Do you have something else in mind?"

"Yes," Wes answered as he mounted his bike. "My mom isn't Jewish. But she's been on her own for ten years, working day and night in the financial world. She took care of me through college, receiving no help from anyone. Half her family cut her off completely for marrying a Jew, and the other half threw it in her face when my dad left home. Even now that she has a decent-paying job, Mom's always trying to keep her head above water. I want to help people who are in her situation."

"Your mom doesn't have to be Jewish to be considered an honorary member of our family. After all, she had you. And, Wes, you are a part of the greatest story that's ever been written."

"So, what are you saying?" Wes asked.

"Please give me her mailing address," Rav said, plucking a Palm Pilot from his jacket pocket. "If you want to help people in your mother's situation, then I suggest starting with her. That will be my gift. Consider it done."

"Rav, are you sure?"

"Harry Jarsdel has been very generous to our shul, making it possible for us to hire you. I would like to give something back."

Wes looked at Rav with joyful disbelief. "I don't know what else to say. Thank you."

"Go take care of yourself," Rav whispered to Wes as they hugged. "We need you here."

Afternoon sank into evening as the brightest part of town saw a lion's share of the action. The yeasty, earthen aromas of baked bread and whole coffee beans melded with an array of other, sweeter scents. From across the dim sidewalk, Wes spotted a figure who seemed oddly familiar. He had to look twice before realizing it was Lars, overdressed in a scarf and pea coat. Holding a long, wrapped baguette against his shoulder, Lars walked across a stony path, bread in one hand and a silver bottle of Dutch gin in the other. Wes waved to Lars, a jerking motion that almost grazed a passing bicycle basket.

Lars focused his empty eyes forward as he shuffled across the street, aloof and alone. The newfound estrangement made Wes feel like an alien stuck living with an earthling who no longer recognized him. And despite Wes's waving and calling, the artist of the Prinsengracht walked on as though the last three months of communal living had never happened: the expense sharing and art lessons, the coffee mornings and the mushroom nights, the what's-mine-is-yours sentiment that had defined their lives until recently.

On the day before what would have been Zayde's ninety-fifth birthday, Wes finished scribing the final book of the Hebrew Bible. Without stopping for rest, he worked through the entire night, catching sporadic power naps on the couch of the synagogue's better-ventilated library. A crew of hired hands with heavy tools had hauled heavy gear into the worn, wooden sanctuary, their clunky devices blowing air as hot as Venus into stained walls and floors.

Wes stood in front of the desk with his arms folded, serious and scholarly, yet not knowing which way was up. As the last of the ink settled into the *klaf*, Rav entered the room with a group of five Yeshiva students—young, still-beardless boys in wide-brimmed, black woolen hats.

Wes hardly could remember the last time he'd looked in a mirror. But it didn't seem to matter. People he'd never met rushed into the crowded sofer room to greet him like a rock star. With every handshake, Wes endured a mild burn from blisters lining his palms. His growing fingernails now looked like claws on a feral creature.

Aviva had once told him what to expect when scribing up close for long stretches. The halos and headaches are temporary, she'd said to Wes on the day they met. But the *Sefer* Torah will last forever. Beside the desk, Rabbi Rav Cohen chanted with Wes the last of his scribed text. Wes then led the congregation outside, where two congregants had set up a table of Medjool dates, cubed cheese bites on toothpicks, and sliced challah loaves. Moms and dads had left work and let their kids take the day off school, pulling out every stop to witness the unveiling of a new bride, the sacred Torah scribed by the grandson of Holocaust escapees.

At eleven in the morning, they gathered around the buffet table in the garden. The congregation coalesced around the Torah, sipping red wine from plastic cups. Wes rested the scroll on his shoulder, at first surprised at how heavy it bore against his chest. The chanting in Dutch and Hebrew subsided, with all eyes now on Wes and Rav. The rabbi introduced the scribe as a hard-working American, someone who might've set the Guinness Record for the world's fastest-scribed Torah. The congregation laughed heartily. At that, Wes twisted out a gracious smile even as he struggled to keep awake. The joints in his arms and hands ached like someone twice his age, and as his eyes twitched, Wes stood before the congregation one blink away from a lucid dream. The long hours and sleepless nights had caught up to him. Wes didn't have a speech prepared when Rav prompted him to say a few words to Amsterdam's Jewish community.

"I only wish my grandparents could see this," Wes slowly began. "Isaac and Malca Levine, of blessed memory, were born in the North of Holland and the South of Italy. Bubbie and Zayde lived here in Amsterdam until 1940, when they left on a ship financed by a British executive named Alfred Jarsdel. By an unbelievable stroke of good fortune, I ended up meeting Alfred's great-grandson Harry in New Zealand, where his aunt, Linda Sorensen, is a rabbi with a pulpit. I almost decided to stay in Auckland to scribe a Torah there. But when Harry pointed to Amsterdam, I knew it was a chance to preserve the legacies of those who came before me. While I always knew I'd scribe a Torah in my grandparents' names, I had no preconceived notions of doing it here in Amsterdam. Through this port city, Bubbie and Zayde left the Netherlands to escape the fate that the bad actors of the world had planned for them. I wouldn't be here otherwise. Now, Isaac and Malca Levine will have a legacy in Amsterdam for generations to come.

"In my life, a lot has been taken a lot from me. My father disappeared when I was sixteen. From then on, it was just me and my mom. Then, Bubbie and Zayde died only a year apart. They had been married for fifty years. And while sitting shiva for Zayde, I remembered the Torah that he'd always asked me to write for him. In all those hours spent mindlessly penciling letters into my sketchbook, I never dreamed that one day, I'd be the only Hebrew scribe in the city where my grandparents had fled by boat at midnight."

Wes stopped speaking, realizing the tears in both his eyes and in those of the congregants. They nodded in appreciation, and Wes, bone-tired and emotional, knew that he had said the right thing to honor not only his grandparents, but Amsterdam's Jewish community as well.

The celebration spilled into the Jewish Quarter, the procession tightly passing through the street like a demonstration march. In the middle of it all, Wes bolstered the rolled-up Torah on two wooden poles. As they carried it into the heart of town, the congregation chanted joyful melodies in Hebrew, their voices ringing out for all to hear.

Back in the sanctuary, Rav and a few of the Yeshiva boys shuttered the Torah behind the wooden doors of its new home behind the bimah. Wes sighed, feeling the weight of history finally taken off his shoulders. The dream that died with Isaac Levine, now two-and-a-half years into World to Come, was safe inside of the ark at last.

When Wes was able to return home, he gazed at the curtained windows which lined the Prinsengracht canal. The entire neighborhood of narrow, brick townhouses, it seemed, had been early to turn out the lights. At his own home, sitting on the stoop, he found Toy resting with her head against her folded arms.

"You promised you were going to talk to him," Toy said slowly as Wes approached the front door. Her tone dripped with disappointment as Wes stared at her. In the time Wes had come to know Toy, he'd never seen her so crestfallen.

"I swear, I told Lars to stay away from Roos. Toy, what happened to your eye?"

"Earlier today, Lars showed up in the District and picked a fight with a trick who was in the middle of fucking Roos. He broke into her cabin. Things got ugly."

"Oh, no," Wes exhaled.

"When I saw Lars choking the trick in the alley, I stepped in to separate them, and another bitch came out and attacked us both."

"I'm sorry you got hurt. But I talked to Lars, I promise. I just wish I could've done more to help."

"Don't you get it?" Toy shot back, standing as though ready to strike him. "Lars is costing all of us a lot of money, and a lot of peace. I can't do my job looking like a battered wife."

"Just tell me what you want me to do," Wes said, extending his arms. "What can I do?"

Toy walked over to her bicycle, swiping it from the brick wall before straddling the saddle. She withheld a response until she'd peddled across the canal.

"If you'd really wanted to help, you would've talked some sense into your boy."

"I tried!" Wes exclaimed. "Now Lars acts like he doesn't even know me."

Toy shook her head. "This was the last straw," she told him, firm and final. *"Adieu."*

"Take care," Wes uttered to no one as Toy steered her bike over the paved brick road, too far away to hear him.

Wes sighed and turned his key into the front door. Kayla stood motionless in the foyer, her lips barely moving as she uttered two faint words.

"Lars," came her whisper. The next whisper took a moment longer. "Died." Somewhere in the city, a sad bell tolled on the hour.

"What?" Wes stared at her and then started to enter, but Kayla shook her head, the sudden motion so rapid and severe that he recoiled.

"You don't want to go in there," Kayla said, her voice quivering. She stepped outside, firming the entrance shut. "He's hanging from a rope. A rope. He's hanging. Dead, Wes. He's dead."

An unnerving siren wailed closer to the canal like eerie grace notes. First came the police van, detectives in latex gloves and medical facemasks charging through the already-open front door. In the studio, Wes took a brief and pained glimpse at the floor, at the now-lifeless Lars, his body contorted like a rag doll. Lars's pinkish cheeks and wide-open eyes almost endowed him with a hint of animation, one last tease that he might still be alive. But he wasn't, the medics declared as soon as their gloved hands detected no pulse on his wrist or neck.

Wes rushed to Kayla, holding her extra tight in his arms as they wept in a private corner. To the scene came two more detectives, grown men on their hands and knees examining the body outline they'd drawn with magic markers on the hardwood floor. The evidence, the detectives concluded, was in the plastic tins of spaceships and fire-breathing dragons found in Lars's recycle bin. When one of the detectives looked stunned as he counted out the magic mushroom tins, Wes wanted to assume some responsibility for the doses he'd eaten with Lars.

"For whatever it may be worth," Wes started, but Kayla shushed him before the confession could slip past his lips.

Kayla and Wes sat on a step at the bottom of the staircase, taking deep and heavy breaths where no one else could hear them. When Wes had last seen Lars, he'd acted like a total stranger as their paths crossed one last time. Just like that, Lars was gone. Lars, the free-thinking fashionista who could pull off any look. The abstract virtuoso who taught the inhibited scribe to loosen up and express himself in art without structure or expectations. It was still almost impossible to believe.

Lars had left a note, which Kayla plucked from the studio when she discovered the body. Before handing it over to the detectives for evidence, Wes read through the contents, still too frozen to process the hopeless desperation in Lars's last words to the world.

"All the signs were there." Wes broke the awkward silence as somber-looking medics rolled the gurney into the studio.

"I just can't believe our roommate is dead," Kayla sobbed.

"Toy warned me. She was here, you know. She'd taken a punch to the face." Wes recalled the bruise on her eye. "As a sex worker, do you ever feel at risk for violence?"

"All the time," Kayla said softly, and then gently tapped her blue jean pocket. "That's why I never leave home without my switchblade."

"Guess you never know what kind of clients you'll get."

"Clients?" Kayla scoffed. "Most of them are weaklings. I'm more worried about the other girls competing for tricks."

"You should do whatever makes you feel safe," Wes said.

"That's why I've decided to stop working in the Red Light District," Kayla shared as the stretcher carrying Lars came rolling out of the house under a white sheet. "It's all about the money, Wes. Money and nothing more. I can't live that way."

"Hopefully you enjoy your work a little," Wes added curiously, thinking about his first encounter with her. "Don't you?"

"Maybe a little," Kayla admitted. "Some guys have even paid extra if I let them go down on me. I once made five hundred euro just for peeing on a man. Sure, it's good money. But I just can't piss on a man for the rest of my life."

"In all labor there is dignity," Wes stated matter-of-factly. "But if you're going to stop working in the District in order to be safe, then that's what matters. And we can find another place."

"My stepdad owns a lot of hotels. L.A., San Fran, New York, and one right here in Amsterdam. We can move out of this place and stay for free."

Wes cringed at the sight of Lars's marker-drawn outline on the studio floor. "This place no longer feels like home, anyhow. Now it's more like a haunted house."

Kayla nodded, but then led Wes upstairs to her bedroom. "Let's spend just one more night here," she suggested, lighting up a full candelabra at the footboard.

The sirens sank into the sunset. Outside of the brick townhouse, Wes could hear the booze-soaked laughter as glass shattered. Just another batch of would-be hoodlums cutting loose on Amsterdam's cobbled canal side streets. But none of that commotion mattered much as Wes followed the candlelight trail like a map to Kayla's bed, a resting stop after the hell they'd endured.

Chapter Thirteen

"Did you read the entire letter?" Kayla asked Wes as she held an attendant candle across the eighth, terminal wick on a brass menorah. The footboard looked like a fireplace, and Wes balked at the constellation of flames surrounding the mattress like a standing army.

"It was a lot to take in," Wes answered from the bedside. "And Kayla, I am really not sure if I want to go to sleep on Candle Island here."

"Who says anything about sleeping?" Kayla whispered into his ear. "Let's stay up and try to remember the good times."

"All right," Wes agreed as they sat up to face one another. "But I just can't imagine what was going through his mind. He wrote down those final words and watched himself die. It seems so—helpless."

"Lars made choices," Kayla said. "Yes, he was our cute little landlord who kept to himself and painted every day in the window. But to Roos, he was a nightmare who wouldn't take 'no' for an answer. I think it's complicated, not helpless."

"Well, I guess this is the candlelight send-off Lars asked for in the note," Wes said to Kayla as they kissed, their looming shadows on the wall merging into one fluid shape.

Before moving to his uncle's canal house in the heart of Amsterdam, Lars had spent his youth in a northern fishing town. His family had a house in historic downtown Groningen, not far from the city's harbor, where houses every color of the rainbow had sparked Lars's early interest in art. At nineteen, Lars moved to Amsterdam with an older woman who'd picked him up when they met at an art exhibition. She provided him a studio space between a hair salon and a coffeeshop. But when passions fizzled and they parted ways, Lars's uncle offered to set him up with the canal house on the Prinsengracht. Now, that house would forever be haunted by Lars's untimely death.

From the bed, Kayla took measured steps through the candlelit maze. She tiptoed, an inch at a time, to not touch or tip over the flames at her feet.

"Before I put out the candles, tell the universe what you want," Kayla told him. "If it's to be, then it'll be."

"Wherever you are is where I want to be," Wes wished out loud.

"That's what I asked for too," she said as she swiped a brassy, antiquated-looking snuffer from the nightstand. "I'll put out the candles now."

By morning, an acrid smell lingered in the room. As Wes coughed into the pillow, Kayla stirred from bed to tiptoe around the blackened wicks and puddles of burned candle wax. Tattered, yellow police tape still clung in the doorway. Wes followed, looking to the curtained front window where he expected to glimpse Lars standing beside an easel with a paintbrush.

"What are you doing?" Wes asked Kayla when she locked up the door as they left. "He's in there."

Kayla looked at Wes, her eyes turning weepy. She touched Wes on his arm, as though tethering him to reality. Wes stared numbly into that vacant window where Lars no longer painted.

"Lars is gone." Kayla's voice cracked, guiding Wes through a stage of grief that she herself had already surpassed.

They crossed the canal by footbridge and followed a sweet, buttery aroma to an open-door café, an espresso bar with golden, glazed croissants rising in a front counter oven. Wes and Kayla sipped their cappuccinos and chatted like robots about the weather, attempting in public to pretend their lives were perfectly normal.

"Did you call your stepdad this morning?" Wes asked.

"We've got a room waiting for us at one of his partner's hotels," Kayla said. "The Renaissance. We can stay there until I run out of vouchers."

"I've been thinking about this, and I'm not sure if I want my old job back in Bangkok," Wes confessed. "I thought I did, but I'm not so sure now. At the company where I worked, Nazis outnumber Jews."

"Here's a thought," Kayla suggested, flicking at the rim of her espresso cup. "Do you want to come with me to California?"

"Yes," Wes quickly replied. "Which part?"

"I've got a little cottage way up in the canyons of Topanga. We can stay there for as long as we need to."

They leaned across the table. She kissed him first. Until now, Wes had not yet connected romance with Europe, where his grandparents had been denied a honeymoon and instead spent the first three years of their marriage in hiding.

"But Toy's in some trouble." Kayla kept her voice low among all the people in the café. "She's deeply in

161

debt. Some very shady people are looking for her. Toy is like a sister to me, and she's been marked."

From across the small table, Wes gave Kayla a perplexed look. "Marked how?"

"Marked for death," Kayla replied somberly. "So, I hooked her up with some vouchers for a room at the Renaissance. She's going to have to hide for a while."

"Then there's only one thing left to do," Wes proposed. "We'll take her to California with us, if she agrees to it."

Kayla sighed as she gave Wes a small, sweet smile. "I love you, Wes."

"I won't give up," Wes returned, looking into her eyes with conviction. "Because I love you, too."

Throughout the day, the canal house turned into another Central Station as cousins came over to claim whatever had belonged to Lars. Wes and Kayla gave thanks quietly that the landlord uncle drove off without asking for their late rent payment.

Strangers swooped like vultures to grab all the bits and pieces, skimming the gallery for paintings, the cupboards for dishes, the sofa cushions for loose cash. An ex-girlfriend helped herself to some of Lars's canvases while tending to a toddler strapped across her chest. The uncle apparently had sent a pair of burly moving men who spoke only Dutch as they boxed up the coffeemaker, the record player, even the plunger behind the toilet. The movers had also walked out with Wes's blotchy impression of the Prinsengracht, that last remaining artifact of his friendship with Lars, the teacher and abstract master. As Wes watched through the window at the house being emptied into a small truck parked along the water, he remembered the collection agents that cleaned out his childhood home before his dad skipped town.

The Nokia ringtone echoed in the empty gallery. The sound startled Wes, who quickly looked at the phone and found Harry's London phone number flashing on the screen.

"Hey, stranger," Wes said, clicking into the call. "What's going on?"

"Stanley Levine has been crossing the Cambodian border," Harry spoke plainly. "Every other fortnight, he picks up a new stamp on his passport at Siem Reap."

"That makes sense," Wes replied, turning his attention to the rapidly depleting battery bar blinking on his cell phone screen. "Without a visa to work, *farangs* usually exit the country every thirty days."

"Then catch him while you can," Harry returned, cold and firm. "He's on the move."

"Kayla and I are ready to leave Amsterdam," Wes said hesitantly. "For L.A."

The line went silent. "I see," Harry finally responded tersely.

"It's time for a fresh start," Wes said. "What's wrong? You don't seem happy about it."

"So, you think you can afford California on a teacher's salary?" Harry asked.

"Who says that's what I'll be doing there?" Wes shot back. "Besides, I'm sick of this overcast weather. I'm sick of the tourists. And I'm sick of the drama that's been going on."

"You know something, Wes? You're pissing away everything I'm trying to do for you."

Wes pulled the cell phone from his ear. "Look, I appreciate how you and your dad have helped me. But I came here to do what I needed to do. I don't want to go for a second citizenship. Why do you care so much, anyway?"

"At the fruit farm, you saved me from wasting a big chunk of my birthright. Now maybe I want to help you reclaim yours."

"That's kind of you. But this place isn't for me. It wasn't for my grandparents, either."

"Your grandparents left Europe in duress, not because they wanted to. Face it, Wes, you were never meant to be a Yank."

"Maybe I'll try again later."

"How much later? When America goes full-on fascist and closes its borders?"

"Come on, Harry. That's ridiculous," Wes sighed. "Besides, you didn't answer my calls for weeks. I worked day and night to finish scribing that Torah before my ninety-day tourist visa expired, when I should've had a whole year to do it."

"You would've had more time if only you'd lodged the application upon arriving in Amsterdam, as I'd advised you to do."

"I thought you were pissed that I mailed those documents to your dad without going through Oliver."

"It doesn't matter, Wes," Harry stated. "But my dad had to pull some strings to pinpoint Stanley's whereabouts in Asia. And now that you've found a piece of ass, you're giving up on him?"

"Harry, I'm sorry. But I've become close with someone who is not just a piece of ass, and we need to get the fuck out of dodge. Kayla and I are no longer safe in Amsterdam."

"Kayla and I," Harry said bitterly in his deep, Cockney accent. "As of late, seems like it's all been 'Kayla and I.'"

"If it's okay, Harry, I'd like to offer you a suggestion."

"Oh, please do," Harry replied sarcastically. "It's what I've been waiting for."

"I'm being serious. First thing I'd do is cut your cousin off completely. Oliver is a greedy bigot who convinced your gramp's lawyers to write you out of the will unless you were married, knowing full well that, as a gay man, you'd be out in the cold. Meanwhile, you're having all these problems transferring money to

Thailand. If you and Oliver use the same financial planner, I'd get a new one."

"I probably should have suspected Oliver all along," Harry conceded. "But Wes, come on. Are you sure you want to leave Amsterdam and waive your right to claiming citizenship?"

"Believe me, I'm sure," Wes answered. "That drama I mentioned earlier? Well, just last night, we found Lars dead in his art gallery with a rope around his neck."

"God, I'm sorry. What do you think made him do it?"

"Lately, there's been a lot of bad blood in the Red Light District. The writing is on the wall. We're no longer welcome here."

"Fine," Harry said, detached. "Go bugger off and enjoy all your phony cocksuckers in Hollywood."

"Are you feeling all right, buddy?" Wes asked, checking the screen as it blinked out on a dead battery.

After packing up his clothes, Wes crawled across the hardwood loft in search for his Nokia charger, thinking maybe someone in Lars's circle had repossessed that, too. He had to call Harry back. There was no way he could let their conversation end on that note.

Beside his bed, Kayla sat on the trunk suitcase, crossing her legs as she stared out the arched window. The comped room at the Renaissance Hotel awaited them. All they had to do was call for a ride. The rain and wind didn't favor dragging luggage across town, and it poured sideways into the canal, stirring the water. That morning, Wes and Kayla had cautiously worn flat shoes, but they tracked their wet footprints up the stairs when gathering their belongings.

Reaching behind the suitcase, Kayla pulled up the charger wire. She dangled the device like a hypnotist's pocket watch. Wes's eyes lit up as he swiped it from her, thanking her with a rushed kiss on the forehead.

"I'll be right back," Wes told her, springing for the closest wall socket to charge up his Nokia. "And I'll mop

165

up the trail of prints we dragged in. Is the bucket still on the second floor?"

"I think one of the cousins took it." Wes thought he heard Kayla say something about Lars's family from across the loft.

Wes pulled open the stairwell door, and he started to lose his footing on the wet step. On the second step, even slicker on his bare foot than the first, Wes fell forward. He slid and tumbled all the way down, clutching for the handrail in a furious panic without realizing it was too late to break his fall. The bottom stair collided with his leg, then ass, and then, his shoulders and head.

From upstairs, Wes thought he heard Kayla call his name, but he wasn't truly sure of anything. Never had Wes felt so banged up, and for good reason: he hadn't ever been this injured, as he'd been fortunate enough to have avoided a broken bone all his life. He ran a shaky, slightly bent finger over his teeth, finding no blood and nothing loose or missing.

Something sharp poked Wes below the knee on the inside of his trousers. From the base, the flight of stairs looked insurmountable, like a staggering mountain requiring special equipment to scale and climb. Alert one moment and woozy the next, Wes faintly heard Kayla calling him again from the top stair.

"Wes, are you okay?"

Wes watched in a slight stupor as Kayla descended one stair at a time, and he felt like an idiot for hurrying on those slick, steep steps. For not holding the rail, for not remembering his slippers, for not foreseeing an avoidable accident on moving day. For everything. When Kayla reached the bottom, Wes saw the horror on her face as she dialed one-one-two for an ambulance.

"I think his leg is broken," Kayla's voice wavered as she timidly touched the throbbing bump on Wes's forehead.

"Has the victim fallen in his home?" the operator asked, her voice echoing from the speakerphone.

"Yes. We were moving out, though, and he slipped," Kayla said rapidly into the receiver. "Please send help quickly."

An engine purred closer to the house as responders in neon jackets stormed the narrow stairwell. The medics grittily counted backwards. *"Drie, twee, één,"* the broad-shouldered Dutchmen grunted in unison, steadying Wes on a gurney. A yellow ambulance occupied the tiny, cobblestone walkway, the last barrier before the waters of the Prinsengracht canal. Like the other cars perched on the edge, the emergency vehicle looked close enough to tip into the canal.

The ambulance interior, a cluster of screens and tubes, afforded no room for Kayla, who pleaded with the medics to let her ride along. A medic close to the rear door shook his head, blurting out the name of the hospital as he pulled the ambulance doors shut. Wes hadn't heard of the facility, either, having never needed medical attention while abroad. Now a paramedic was securing a needle with clear tape on the inside of his elbow, and the sudden shock of it all made Wes gasp. Pain returned with a vengeance to his lower extremities. One look at his lopsided leg, and Wes turned to vomit into the plastic bin that another medic held on standby. After he finished and was properly positioned back on the gurney, his vision grew blurry as the medic pushed a fluid-filled syringe into the inserted needle and tubing in his arm. Liquid surged through the tube and into his vein, flooding Wes's body with instant relief.

"Waar is Kayla, mijn vriendje?" Wes mumbled to the paramedics, who didn't respond. "Please. My girlfriend."

During the ambulance ride, Wes drifted in and out of consciousness, waking slightly as they hauled him through the automatic doors of patient intake. Wes nearly vomited a second time when he looked down and saw the splint, a long, thick plastic shield holding his leg in place like a prosthetic.

"I'm George Washington," Wes joked to a steely-eyed technician in blue scrubs who didn't get it. He closed his eyes as the tech aimed a boxy, handheld X-ray generator at Wes's leg, pointing it like a gun. In a flash, the impression processed on a big screen. The bone looked curved and jagged like the California coastline.

"That's not what a leg should look like," Wes muttered weakly.

"I'm not the doctor," the young-looking tech began. "So, I'm not supposed to discuss a diagnosis with you. But I'd say the bottom of your leg is broken. Above the knee looks perfectly fine."

"When can I walk again?" Wes asked without getting a definitive answer. The tech's image grew hazy as Wes fell into another deep sleep.

Wes later woke to a man and woman in matching blue scrubs greeting him at the side of the upright hospital bed. The female nurse carried a shallow plastic basin with a sponge floating over soapy foam. She squeezed out the water, nodding to her counterpart as he scrubbed Wes. The sponge tingled underneath a thin, sanitary gown. At first, it felt strange, being this exposed, having his junk out in front of people he'd never seen before. A bristle on his thigh awakened his senses, and he clutched the exposed parts between his legs and apologized.

"It's all right," the nurse said, lowering her face mask. "Nothing we haven't seen before. We're just here to look after you."

"For a second there, I thought I just woke up on the set of a porno," Wes responded, his voice a jumbled blend of medication and hope.

"Well, it's great to see a patient getting their sense of humor back," the male nurse commented.

"How long was I out?"

"Only for a short bit," the male nurse reassured Wes. "You're on a morphine drip, so hopefully you're not feeling too much pain."

"I actually can't feel much of anything," Wes whispered, nervously eyeing the needle taped into the crook of his arm.

"Good. For right now, that's good. Your left leg was broken when you fell down the stairs."

"Will I walk again?"

The female nurse looked him over. "Yeah, you'll walk again. The question is when, and that's really for the doctor to answer."

"Please," Wes said. "Any ideas?"

"How old are you?"

"Twenty-five."

"Well, if you were student in Primary who took a fall on the playground, I'd say you'd be on your feet again in three to six weeks. For someone twice your age, the prognosis might be three months or longer," she said, staring into a chart on a plastic clipboard. "Your healing time is likely somewhere between the two."

"Is my right leg broken, too?" Wes asked.

"Not at all," the male nurse responded, pointing to another X-ray image on a computer screen overhead. "Your left shinbone suffered the most upon impact. This is called a tibial shaft fracture, which means that the injury has affected only parts of the leg below the knee."

"Am I going to need a wheelchair?" he asked, his voice cracking. Wes didn't have an issue with mobility devices, but thought about how he needed to leave town with Kayla and Toy as soon as possible.

"No, that won't be necessary. You'll have a much easier time getting around on a knee scooter until you're all healed up. But again, all of this will be up to your doctor." The female nurse gave Wes a small smile before rubbing her eyes. "Why don't you get a little more rest? After the doctor comes in, we'll show you how to use the scooter, and then, once you're cleared, you can go home. But for now, rest. It's good for you."

Wes took the advice as another stream of morphine hit his system, and he alternated between restless sleep and brief conversations with a rushed doctor who showed Wes how to use the knee scooter. It was a sleepy, shaky venture, and the overwhelmed doctor finally sighed and said, "You'll figure it out. In a few moments, I'll have one of the nurses bring in your discharge paperwork." Then the doctor left the room, never to be seen again.

As Wes struggled to saddle his way on the knee scooter, his arms trembling from lifting his body weight, Kayla rushed into the room and greeted him with a prayerlike bow. One of the nurses followed with a stack of papers and two small bags of pills for the pain, presenting both items to Kayla. Wes watched as she nodded, signed the paperwork on his behalf, and then, Kayla kissed Wes on the cheek and slowly helped guide him through the hospital doors.

Boarding the tram was made easier by a ramp. When they returned to the canal house, Wes looked up the staircase that had caused him so much pain and settled for the ground floor, which still smelled of paint and ashtrays. The stale air reminded him of Lars, always with his brushes and cigarettes.

Kayla walked in on Wes weeping into his palms when she returned with tasseled pillows to elevate his leg. She sat on the bedside of the old cot she'd moved from upstairs into the ground-level room, careful not to brush against Wes or his broken, cast-bound bone. As he knocked back another pain pill with Evian, Wes dosed off with Kayla running her fingers through strands of his hair.

"I really fucked things up," Wes whispered to Kayla. "We were just about ready to leave."

"It's okay," she replied. "We can stay at the hotel until you feel ready to fly."

"What's happening?" Wes asked, his voice shaky and out of touch. "Everyone is leaving town. It's like the canals are rising, and people are getting out of here while they still can."

"Sweetheart, this is Amsterdam," Kayla replied, her voice loving yet cynical. "There are always people leaving. They're called tourists."

Wes twisted out a half smile. "You know what's weird? Ever since the medic gave me that needle in the ambulance, I've been getting visions of a huge flood. What if Amsterdam becomes like Venice? You know, little boats, and no room for cars since the paved roads have all been washed over?"

Kayla looked down at her lap, cracking a pained smile as Wes felt himself drifting in and out of consciousness.

"Try not to worry too much about the future," she told him. "It'll get here soon enough."

Everyone did seem to be leaving all at once; even boathouses that during warmer months had lingered along the canal no longer docked on the Prinsengracht. The nearly emptied-out dwelling felt abandoned, too, hollow and exposed to the watching world treading along the walkway daily.

There was no getting Wes up the narrow, staggering steps, not while bound to a knee scooter. While Kayla went upstairs to the loft and collected Wes's belongings, he waited alone in the room where he and Lars took magic mushrooms and laughed the night away. How long had it been since they'd become friends? Time seemed unreal, like an abstract concept, and Wes shook his drug-addled head as he struggled to

171

sit up on the cot. It was all too much, too fast. Too much loss, too much fear, too much suffering.

Kayla came back with the heavy luggage, cursing Lars by name as she plodded slowly down the steps that broke Wes's leg. In their grief, Wes and Kayla went back and forth, almost never landing on the same page. It was now Kayla's turn to despise Lars, just as Wes was turning to marshmallow over days gone by.

As soon as his phone held a charge, Wes reached out to Rav Cohen, and the rabbi drew two volunteers from the congregation to haul the luggage into a van. Rav commissioned a driver named Ahmed, who shuttled Wes and Kayla to the Renaissance Hotel.

"I ask Allah," Ahmed called to Wes from the van's window, "the Lord of the Mighty Throne, to cure you."

"Thanks for the ride," Wes politely replied, his focus more on testing out his knee scooter on the hotel's brick and cobblestone sidewalk.

A world of visitors passed through the marble-floored reception area, an unseemly, walking conglomerate of stoners and businessmen. Wes and Kayla gave their full names to receptionists behind the front desk. And just like that, a bellhop with a brass cart was loading their luggage into the elevator and escorting them to the second-floor suite: a bed the size of a planet, a view of Amsterdam's busiest street, a bottle of wine with a welcome card attached. Wes swept his foot on the carpeted floor. On the smooth surface, he tested out the knee scooter, going corner to corner like a kid at a carnival. The medication was making him giddy now, and he laughed a bit as he rolled about. But he stopped in his tracks when Kayla came out of the bathroom wearing nothing more than a towel. Wes clenched the handlebars and listened for her words of wisdom.

"Whenever you're finished playing with that little scooter," Kayla spoke in a honeyed drawl as she dropped the towel and draped herself upon the California king mattress, "I've got another carpet I could roll out for you."

CHAPTER FOURTEEN

Kayla helped Wes hobble off the scooter and into the sheets. Then, the questions came all at once, like a wave crashing ashore to topple their sandcastle illusions of each other.

"What if I told you that I'm running from human traffickers?" Kayla asked him point blank.

For a moment, he couldn't muster a response. "Are you?" Wes asked, wondering if he'd imagined Kayla's words. "Does your family know?"

"They do," she answered frankly. "But none of them can help. They've got their own skeletons to deal with."

"Can you tell me more about the traffickers? I mean, who are they?"

"My stepfather had a business partner who introduced me to friends of his. Big money, big lifestyles. I mean, what could go wrong, right?"

Wes pulled off a forced, accepting smile as Kayla described sordid interactions with men three times her age.

"Did anything go wrong?" he finally asked.

"Not until I moved to Amsterdam," Kayla bluntly replied. "When I made my own way into the world, that really pissed off the wrong people. Some of them are still in my dad's orbit."

Wes turned on his side to face Kayla, their heads now resting firmly on one pillow as he looked into her eyes. "I promise you. We'll get out of here and start our lives over again. My grandparents did that in the middle of the war. Escape is in my blood."

"Don't you get it?" Kayla sighed and pushed away his hand. "Powerful people want me dead."

"Then it'll be you and me against the world," Wes spoke with a cocksure grin that turned Kayla's frown to a partial smile.

"By any chance, did you happen to major in martial arts?" she asked.

"In high school," Wes began. "I trained with Masada. Ex-military Israelis. But when I took a gap year and learned to scribe, I became more patient. Suddenly, I was brimming with all this empathy, but knew I wasn't going to be making the world any better with a quill in my hand. So, at university, I majored in liberal arts. Martial arts is in the past. Now I'm a lover, not a fighter."

Kayla locked eyes with Wes. "Cute," she commented coyly.

"I know you told me, but I forgot. What did you study at UCLA?" Wes returned the question.

"Anthropology and Environmental Science," Kayla answered. "Did you know that human beings are the only species in the entire animal kingdom to face each other during sex?"

Wes smirked. "Guess I never thought about it."

"And here we are at last," Kayla spoke across the pillow, fingering the notches on Wes's belt.

"But what about the traffickers?" Wes repeated as she blanketed his neck with ticklish kisses. "Didn't you want to talk about that first?"

Kayla's smile turned childlike, too playful for the question, and Wes wondered if she was simply trying to avoid her truth. But she giggled like a cute cartoon character as she slowly stripped Wes of his clothes. She tended to his legs, sliding a pillow underneath the broken one. After a good ten minutes of bouncing for a comfortable position, Wes and Kayla finally came together, belly to belly. Even as Kayla sucked him, her fingers trailing up and down the uninjured smoothness of his abdomen, Wes still rambled on about the human traffickers.

"Look, it's just that I care about you," Wes said, his voice tense as he wrestled with both pleasure and pain. "I want to know who's a threat to you."

Once Wes was hard, Kayla inched her way on top of him. "Baby," she whispered urgently. "Just shut up and fuck me already."

They didn't come out of their room for a few rainy days. All the sunshine in Amsterdam was in that hotel bed. Wes and Kayla fucked until fucking became more intense and powerful, turning the carnal act into more than just sex. They were making love, moaning with delight and toying with the notion of forever, refusing to leave the bed and ordering all their meals from room service until the squeaky little guy and his pushcart stopped showing up.

After that endless, overcast spell, Kayla turned back the curtain one morning to a warm, panoramic window. Across the street, the old, brick buildings glowed with the sun. Their hotel room smelled of sex, whiskey, and the charred stench of leftover filet mignon. Once outside, the fresh air tasted like heaven.

Wes glided into the bike lane as Kayla kept the pace beside him. They turned on Haarlemmerstraat, passing bakeries and espresso bars and the faint scent of what filled the display cases: oversized pastries, mountains of whipped cream, and colorful icings. After stopping for rest at a bench overlooking a narrow sluice, Wes stared at his reflection in the low water, wondering if a bigger body might someday refresh the canal, flooding all that lay in its path.

The long, cobbled walkway looked more similar as they ventured deeper into the shopping district. Wes and Kayla settled on an ordinary Central Amsterdam café, one of a thousand open-door joints with Belgian waffles and frosted donuts in a glass display.

"I was thinking about something," Wes suggested as they settled into seats far from the other customers. "How would you feel about going to Thailand before California?"

"Have you been able to get into touch with your dad?" Kayla asked.

"Not yet," Wes answered. "But he's definitely there."

"When I lived in Shanghai," she began, looking at Wes across the small, two seat table. "I was supposed to go to Thailand, but the trip got cancelled because of SARS."

"I remember that. My mom was begging me to come home. But I wasn't about to leave Asia. That's where English language classroom jobs grow on trees."

"They sure don't here," Kayla quipped. "But can we think about it?"

Wes smiled agreeably. "Sure. It could just be a quick stop in Thailand. We don't have to stay for too long."

"Glaciers in Antarctica are on the verge of collapsing," Kayla suddenly warned. "Sea levels are about to rise."

As his eyes sprung alive, Wes felt lines form across his forehead. "What? Where?"

"Vulnerable locations near water. Not all the way up here in Amsterdam, where Arctic melting poses its own threats. We're talking anywhere around the Equator and below."

Wes dry swallowed, shrinking back from the table to process what the changing climate meant for the world, as well as for *his* world.

"If we had to, we could just stay here," Wes replied. "My friend Harry, the one from London, will help me get European citizenship."

"But we don't have jobs in Amsterdam," Kayla reasoned. "Plus, sooner or later, my stepdad's hotel vouchers are going to hit a limit."

"Maybe we can ..." Wes paused, knowing that he was out of answers, and the world was closing in on them.

"Let's just go to Thailand," Kayla reconsidered, her voice hot with haste. "I've got enough traveler's checks to knock around for a few more months."

"Would you rather sleep on it?" Wes asked.

"No. We can do this," Kayla insisted with spirited poise. "Now why don't we book those flights to Bangkok before I overthink the climate crisis and change my mind."

"I know it's barely noon," Wes said, a little winded as he leaned on the handlebars. "But I could use a drink."

Kayla looked him over. "Are your pain meds helping at all?"

"I'm trying really hard not to take any more," Wes replied, wincing with discomfort. "Came this close to flushing the whole vial down the toilet. I don't want to get addicted to anything. My pain is mild, nothing a little whiskey can't handle. If I'm not taking the pills, I can take one shot."

Wes and Kayla returned to the hotel and settled on a table across from the bar dimmed under soft neon lights. Hotel guests passed through the lounge area. Kayla spotted Toy and pointed her out to Wes, and without a word, they both nodded. They approached

Toy as discreetly as possible as she sat alone at her cocktail table, head hanging low, no drink in sight. Kayla stopped short of an embrace, taking a cue from Toy that she didn't want to draw further attention.

"How are you holding up?" Kayla asked Toy.

"I haven't been outside of the hotel for over a week now," Toy replied distantly, eyeing a trio of young men in hoodies sipping cocktails on the other side of the bar.

"That sucks," Wes said.

"Not really," Toy shot back, tongue running across her front teeth. "I make more out of my hotel room than I ever did in the District."

"We're leaving for Thailand as soon as we can," Wes said, shifting the subject. "I've been thinking about your safety, and Kayla and I thought that maybe you could come with us."

"That's very sweet of you, Wes. And hey, look. I didn't mean to tell you off that day at the house like that. I'm sorry about Lars. Did he ..."

"It looked like it," Wes answered quickly. "He left a note, but the police didn't do a very thorough investigation. Kayla and I just didn't feel safe there anymore."

"How long are you staying in Thailand?" Toy asked.

"Maybe a few weeks," Kayla answered. "After that, we're off to L.A. And we could use an extra roommate if you'd like to come with us."

"I'll have to think about that," Toy said with a glimmer of hope in her eyes.

Wes grimaced uncomfortably, adjusting into the scooter saddle supporting his broken leg. He stared into his cocktail glass at ice cubes slowly melting into a watered-down bourbon puddle. Jack Daniels wasn't doing the job, and Wes had left his tablets in the room.

"I think I should go lie down for a while," Wes groaned. "My leg needs to be elevated."

179

Kayla bit her lip as she looked to Toy for approval. "I'll get him settled in bed, and then we'll go shop the flights. See you in the lobby in twenty?"

"Whenever you're ready," Toy said to Kayla, slipping her a plastic keycard. "Come get me on the fifth floor."

Back in their room, Kayla helped Wes off the scooter and stacked a few pillows around the broken leg. She tried turning on the television with a fickle remote control, but it didn't work. Exasperated, she left the remote on the bed with Wes. Then Kayla departed rapidly, her appointment with the travel agent a twenty-minute bicycle ride on the other side of the Central Station.

After she left, Wes settled further into bed and reached for a vial on the nightstand, knocking back a much-needed tablet for the pain before closing his eyes.

But his medicated sleep was stilted, broken by bad dreams and visions of people drowning in chaotic, crashing waters. Unable to truly sleep, he opened his eyes to Woody Woodpecker cackling away on a TV Wes didn't remember turning on.

"Kayla?" he called out. "Hello? Is someone here?"

No one answered. Then, Wes heard a noise by the door, and he froze. After a beep from the keycard reader, the door clicked opened, and Wes sighed with relief as Kayla entered the room. Nothing was wrong, Wes quickly realized, and he'd probably just rolled on the remote.

"Hey," he said as Kayla approached the bed. "How did it go?"

"We need to talk."

Wes felt sweat beads form on his forehead as Kayla reached for the remote and switched off the TV. As she held out the travel itinerary, her glassy eyes spoke volumes in pure radio silence. The party, as Wes knew it, was coming to an end.

"L.A?" Wes uttered the destination like a secret password.

Kayla nodded. "Toy didn't have a good feeling about Thailand. And the bird migrating patterns there are freaking me out. I don't want to go."

Wes stared quizzically at the blank TV screen. "Bird migrating patterns?"

"It's the first telltale sign of an environmental disaster."

Wes scratched his beard and sighed. "Okay."

"I'm serious about this, Wes. The seas are rising, and the answers are with the animals. As a region, Southeast Asia sees massive devastations in hundred year cycles. This could be the year when a major disaster strikes. You mentioned having visions of a flood. And I'm convinced that vision is connected to an historical pattern."

Wes swallowed hard, thinking about the dreams he'd just had. But he decided to keep them to himself. After all, the medication caused side effects. He couldn't rely on what he saw. "I can't predict the future." Wes began. "You know that. Why base your decision on something stupid I might have said when I was zonked out at the hospital?"

"Everyone has psychic abilities," Kayla replied. "Besides, you lived there for a year, so you're even more in tune with the weather patterns. Maybe, somehow, you know of what's to come."

"It's not like I'd be going back permanently," Wes replied. "Besides, Bangkok is far enough from anything coastal."

"Why do you have to go back to Thailand at all?"

"My dad needs to know what happened to his parents. Before they passed, I made them both a promise. He's still there, and I've got to find him."

"And I don't want to stand in your way," Kayla said softly, touching Wes on the wrist. "Toy's coming with me to L.A. When you decide to leave Thailand, you can stay at my place."

"Guess I'll try to be there as soon as I can," Wes replied, deflated.

"Pay attention to what animals do while you're in Thailand," Kayla advised him. "I'll pick you up at LAX whenever you can get there. That is, unless maybe you forget all about me and fall in love with a Thai girl first."

Wes blushed. "I doubt any Thai girl wants to get stuck with me and my elephant leg."

Kayla cracked a smile that quickly shrunk into a frown as she set an envelope of her travel itinerary on the nightstand. Looking downcast, Wes turned around in his scooter, knowing their time together was slipping away. He'd once been let down in a long-distance relationship. A border was one thing, but an ocean, another thing entirely.

Morning came. His Nokia buzzed between all the vials and bottles cluttered across the nightstand. Alone on that giant bed, Wes ran a hand across a crescent-shaped crease where Kayla once slept. Wes hazily recalled her saying something about taking the other bed in Toy's room, but the whole night seemed like a blur. To stay ahead of both his physical and emotional pain, Wes was popping pills and pounding booze in ever-shrinking intervals. Eight hours became six, which soon turned into four, and now, he was waking up just to knock back whatever awaited him on the nightstand.

"Good morning," Wes answered the vibrating phone that had rattled him from sleep.

"Wes, can you hear me?" Kayla's voice cracked in despair, the call echoing like she had rang him from inside a tunnel. "Wes. Listen to me. One of the traffickers is staying on Toy's floor."

Wes held the phone back from his ear. "Where are you right now?"

"I'm calling from Toy's room. We've been sheltering in place ever since he gave Toy a creepy look in the elevator."

"We should report to the authorities that a known human trafficker is staying at the hotel," Wes said. "Do you want me to make the call?"

"I'm not going to do that, Wes, and neither are you. He's one of my dad's business partners. Now I'm caught in the middle."

"Can I come see you in Toy's room?"

"Not for at least a couple hours. Toy's got a client who's on his way. I just want to be upfront with you because he might ask me to join in for more money."

Wes felt his heart pound like a hammer banging upon an anvil. "I understand," Wes said resignedly as the weight of the world sank into his chest. "I'll go kill some time at the bar."

"Even if I do something with someone else," Kayla told him. "I only truly love you."

Wes didn't answer, not right away, hesitating long enough that they disconnected on a terminal beep. He wished that she'd rang him from her cell instead of the room phone. Every call sounded open and exposed, timing out after five minutes of a strange background static interfering on the receiver.

"I guess," Wes spoke to the dial tone. "And I love you, too."

CHAPTER FIFTEEN

Wes steered the knee scooter across marbled tiles, the rubber tires screeching as another spasm struck his broken leg. Those bitter tablets he'd been prescribed for pain had turned his tongue into a stick of chalk. Rolling past the barstools of young women in form-fitting dresses, sipping their Cosmopolitans, Wes squeezed the handlebars to brake at the bartender's station and ordered a tequila neat.

"Oh, damn. Sorry," Wes said, patting his wallet pocket. "Left my drink vouchers on the second floor."

"Give me your room number," one of two bartenders suggested. "You can start a tab."

From the seat beside Wes's knee scooter, someone reached down to pass him a cocktail glass. "It's tequila," a man said. "I didn't drink from it. Go on, please. Take it."

Wes suspiciously looked at the golden hue, tequila straight, finding no fizz or visible traces of foreign particles. He held the drink to his lips, sipping it slowly.

"Don't worry," the stranger assured him. "I didn't put drugs in it or anything."

Flummoxed, Wes nearly forgot which leg was the broken one, and said *fuck it*.

"Come to think of it," Wes quipped, knocking the shot back. "I wouldn't mind if you did."

"Interesting choice. Do we happen to know each other from somewhere?" the older man asked.

Wes took a long, hard look at the silver-haired shaker in a slick suit, drawing a blank. "I might've seen you on TV."

"Probably not. I haven't been on a screen since Forrest Gump."

"Really?" Wes responded, at once animated. "I'm Wes Levine. What's your name?"

"Donnie Grabinsky," he answered. "But you won't find me in the credits. I was an extra."

"So, you've met Tom Hanks?" Wes asked.

"He wasn't in my scene. But it was my elbow, all right. How about that? I was in an Academy Award-winning film, and didn't even have to blow the director."

"Sure," Wes replied, awkward and breezy. "We have a comedian in the house."

"What state you from?" Donnie asked.

"Maryland."

Donnie stifled a shit-eating smirk. "You're Jewish, aren't you?"

"Yes," Wes answered. Masada Wes, the one that could hand someone their own Adam's apple if he was that kind of man. "Why do you ask?"

Donnie grunted, reaching for another cocktail glass. "You're a sensitive guy. And that's exactly how Kayla roped you in."

All the fire and pain in Wes's knee transferred to the space between his eyes. "Where are you from, exactly?"

"New York," Donnie responded firmly. "Most of my business is in California."

"And how do you know Kayla?"

"I don't know her personally. Her father is a former business partner of mine."

"Why former?"

Donnie grinned slyly, looking Wes up and down. "Well, you sure have a lot of questions."

"It's a legitimate one," Wes pressed. "What happened between you?"

Donnie sniffed his tequila without sipping. "He fucked me out of a lot of money."

"So, what's that have to do with Kayla?" Wes asked.

Donnie didn't answer. He downed his shot and signaled to the bartender for another round. "I'm here to help you, Wes. Trust me, I know how this business works. Kayla's setting you up to take the fall."

"The fall for what?"

"I'm afraid you'll hate me for telling you this," Donnie began, a forced expression of compassion streaking across his face. "But Kayla's selling you the California Dream. I'm sure you're aware that she's always got something to sell. I'm asking you to think carefully before putting your neck in a golden noose."

Wes recoiled from the barstools, backing up in a hurry. "You're really talking nonsense, and I'm leaving now. Out of my way."

"Hate to say I told you so," Donnie drawled. "Kayla's good for business, but she's not good for you. Trust me on this."

Wes turned his scooter around. "Look, just because we had drink together doesn't mean you know me."

Donnie cracked a toothy, conceited grin. "I'm doing you the biggest favor anyone will ever do for you, Wes. If you care about your life, you'll roll that scooter of yours as fast as you can in the other direction."

"What if I—" Wes's voice cracked, the tequila kicking in as his eyes burned with tears. "What if I really love her?"

"Then you have my condolences," Donnie offered emptily, passing Wes a highball glass, a darker whiskey on ice.

"What you're saying sounds ridiculous. Why would Kayla accuse her own boyfriend of trafficking?"

"Ha! Is that what she calls you?" Donnie stifled a cold, cryptic chuckle under his booze-soaked breath.

"Kayla and I are in love," Wes enunciated, trying to believe his own words. "So, I'm calling you on your bullshit, Donnie."

Donnie twisted out an indifferent smirk, raising his glass to toast. "Hey, buddy. It's your life. Here's to you. *Lah-chaim,* isn't that what you say?"

Holding the glass close to his chest, Wes clinked the untouched booze on the tabletop. He stared through the gold, foamy surface of his drink, downing it in a hurry.

"Thanks for the drinks," Wes said, backing away from the bar. "But when I want advice, I'll ask for it."

After retreating to the white leather deco sofas around the lobby's faux fireplace, Wes dialed for Kayla on all the numbers he knew. Then he rolled through the revolving front door, hoping Kayla or Toy might turn up.

The light breeze turned blustery as Wes scootered across the bumpy stone road to scour the bright, rose-tinted doorways of women working in backstreets around the hotel. A prescription vial poked out from his flannel shirt pocket. Wes knew that he looked like a wino, the straggling hair and caveman beard that hadn't seen water in days, but he had a hard time caring about that. Most of the working girls smiled and blew air kisses at Wes, who knew he wasn't going to find Kayla, not anywhere so exposed as these angels in lingerie. As a dim street turned into the Red Light District, the main canal's brothel cabins appeared to Wes like a light in the dark. Central Amsterdam only felt excessive when crowds flocked, which happened at least once every night. The alleys swelled with passers and Wes had to maneuver deftly on his scooter, going around them to scan the red-lighted windows.

"Hello, handsome," a blonde in lacy white leggings said through a cracked open door, looking straight at him. Her deep blue eyes held him captive. "Come in," she offered. "It's cold out."

"Hi, hello," Wes responded, overly polite. "I'm looking for my friend."

As she squeezed her boobs together, a nipple casually slipped out. She shrugged. "I can be your friend. Fifty euro, and I'll take my top off."

"I'm dealing with something urgent right now," Wes went on, turning the scooter around. "Stay warm."

"Stay warm?" she returned, rubbing her bare arms and looking at him with disdain as he steered out of the alley. "Fucking asshole," Wes could hear from the other side of a neon-lit window.

Rolling back through the hotel door, Wes cruised on the knee scooter that, by now, felt more like a natural extension of his leg. At the bar, Donnie Grabinsky sat between a group of women. Kayla's disappearance left Wes second-guessing the soundness of his own judgment; first, for falling in love with a sex worker and then seeking the advice of lecherous know-it-all. Wes scootered closer to Donnie's lair, hopeful that with women around him, he might not play like such a jerk.

"She's not picking up her phone," Wes said, calm and discreet. "Just thought you might have some insights."

"This doesn't take a crystal ball," Donnie replied from the barstool. "Have another drink and find someone new. It's not like she's the only girl in Amsterdam."

Before Wes could feel irritated by the comment, one of those women slipped from her barstool to greet Wes with a warm smile.

Wes responded with a shrug, shaking his head. "Thanks, but I'm not looking for any company right now."

As Wes steered in the other direction, Donnie stood before the scooter wheel. "Hey, buddy. I'll buy you a drink. Just let Kayla go."

Wes glared bitterly at Donnie, accepting the drink despite his instincts. As quickly as Donnie twiddled a finger at the bartender, Wes had a stiff vodka highball over ice. Wes knocked it back, thirsty for relief. The booze went straight to his inflamed knee, relieving the pain while the room spun around him like a dreidel. Losing balance, Wes nearly tipped off his scooter. Steadying himself with handlebars, Wes wiggled his way back to the saddle center, knowing without turning around to look that all eyes at the bar were watching his every wayward move.

Of the four women around Donnie, Yvette was the distant one. The brunette who spoke only French didn't put much into the banter. She stepped out of the group, offering to guide Wes to the closest elevator. On the brief lift to the second floor, Wes worried their path would cross with Kayla's as Yvette spoke sweetly to him in a language he'd studied in high school, revealing to him that in Paris, she worked as a nurse. His throbbing heartbeat went into double time as the elevator stopped. Yvette's soft brown eyes sparkled through long, lush lashes as she protectively stood in between the sliding doors, enabling Wes a safe path through. Yvette tousled back her hair and offered to come in and help him get situated in bed, and with only a moment of drunken reluctance, he agreed. On the third try, Wes opened the door with his malfunctioning keycard. Yvette turned the knob and pushed forward as Wes rammed his way into the room, everything hazy from the barrage of booze and pills in his system. She held his hand as he dismounted the scooter, their fingers still entwined as Wes retreated to the pillow. Yvette smiled warmly as her thumb traced circles on his palm.

"*Voulez vous coucher avec moi, ce soir?*" Yvette said, words Wes had heard somewhere before, and she placed her hand on his belt buckle.

"*Merci quand même,*" Wes thanked her, turning down her offer in the best French he could conjure. "*Tu es tres belle, mais j'ai une petite ami.*"

"*D'accord,*" Yvette spoke in a melodic tone, taking slow backward steps to the door.

After Yvette left, Wes reached for the vial of pills, helping himself to two more white tablets. All he needed, he thought, was to be knocked out cold. Just for a while.

Waking from his stupor, Wes first thought of Kayla. He called her name a few times, naively hoping she might emerge from the shower, or otherwise appear out of thin air. When no one came, Wes bounced on a pillow into never-never land. For an hour or two—or, for all he knew, it might've been a day or two—he sank into a deep, dreamless sleep, almost like being dead. He remained still with slumber until finally awakened from the silence by his Nokia's ringtone, which vibrated with urgency from beneath Kayla's vacant pillow.

"Kayla?" Wes groggily uttered into the receiver. "Is that you? Sorry I missed your calls. I was out of it."

"Are you in the room?" Kayla asked urgently. "Toy and I tried getting you on the room number."

"Can I come up and see you in Toy's room?"

"We're not there. I need you to bring me my passport. It's in the nightstand."

Wes pulled the drawer open, feeling through a stack of brochures for Kayla's travel documents. "Okay, got it. It's right here. When are you going to L.A.?"

"Toy and I want to take the train to Schiphol. We'll stay there until our flight," Kayla said. "We just don't feel safe in Centrum with a trafficker staying on Toy's floor here at the Renaissance."

"Who's the trafficker?" Wes asked urgently. "Can you give me his name?"

"I can't talk about this right now," Kayla said, her voice muffled. "You can stay on the second floor until you fly out to Bangkok next week."

"Maybe we could get a room together near the airport," Wes suggested. "Our bags are already packed."

"That's not a good idea," Kayla gently replied. "For your own safety, Wes, you should stay where you are."

Wes took her suggestion like a punch to the gut. "Tell me what's going on. Kayla, please."

"I'll be in front of Hekelveld Square in fifteen minutes. Me and Toy. She has her passport. Once I have mine, we'll be on our way."

"What about your luggage?" Wes asked. "I can send someone to bring it for you."

"Wes, I'm asking you to understand that I need space. When I get back to California, I'll call you, and we'll talk all about it. It's complicated right now. I can't get into too much detail. Toy and I will be a lot safer at the airport hotel."

Wes breathed deeply. "Kayla," he said on a sigh, "I love you."

"Sorry, I have to go," she whispered, clicking out as Wes spoke into the air, to no one. "Is it Grabinsky?"

Wes rolled to the elevator on one knee, rushing past the stoic bellhops in red Nutcracker suits. From the access ramp in front of the Renaissance, he inched across the street to stop at the brown brick Hotel Sint Nicolaas building. A chiming, Dam Square-bound tram glided on an overhead cable, the clenching brakes screeching lightly against the track as Wes swept his foot to cross the bike lane at Hekelveld. The main artery split at Sint Nicolaas into two streets.

"Hey," Kayla's voice echoed from somewhere on Spuistraat as nearby, another cable-bound tram chugged along the city's central artery, a precursor to the city's brightest bustle. The neon storefront signs of steakhouses and coffeeshops blazed a path into the heart of town.

"Kayla?"

"That was a close call." Wes could hear Toy's voice as he turned the scooter around, doing the best he could with the cobbled sliver of sidewalk, a tiny island beside whizzing traffic.

Wes embraced them both. "Just glad you're okay. I missed you."

"Thanks for bringing my passport," Kayla returned, touching Wes briefly on the wrist. "We've got to get out of here."

"Let's go to Central Station. Now," Wes suggested.

Kayla held an arm on the knee scooter. "I don't want to put you in danger, Wes. It's better if we're not seen together."

"I'll call Rabbi Cohen to send for a driver," Wes offered. "Ahmed can take you in a tinted van. No one would see you."

"Yeah," Toy supported the idea. "Better to take a van than the train. That would be cool of you."

Wes sent a text message to the rabbi, who promptly dispatched Ahmed to pick them up at Hekelveld Square. As they waited for the getaway ride, a motorcycle engine rattled from across the street.

"What do you want, Grabinsky?" Toy spoke over the growling engine. When Wes heard that name, his eyes shot straight up as he ignored the stabbing pain in his knee.

"I don't know," Donnie dumbly answered as he parked. His wrinkly, old eyes looked her up and down.

"I never been with a Black girl before. What do you say, Toy?"

Toy stared deadpan at Donnie Grabinsky. "What do I say. Huh, what *do* I say? I think the words would be 'go to hell, creep.'"

"Toy," Kayla whispered, her tone cautious as she positioned herself protectively in front of her friend.

Donnie cracked a conceited grin. "Suit yourself, ladies," he said, twisting the throttle to ride the bike lane to Central Station.

"Grabinsky. I knew it," Wes confessed to Kayla. "I saw him at the hotel bar. Strange man. He said horrible things to me."

"What exactly did he tell you?" Kayla asked.

Unconcerned, Wes shook his head and smiled. "None of it matters, really. It's not true."

"It *does* matter," Kayla said, pressing her palm against her forehead. "Wes, Grabinsky is the trafficker."

"The trafficker?" Wes asked, bewildered. "He told me he was one of your dad's business partners."

"Is that what he told you?"

"Don't worry, Kayla. I don't believe a word of it. Ahmed should be here any minute, and he'll take you wherever you want."

"I hope you didn't accept a drink from him," Kayla added. "It'll put you to sleep. He gives those pills out like Skittles and convinces you it's in your best interest to take whatever he offers."

"Last night, I slept really hard," Wes said. "Feels like I lost a whole day. I should have known."

"That's also what happens to women and girls who end up in his bed," Kayla put in. "You're lucky he didn't try to have his way with you."

"Hello, Kayla."

Wes jolted as he heard the voice, *that* voice. Donnie had returned, competing with the din of his motorcycle still purring on the street corner. "Hear me out. I can

193

look past the difficult business relationship I've had with your dad, and I'd be willing to cover your debts to anyone in the Red Light District."

On the cobbled sidewalk island in front of Sint Nicolaas and Centrum traffic, Donnie advanced closer to Kayla.

"We don't have any debt," Kayla told Donnie as his hands clasped her hips. "Take your hands off me!"

"Come on," Donnie grunted in her ear. "One night with me will solve all our problems."

"That's my girlfriend you're talking to," Wes warned, standing firm on his good leg.

Donnie looked Wes up and down, turning around to drag his cheek close to Kayla's. With Donnie breathing on her ear, Kayla reached into her back pocket, flipping open a switchblade. The steely, clinking sound alone was swift and sudden enough to send Donnie scampering back to his still-running motorcycle.

"Piss off!" She brandished the blade defiantly, ready to fight her attacker, as a pair of giant, black horses carrying uniformed men stopped at the corner. Smiling politely, Kayla quickly stuffed the illegal, spring-ready knife under her shirt. The hooves clacked leisurely on cobbled stone as the Friesians slowly passed them by.

Wes watched as Kayla held the concealed knife against her abdomen, feeling around for the elusive handle on the outside of her white cable knit sweater.

"I've got to get rid of it," Kayla spoke secretively to Wes and Toy, who both looked on in horror as she moved to cross into the bike lane.

"Kayla, careful," Toy said, and Kayla stepped into the path of a woman on a bicycle.

That woman happened to be a nurse, with a first aid kit sitting in her bicycle basket. Wes watched as though disconnected from his body as it all happened: the scream, the collision, the blade sliding up to puncture Kayla's side.

"What?" Kayla mumbled to the panicked nurse. "Why are you screaming? Nothing's wrong." And then, the knife tip fell out of her, and as Kayla glanced down, she began to sway.

The nurse guided Kayla back to the sidewalk, laying her flat to lift her sweater. As Kayla looked herself over and panicked, the nurse ordered Wes and Toy to shield her from any signs of trauma: her white Kashmir that was heavily blood-stained, the toppled bicycle, the onlookers with concern upon their faces. In the urgency of the moment, the nurse banged her first aid box against the curb, the medical supplies spilling to the sidewalk as she quickly patched the left side of Kayla's stomach with gauze and tape. One layer quelled the bleeding until more blood seeped through, and the nurse pressed a larger bandage upon Kayla's side.

"Call one-one-two!" Wes shouted at the dead-silent, statuesque pedestrians hovering around the horrific scene. "What are you waiting for? What's wrong with you? She needs an ambulance!"

One person stepped out of the dumbstruck throng, a purple-dreadlocked budtender working nearby at Resin Coffeeshop, who came forward with a cell phone. Ahmed turned up before the ambulance, and the nurse stayed around to hold Kayla on her way through the sliding door of the van.

"I guess you're wondering what I was doing with a knife under my shirt," Kayla said to the nurse, her voice faint and tremorous.

"I saw what happened," the nurse replied in a lilting brogue that sounded more Irish than Dutch. "I'd have pulled that knife on the pushy bastard, too."

Wes and Toy climbed into the van to coalesce around Kayla, helping her lay flat in the hatch.

"Thanks for fixin' me up," Kayla called to the nurse, who scoured the sidewalk for her belongings as the crowd dispersed.

"Are you okay?" Wes asked, fearing that Kayla didn't grasp the extent of her injury.

"It's just a scratch, Wes. A scratch. It's just a scratch," she repeated in childlike delirium until Wes was in tears.

Kayla walked herself out of the van, one hand on her bandaged side and the other clasping fingers with Wes. A stretcher became available at the front doors. A burly guard blocked them from the emergency room, where a squad of white coats gathered around Kayla under a celestial bright light. As the double doors swung shut, Wes and Toy trailed in the other direction to a room outside of patient intake. They sat for a few minutes in shock and silence.

"She's going to be okay," Toy said gently. "I've seen people survive worse stab wounds."

Wes covered his mouth, his eyes stinging with tears just as the leg pain started to taper off. "I can't believe this happened to Kayla."

"She was ready to leave it all behind and start over," Toy said as she plucked a pocket mirror to check the faded bruise under her eye. "The Red Light District is full of creepers. Clients are more generous in the comfort of my hotel room."

"Is that safe?" Wes asked. "I mean, what if one of them tried to do something you didn't want to do?"

"That only ever happened to me before I went self-employed," Toy answered. "The guys I take to my room are mostly hotel guests. They know not to step out of line."

"Kayla told me that Donnie Grabinsky was staying on your floor." Wes didn't know what he was digging for, but only knew the man was a vile, self-dealing scumbag.

"We avoided him most of the time," Toy recalled. "After bumping into him on the elevator, I stopped coming out of my room."

"Did Kayla feel threatened by him?" Wes whispered to Toy.

Without answering, Toy averted her focus to the swinging doors to urgent care, through which a seasoned medical practitioner with a stethoscope around his neck stepped somberly towards the magazine rack.

"I'm really starting to miss her," Wes said, his voice empty and desperate.

Toy looked at him strangely. "Miss who?"

"Kayla Hagen?" the doc called out.

Wes nearly hopped off his knee scooter. "Yes, we're with her," he replied eagerly.

Doc sighed through his nose. "I want you to know that we did everything we could to keep her comfortable. But Kayla's blood loss was significant enough to cause a hemorrhage, and her heart was unable to pump blood quickly enough. I'm so sorry, but she didn't make it."

Wes looked at the doctor like he was speaking Greek. "What?"

"Kayla died this afternoon at four-twenty."

"Four-twenty?" By now, Wes was as dazed and confused as ever.

"Yes. I'm so sorry. Take all the time you need to process what's happened, and please let us know if you have any questions," Doc said, patting Wes on the shoulder as Toy sank into tearful disbelief.

Wes stared numbly as a hospital attendant handed over a zipped plastic bag with Kayla's leather handbag, blood-stained even through the thick designer material.

"What did the doctors do to her?" Wes asked, slipping into a state of delirium. "She was so alive in the van. She was. You know she was!"

While Wes wept, Toy snagged Kayla's knife, still smeared in blood. A young-looking nurse in a sky-blue hijab nodded grimly, guiding Wes and Toy to a steel corridor, where they exited the hospital through an automatic doorway which looked as bright and airy as a heavenly gate.

"She might still have a chance," Wes whimpered, hopelessly in denial. "Right?"

Toy momentarily covered her eyes, unveiling a trail of mascara. "Honey, she's no longer with us."

Wes stared into the city skyline. "You mean the blood on that knife is Kayla's?"

"Kayla died, honey," Toy spoke with strength. "And now, we have to get out of here."

"I texted the driver," Wes said, pointing to the headlights of Ahmed's van rolling over cobbled stones.

Wearing a denim *thawb* hanging over his blue jeans, Ahmed told Wes that he had just returned from that day's Jummah prayers, where he petitioned to Allah for an outcome that was not to be.

Ahmed lifted Wes into the van, hauling the scooter into the hatch that still smelled of Kayla's perfume. At the dawn of winter, birches and elms that once sparkled with golden leaves now looked old and dead, with bare branches outstretched into bitter air and vacant space. Through the window, Wes glimpsed clusters of seasonal lights that replaced the last lingering traces of fall foliage. A towering Christmas tree overlayed the national monuments at Dam Square, casting a silver metallic light into the Amstel River's most trafficked plaza.

"I am very sorry," Ahmed offered his condolences as he steered to the cobblestone curb outside the Renaissance Hotel. "My prayers were not enough."

"I guess there was nothing the doctors could do to save her," Wes responded slowly, adjusting his broken leg across the backseat where Kayla had spent her final moments.

Toy ran her finger across Kayla's knife, tracing the now-dried blood that had caked into the blade. Pointing the knife, she traced Donnie Grabinsky's initials into the air. Ahmed flinched in the driver seat as Toy flashed the armadillo scale handle flecked with tiger spots, and kept glimpsing at her motions in the wide rearview mirror.

"Take good care," Ahmed finally said, his voice wavering with trepidation as they turned around at the revolving door entrance. "Revenge is not the answer."

"Every working woman in this town should carry protection," Toy replied from the sidewalk as she twirled the knife handle like a drumstick. "Kayla knew it, and I know it. I never leave home without it. After all, you never know what's gonna happen, now do you?"

CHAPTER SIXTEEN

Wobbling across the marbled lobby of the five-star hotel, Wes clenched the scooter handlebars to brake. As the sharp pain invaded his broken leg, Wes parked himself between two matching bellhops who didn't stir a muscle. Soon, the pills started doing their job, and he rolled past barely-breathing statues staring emptily on either side of him.

Wes didn't care if they saw his tears, but the aging luggage handlers had possibly been the only unfazed workers at the Renaissance. By now, most of the other hotel staff already knew what had happened to the guest on the second floor. The daughter of a hospitality industry giant who'd furnished hotel vouchers for her stay, an underemployed language instructor and occasional sex worker tragically taken down by a bicycle and a switchblade. Toy buried that blood-stained knife deeper into the clutter of her oversized leather handbag, retreating to the fireside sofa with her cell phone. She dialed out to cancel an appointment with an expectant client whose phone grumblings Wes could hear from across the lobby.

On the way to Toy's fifth floor room, a drowsy spell came upon Wes at once. His eyes fluttered as the meds kicked in. The last bitter-tasting tablet he'd swallowed zapped his energy, quelling the pain enough to facilitate sleep. They arrived in Toy's room, where Toy offered Wes one of the twin beds and sprang for the shower. Wes faded fast, drifting soundly to sleep as the water ran. When the bathroom door clicked open, he came alert to Toy in a bathrobe.

"Maybe we can get some fresh air?" she asked.

From bed, Wes grappled with a sharper new pain that had returned to his knee. With booze and pills failing him, he needed a shot of something stronger.

"Would you like to come with me to Vondelpark?" Wes asked, wiping the sweat from his brow as Toy looked him over.

"Are you sure you're feeling up to it?"

"I think I am."

"Vondelpark is sketchy as hell," Toy bluntly replied. "What's there, anyway?"

Wes shrugged, knowing full well that the park was a last-ditch resort, a flat-out cesspool of junkies and dealers who lacked connections to the high-quality dope in Amsterdam.

"Nothing really," Wes said. "I went with Kayla a few times, and felt like going back."

Toy teased the strings on the fleece robe belt, slowly stepping to the bedside. "Let's stay here tonight. I'll take care of your meds, and get you whatever you need."

Wes winced, trying to respond with a smile as all the flaring in his body rushed to the central joint of his broken leg. "That's very kind of you. Hope we'll see each other again."

Toy looked downcast. "I don't know," she said with doubt in her eyes. "In just a couple days, I'll be in L.A., and you'll be in Thailand. All we have is the here and now."

Those words sang to his soul, *the here and now,* ringing true like a sole kernel of truth in a Bible full of unbelievable bullshit. With his weary head nested on a pillow, Wes looked with one eye open at Toy, who tugged the knot on her fleece belt, opening the robe in slow motion as she bared herself to him.

"It's just the two of us here tonight," Toy whispered, inching her way to the bed. "Let's make love."

"I'd like that," Wes replied with unexpressed enthusiasm, woozy from the pain meds and delirious with grief, but still unable to deny that he was rock-hard at the sight of her.

Toy let the robe slip from her body. Since he'd broken his leg, Wes had been experiencing random, horny bouts that waxed and waned around the haphazard timing of his doses. This, Wes could tell, was one of those bouts.

With skilled, careful hands, Toy slowly relieved Wes of his clothes except the pants, which dangled from his broken knee. She banked his broken leg between piles of pillows and mounted him like a horse. Wes thought he saw a tasseled cowboy hat on the goddess riding him cowgirl, but was surer of the fireworks bursting over the bed as they finished, a sweaty mixture of pain and sorrow and pure need pushing them into overdrive.

Toy sighed gently, breathing sweet breath on Wes's neck as he cuddled his head between her comforting breasts. Before long, Wes was out cold.

He woke up drenched in sweat. In the other bed, Toy laid in her silky pajamas, waving a remote at the TV, tapping the batteries to make it work. Wes wanted to scream, but instead bit down on his lip. The pain meds had worn off again, leaving him to teeter on the edge of agony.

"I think I need a drink," Wes mumbled from bed. "Already took too many pills today."

"Just so you know," Toy said, flipping through channels. "My room doesn't have a minibar."

"To the lounge then?" Wes asked on a decisive hop into the knee-scooter saddle.

Toy slipped under the bedsheets. "I'm staying in tonight."

"Okay," Wes agreed, turning his head to the door. "Call me on my cell if you want to talk or whatever."

Toy smiled at him, kind and affirming. "We only slept together, Wes. I don't want to be anyone's keeper."

Wes fidgeted on the scooter as he rolled to the door. "I get that. I just thought that—"

"You don't have to tell me what you're doing or where you're going or who you're doing it with," Toy crashed into Wes's sentence. "If I'm still up when you get back, and if you're in the mood, then I'm all yours."

Wes cleared his throat again, deferring respectfully to the goddess offering another trip to paradise while his toes still curled over the first.

"Thank you for being so patient with my leg and all," Wes responded, a little bashful. "I didn't mean to just lay there the whole time."

Toy looked like she wanted to laugh. "You're thanking me? I enjoyed doing most of the work. My clients are usually all over me. It gets tiring."

"Understood. So, I'll see you after a drink," Wes inarticulately confirmed, second-guessing his way through the door.

"Just one, okay?" Toy cautioned, sitting at the bedside to look Wes in the eyes. "Remember, you're on medication."

"One drink. No more, no less." And Wes meant it. No going out to shoot dope in the park to escape the burning within, or hopping back into bed with Toy after getting loaded on the sly. Wes had taken his last dose hours ago; how many hours exactly, he couldn't say. His inflamed knee screamed out for more than another tablet, another miserable dose with that nasty, metallic aftertaste. A pill would wrestle down his pain, but a cocktail or two would deliver it a knockout punch.

Wes rolled into the lounge during last call, the bar now almost empty. A bartender sat in an unbuttoned tuxedo shirt with his eyes glued on a calculator at hand. Since the start of his stay at the hotel, a late-night gin and tonic had become Wes's regular fix. Something about the taste relaxed him just enough to catch some sleep, waking up to his knee burning like a hot coal.

From the other the end of the bar, Donnie Grabinsky turned up like a bad coin. He ordered grapefruit juice. The bartender dashed out of the kitchen with a big bottle of Ocean Spray and two highball glasses.

"Last call. Ten minutes," the bartender politely informed them, twisting off the cap in a hurry.

Donnie poured the juice and sipped from the rim. "Keeps me regular," he remarked, staring too much at the prescription vial sticking from Wes's shirt pocket. "You should try it sometime. Too many of those pills can give you real constipation."

"I don't want your drink, asshole," Wes stated, his jaw clenched and straining. "Kayla's gone."

"I heard. It's a terrible thing," Donnie mused, too whimsical and detached for authenticity. "All I can say is sorry for your loss. But if I remember correctly, I gave you condolences well in advance. You've just dodged a bullet."

"You just don't know when to shut up, do you? She was done with the Red Light District. We had a future together."

Donnie chuckled wryly. "How can you trust someone who makes money off her body?"

"Everybody makes money off their body," Wes shot back. "One way or another."

"Look, I know you're religious and all, but you can't possibly be that deluded," Donnie went on. "To think that one of these prostitutes would ever have a legitimate relationship with you."

"First of all, I'm not religious," Wes said. "And they're not prostitutes. They're sex workers, and they're human beings who deserve respect and dignity."

"You're being sensitive," Donnie concluded. "Nice quality, though. That's what made you an easy target for Kayla."

"You don't know the first thing about me," Wes shot back.

"Oh, is that right, Mister Torah?" Donnie asked, sipping his juice through a skinny straw.

"I don't know what you're talking about. What are you, a stalker?"

"Don't flatter yourself," Donnie answered, cocky and assured. "I don't stalk guys. I stalk girls. And I can introduce you to some great ones if you just let Kayla go."

"Let me tell you what happened to Kayla," Wes began with a steely glare. "If you hadn't crossed the street to harass her, she wouldn't have had to pull the knife. The knife that she stashes under her clothes to hide from the cops on their horses. And then comes the bicycle. This bicycle crashes into Kayla and she starts bleeding heavily. The woman on the bike happens be a nurse. So, the nurse stops the bleeding, but—"

"Why are you telling me this?" Donnie cut in. "Like it's supposed to mean something to me. She's gone, so do yourself a favor and start remembering to refer to her in the past tense."

Wes gripped the saddle, ready to deck him. "I thought the world of Kayla. We were out of here, ready to start over again in L.A."

"Smart move on her part, I'll give her that. L.A. is America's sex trafficking hub. What do you think she was planning to do, help you launch a movie career?"

Wes shot Donnie an indignant smirk. "Right before she got hurt, Kayla told me something about you. And you know what? I'm starting to think that it's your sex trafficking ring."

Donnie scoffed. "Yeah? Always with the quick mouths, you heebs."

Wes balled his fists. "What did you just call me?"

"She would've ruined your entire life," Donnie diverted, turning his back against the barstool with a finger in the air. "You should be thanking me."

"Kayla told me she was running from traffickers."

"And if you would've followed her to L.A., she would've turned on you in a New York minute."

"I don't get it. Why wouldn't she just expose whoever put her in this situation?"

"Because they are killers," Donnie blurted. "The only reason she chose you is because you're just a nice Jewish boy who wouldn't hurt a fly."

Wes inched closer on his knee-scooter. "I may be a nice Jewish boy. I take pride in that. But this nice Jewish boy could kill you with one hand."

Donnie shrank into his barstool. "Stop threatening me. I've got lawyers."

"You don't know who you're fucking with," Wes spoke, his voice calm and low.

"And you don't even know who you are. Who in their right mind tries to bond with a prostitute?" Donnie asked smarmily. "I only bring this to your attention because I like you."

"Those relationships develop organically," Wes asserted. "But every time I see you, you're always chasing after women. Maybe I don't have to stoop to your level."

Donnie stared down at Wes on the scooter. "All right. Let me ease your pain a bit. I propose an offer to you and Toy."

Wes rolled his eyes. "Yeah, and what's that?"

Donnie motioned a hand toward his pocket. "Ten thousand dollars for two hours. I want to watch you and Toy doing the nasty."

Wes cracked a disbelieving laugh. "Are you kidding me?"

"I have no qualms with Toy. She's not fond of me for whatever reason. But all I'm asking for is a seat in your room while you two do your thing."

"What makes you think Toy would be okay with that?"

"Ten thousand dollars is what makes it okay," Donnie declared, solemn like an oath. "You can take it or leave it."

"I need to get some air," Wes said, rolling on his scooter in reverse.

"Don't wait too long," Donnie called from the bar. "I'm back in New York the day after tomorrow."

Wes left the hotel feeling drained, when all he wanted was a drink and instead got Donnie Grabinsky. Alone on the scooter, he crossed the tracks for the nearest tram stop. A ramp lifted him aboard the cable-bound ride to the grassy side of town. Wes clung to a rail and people-watched: tourists smelling like a bong and residents toting briefcases and laptop bags, or maybe the other way around. Wes wondered if anyone else on the bus was going out to cop dope. A woman with two small kids looked on with suspicion as Wes checked his pocket for the spoon he'd swiped from the hotel dining room. Sure, it might also have been the knee scooter that raised eyebrows, with no one on board but Wes getting around on wheels, but he

207

considered it doubtful. He continued to watch through the window at passing traffic lights until the ride stopped at Vondelpark, when a platform lifted from the tram floor to drop Wes and his scooter into the dark of night.

Wes scoured for a spot under an acacia with wide branches and pointy leaves overhanging like a giant umbrella. Across the way stood a tree with bunches of leaves drooping to the ground, long and dreaded like hippie hair. Kayla's favorite spot in the park was Tulip Island, a tiny patch with a little crossing bridge and a gazebo banked by a flowerbed.

After sunset each night, out came the junkies in their thick, corduroy pants and oversized trench coats. Kayla used to converse with them in fluent Dutch as they tied off on park benches. She'd warned Wes *Nederlands te spreken in het park* so that gangsters within an earshot wouldn't pick up on the tourist tongue. While Toy had never been a fan of Vondelpark, Kayla was forever undeterred by the strung-out souls lingering around benches like zombies without origin or destination.

A man in a black leather topper approached Wes, keeping a distance on the curbside as he glanced and whispered, tapping a finger on the flap of his trench coat.

"Psst," the dealer hissed. "Coca? X? Horse?"

"Is jouw horse goed of niet?" Wes asked.

"Ja, het is goed," the dealer rattled off in Dutch, hopping out of the shadows with a tense dance move.

"Echt?" Wes replied.

"All good, man. This is Amsterdam. Go party. Go have a good time."

Wes slipped the dealer ten euro for a tiny, plastic fold of tightly-packed powder. The dealer took the money into a black-gloved hand. As he smiled, the dealer flashed a gold front tooth before vanishing into a shadowy street void of light.

At the hospital where Kayla spent her last hour, Wes had snagged a syringe from a barrel outside of patient intake. The loss was too sudden and unexpected not to throw Wes off course. Gripping that clinical syringe like a spike, Wes braced himself for something stronger than whatever the doctor had prescribed for his leg pain. He peeled back the plastic and tested the needlepoint against his skin, and prepared himself, both physically and emotionally, to begin.

Wes steadied a plastic Bic lighter under the spoon, doing his best to sanitize it. Stooped over the scooter handlebars, he unlatched his belt, pulling it around his arm to draw out the vein first pricked by the paramedic in the ambulance. Wes pointed the needle, like a weapon, at himself, his eyes wide with dread. As he twitched with anxiety, the syringe shook free from his hand and rolled on the ground. The fix had landed somewhere on the grass. Wes eased to his knees to crawl, scouring the harsh pavement with his hands.

A flashlight beamed straight into his face. Then it went dark again as the light-bringer turned the instrument on a plastic-handled bag. There, a second, taller officer plucked the fallen syringe from the cold, brittle patch of grass.

"I was just in the hospital," Wes said weakly, sitting on the sidewalk with a busted open splint.

"*Spreek jij Nederlands?*" asked the taller officer, his bushy brows arched fiercely at Wes.

"*Maar een beetje.* Very little. I broke my leg," Wes spoke loudly. "I'm in pain."

"*Pijn?*" returned the Dutch-speaking officer. "*Wat voor pijn heeft u?*"

"I broke my leg," Wes said once more, this time through gritted teeth. "And then, my girlfriend died at the hospital. My fucking leg feels like it's on fire. My fucking soul feels like it's on fire. How many more examples do you want?"

"We kunnen je helpen," the shorter officer returned, reaching into his neon green rain jacket to present Wes with a fresh, unopened syringe.

"I appreciate your concern," Wes uttered as a stunned apology. "But I don't need this."

"Take my hand," offered the English-speaking cop, clasping hands with Wes to steady him back on the knee scooter.

The officers assumed positions behind Wes, giving him support to stand while the knee scooter ascended through the rear of a white *politie* van. Upon reaching the Renaissance Hotel, they saw Wes out and propped up a little first aid station on the sidewalk.

"You don't have to do that," Wes told the taller, Dutch-speaking officer who wrapped the splint with medical-grade tape around his aching leg. "I can go to the clinic."

"Don't mention it," the partner responded, holding another factory-fresh syringe in hand.

"Are you sure you don't want it?" the officer asked.

"I've never taken drugs by needle before," Wes confessed. "It was just a stupid idea."

"This is much safer than getting something off the streets," the officer tending to his leg said, suddenly switching to English. "You can always change your mind, you know."

"Well, if you insist it's safer," Wes quipped, reaching for the plastic bag. "But the doctor at the hospital gave me a prescription."

"Glad to hear it. Have a safe rest of your evening, Mister Levine," the driving officer said. Wes saw the name Hoffman on his badge.

"How did you know my name?" Wes asked suspiciously.

"You scribed a Torah at *B'Nai Havurah Kehillah.* My son, Alex, is having his bar mitzvah there next month."

"Small world," Wes replied. "Mazel tov."

"Stay out of trouble." Hoffman winked from the driver's seat as they rolled out.

Wes steered the scooter to the nearest bin, dropping into the trash everything he'd spent the evening chasing: a fumbled needle, a painkilling opiate he'd scored at the park, a plastic-sealed syringe provided courtesy of the Amsterdam beat cops. Beyond the access ramp awaited an elder bellhop in a tight-cut suit with a tufty Santa Claus beard, who pulled the door open as Wes rolled through. With a hand to his forehead, Wes saluted the stoic-looking older man in matching gold threads and a red jacket, and then he made his way up to Toy's room.

As Toy slept in the darkened suite, Wes felt around the nightstand for his prescribed pain medication. A few doses remained, perhaps two or three pills clinking in the vial. In her bed, Toy stirred between the sheets as Wes drank from a water bottle, gulping every drop to mask the awful tasting tablet.

"Hey," Toy spoke softly from bed. "Did you have a drink at the bar?"

"No, I went to Vondelpark," Wes confessed into his pillow. "I'm not proud of it, but I was *this* close to injecting dope into my arm."

"Oh, no," Toy said, sitting frozen on her bedside. "Why would you do something like that?"

"I didn't have a drink at the bar. Grabinsky was there, and on top of that, my knee was on fire."

"Well, I'm glad you decided not to," Toy replied, flipping the switch on the lamp between the twin beds. "I had an uncle back in Chicago who died doing that shit."

"The needle kind of twitched and jumped out of my hand," Wes marveled. "Almost like a ghost stopped me from taking it that far."

Toy arched a brow. "Have you ever done heroin before?"

The question took Wes back to his college days, when he'd played guitar in a band that opened the show for someone big. Backstage at the club gig, he had a long chat with a roadie on tour with the headliners. At first Wes didn't buy the roadie's claim of only once shooting heroin and never picking it up thereafter. But after that night, the seed had been planted. Somewhere along the way, Wes aligned himself with the notion that he too might pull a similar feat, to chase the ultimate high but without any blowback: no sickness, starvation, rehab, or death. *Use once and discard,* Wes remembered the roadie telling him while they passed a joint in the parking lot. One little needlestick wasn't going to turn him into a wilted, carved pumpkin rotting back into the Earth with a pulpy, toothless orange smile.

"No, I've never used before," Wes answered after a long pause. "Guess I just wanted something for all the pain."

"Haven't you ever considered smoking some good, old-fashioned cannabis?" Toy asked. "After all, we are in Amsterdam."

"Yeah, I know. Hey, let's try Resin."

Toy looked wistfully through the window. "That's the coffeeshop next door to the hotel. That one guy who called one-one-two for Kayla works there."

"I won't be able get high for long," Wes stated, talking himself out of it. "In Asia, people get killed over that sort of thing."

"Then just stay in Amsterdam until the pain stops. We have open tickets. Let's stick around a while."

With that, they left for Resin, one of few coffeeshops still open after midnight. The ground-level tenement was connected to the Renaissance Hotel building, a piss dribble away from the Central Station's trains to everywhere.

"I heard about Kayla," the young, white budtender with purple locs said. "I only wish I'd acted sooner."

"You did everything you could," Wes shakily spoke from across the bar. "I still can't believe she's gone. I'll need something for more than the pain in my leg."

With two hand-held spheres between his palms, Bud funneled the grinded-down shake into rolling paper, twisting it up, and served the joint in a plastic cone.

"Don't charge them for this," Bud told the cashier.

"Two Chocomels, please." Toy ordered the drinks, bringing the bottles of Dutch Yoo-hoo into the bewildering ambience of Resin Coffeeshop's evergreen walls.

Wes took the first hit, stunned at how quickly it dialed down the pain in his bad leg. He passed the joint to Toy, who sat closely beside him. They went back and forth on the joint until Wes wrestled down his nerves and told her about Donnie's Grabinsky's offer.

"He's a racist and an anti-Semite," Toy said as she stubbed out the roach in an ashtray. "But how much is he offering us?"

"Ten grand."

"Let's do it." Toy leaned closer, her eyes smiling with mischief. "Come on. What do we have to lose?"

"I don't know," Wes replied halfheartedly. "Maybe our dignity?"

Toy laid a hand on Wes's leg. "Forget about dignity for a minute. Tell Grabinsky half the money upfront, and half after the deed is done."

"It's just weird. Why would anyone pay that much just to watch?"

Toy shook her head, unconcerned. "That's his fetish. Trust me, everybody has one."

"He just texted me back." Wes pointed to the message on his Nokia screen. "Would tomorrow work?"

"As long as he agrees with our terms," Toy spoke pointedly. "Getting ten grand to let some old creep watch me make love to my boo is too sweet and easy to pass up. But if he tries to do anything else, the deal's off."

They exchanged a few text messages; Donnie quickly agreed to all the terms and promptly turned up in Toy's room with an envelope in his hand. Toy counted out the American dollars, laying the cash in five neat stacks on the other twin bed. She dimmed the lights and helped Wes into bed, setting his taped-up splint over a pillow.

"Did you know that my room is across the hall from yours?" Donnie always sounded boastful when he spoke, but Wes found that statement especially unnerving. "After this, I've got more money in the safe that we can play around with."

"We're here to work," Toy flatly replied.

"Then do what I'm paying you to do. To start, I'd like all the lights on," Donnie insisted from the small window table. "For this kind of money, I expect to see as much as I can."

"Yes, sir," Toy said emptily, shrugging as she flipped a switch that turned the ceiling panel into a white-hot spotlight.

On the illuminated bed, Wes and Toy undressed each other with a deliberation and grace quite uncommon in the world's quick-fuck capital. One layer at a time, Wes and Toy turned naked before Donnie Grabinsky. They moved slowly in that twin bed, slow enough for Donnie to check his watch and grumble about the clock ticking away. Wes thought of Kayla and the threesome they'd enjoyed with Toy on one relaxing afternoon, a recent memory now fading like an ocean liner on the horizon.

"Let's take a moment and remember Kayla," Wes whispered to Toy as she finished undressing him. "I wish she somehow could be here with us, enjoying all of this."

214

Toy locked eyes with Wes, sneaking a skeptical glance at Donnie seated behind them with cross, impatient eyes. "Let's not discuss her right now."

With his arms wrapped around her waist, Wes kissed around Toy's nipples. "Let's show him what he needs to see."

Toy nodded, smiling blissfully as Wes puckered a trail of kisses down to her studded navel before going lower to slowly run his tongue along the inside of her thigh. As Toy arched her back, Wes moaned, aching desperately for release.

"Just try to last for two hours," Toy whispered as Wes slid his tongue inside of her. "Don't come too fast like horny teenager, okay, baby?"

"If you keep talking to me like that, I might not last two minutes," Wes said. "Agreed. Let's try to take it slow."

Donnie's frequent trips to the bathroom made it easier for Wes and Toy to get through two hours of kissing, touching, and lovemaking. At the two-hour mark, the Nokia alarm pulsed and beeped from the nightstand. Donnie stood up to clap, pattering his hands together with exaggerated restraint. He reached into his pocket, setting another fat cash envelope on the table.

"Here's the other five thou. Count it if you like," Donnie said, poker-faced.

"It's okay," Toy replied, scooping her lingerie from the floor. "Thank you for your generosity."

Donnie turned to Wes and snickered. "In the safe, there's an extra grand if you let me blow you."

"No," Wes answered bluntly. "I don't play that."

"Suit yourself." Donnie shrugged and lifted his jacket from the table. As he did so, Wes glimpsed a pistol handle sticking from a small holster.

"Holy shit," Wes uttered. "Where did you get that?" Wes wanted a reaction, and so he stared at Donnie, longing for some shred of truth or reason. But Donnie simply shrugged again.

"From the same guy that sells dope on the corner," he said. "This is Amsterdam. Everything here has a price on it."

"I'd appreciate it if you'd take that thing out of here," Wes stated. "Seriously. Now."

"Baby," Toy's voice wavered. "I'm calling the front desk."

"Don't worry." Donnie took a step back, removing the gun from the holster before securing the weapon against his temple. "There's only one bullet in the chamber. And it's for me."

Rising to his feet, Wes stood in front of Toy like a shield and felt the weight of the world collapse on his broken leg.

"Just let me blow my brains out in front of you," Donnie begged. "A final act to this fine night. Please."

"You don't have to do this," Wes pleaded from the floor, the seams on his splint coming undone.

"I don't want to go on living any longer," Donnie said, his voice flat. "But thank you both for giving me one of the most enjoyable nights of my life."

Wes eased back into his knee scooter, eye to eye with Donnie, who was now on his knees and poking the barrel against his lips. "I'm glad you enjoyed tonight. Now I'm asking you to please put down the gun and think it over. You only get one life."

"I've already wasted mine," Donnie mumbled, the statement solemn as though he was speaking his last words. "It's too late for me. There's no turning back."

"Donnie, don't do it!" Wes shouted to the sixty-something man with his thumb around the trigger.

As the door cracked open, Donnie slowly took the barrel from his mouth. A yellow housekeeping cart bumped against the door on the way in. The gun quickly went back into Donnie's jacket, and Toy sighed her relief.

"Hello, sir," a maid's soft-sounding voice seeped from the doorway. "I was cleaning your room and some police came in. They're looking to speak to you."

Donnie laid his jacket on the table, disowning the gun and vest. He closed his eyes, and Wes wondered if Donnie knew what was about to happen as the sudden chaos erupted all around them.

Europol agents swarmed the room, five or six navy blue windbreakers plowing past the housekeeping cart. Local Amsterdam officers bulletproofed in Velcro joined the party, sparing few words as they cleaned up. One of them swooped up Donnie's cash payments from the twin mattress and tabletop. An officer read Donnie Grabinsky his rights, in English with a thick Dutch accent.

With one Europol agent restraining each of his arms, Donnie relinquished autonomy to the handcuffs clinking on his wrists and the muscles standing behind him. The agents rapidly steered him out of Toy's room. Then, the officials vacated the suite as quickly as they had turned it into a crime scene.

An hour passed as Wes stood there on his knee scooter, letting the events sink in as Toy counted out the euro in her purse. Her face sank upon coming up short. "They could have let us keep the money," she said, throwing the purse onto the floor.

"It's blood money, anyway." Wes reached into his wallet pocket. "Do you need anything?"

"I'll be all right," Toy answered, flipping the TV remote. On the news station, reporters behind an anchor desk rattled off what Wes already knew: Donnie Grabinsky had been arrested on a long list of criminal charges, which now included possessing an illegal switchblade in a knife-free zone. As Toy clicked off the news, she apologized to Wes for not being upfront with him about slipping that blood-stained knife into Donnie's jacket while he was in the bathroom.

"I would have done the same thing myself," Wes summed up. "If Donnie hadn't approached Kayla that day on the street, she'd still be alive."

"And that's what keeps me up at night," Toy said. "While Donnie Grabinsky was here in this room, I saw my shot, and I took it."

"I'm glad you did. But there's one more thing I'd like to do for Kayla before we leave," Wes said as he plucked a packet from the nightstand drawer.

"Tulip bulbs?"

"They're from the hotel gift basket. If it's okay, can we plant them in Vondelpark?"

Toy eyed him with curious suspicion. "Is it your pain again?"

"No," Wes answered. "I don't want drugs. I just want to do this one last thing for Kayla."

"Whatever you like," Toy returned. "But I want to stay in tonight."

Wes reached beside the bed for a knob-handled cane. A more manageable pain in his leg lingered, with a Charlie Chaplin cane now taking the place of the knee scooter.

"I think I can handle it."

The tram cruised to the Vondelpark stop, an unusually quiet ride for Friday. At the park where they fell in love speaking Dutch under gazebos and acacia trees, Wes resigned the bulbs into the ground where tulips would bloom come spring. He looked lost and out of place, with thick, Ray Charles sunglasses worn at night, and a walking stick for balance and support. Wearing shades in the black of night, Wes let the tears run their course, knowing it would have been impossible to stop them.

On the slow, hobbled walk back to the tram stop, Wes tapped his walking stick around gleaming puddles of rain, those small, broken mirrors casting their crooked reflections. Though Wes thought he saw Kayla's image on that cobblestone sidewalk, he knew that she was gone.

And when he returned to Toy's fifth floor room, he found a hand-written note scrawled on the back side of a fancy, folded room service card:

Hey Wes! I went to a hotel by the airport. An old client called and wanted to see me tonight. You'll be in the sky by the time I get back to the room. It was fun getting to know you. I'll always cherish those memories of the times we shared. XOXO, Toy.

CHAPTER SEVENTEEN

A rare stitch of December sunlight seeped through the half-drawn hotel curtains of the hotel room. Those piercing rays prompted Wes, on the morning of his departure, to turn the blinds shut. The landline rang, again and again, as Wes hopped back to the nightstand. He picked up the call halfway into ring number five or six, gasping on hello.

"Just thought you could use a wake-up call," Toy said cheerily. "How's your leg?"

"Good, thanks. Better," Wes replied. "I think I'm finally done with the scooter."

"When you leave, don't check out of the room," Toy clarified. "Just leave the spare key card under the phone. I'll be coming back tonight."

"Okay. My flight leaves this afternoon."

"Aww," Toy cooed, just sweetly enough for Wes to feel pangs of longing. "You know where to find me."

Wes smiled. "Maybe in L.A., we could catch a Lakers game some time."

"I'll always be a Bulls fan," Toy declared with a light laugh. "Chicago in the house!"

"If you save me a seat next to you," Wes began, pausing to think of something clever. "I'll root for whoever you like."

"You don't have to do that," Toy replied, her tone turning serious. "My door's always open."

"So is mine. Take good care of yourself, Toy."

"Love you, baby," Toy said to Wes, making him smile once again before she clicked out of his life.

With one hand on the top grip of the Chaplin cane, Wes dragged the wheeled suitcase through the lobby, where a trio of bellhops scurried to assist him. The much-older men in red Nutcracker suits trailed Wes on the sidewalk, seeing him off at the train station. The cozy aromas of rising bread and fresh espresso grinds followed Wes from the hotel's cobbled walkway to the ticket counter at *Centraal.*

The train ride to the airport put the gabled brick houses in rewind. Through wide, panoramic windows, Wes watched Central Amsterdam fade from view as the historic cityscape gave way to newer, taller buildings. When the train glided to a stop at the gates of Schiphol International, the sliding doors opened quickly, as though urgently ushering him to keep going despite the recent tragedies he had survived. With passengers pouring in from all directions, Wes trudged his way to the departures queue, never more ready to hand off his clunky trunk suitcase in exchange for a boarding pass.

The woman behind the counter who took his bags smiled at him the whole time, and she was stunningly gorgeous—dirty blonde hair slightly covering her dark, thickly-lashed almond eyes, with a tiny mole accenting her full, rose red lips—and Wes, in no position to start a romance but unable to resist her beauty, decided to woo her by voicing his opposition to the Iraq War.

"My family is always in grave danger," she replied, her finger landing firmly on her lapel flag pin. Wes recognized the tri-color stripes and stretching red triangle from a banner on the wall at Zayin's Kebab Shack.

"And I stand with Palestine," Wes said as the boarding pass changed hands. As the next passenger approached the counter with a luggage cart, she smiled demurely, dismissing him. Wes shuffled to the next station, queuing briefly at customs, which hadn't held him up too much, he thought. After all, he had nothing left to declare.

The plane landed in the balmy breeze of a Bangkok sunrise illuminating the runway at Don Muang Airport. Beyond the aircraft, palm trees swayed in the sweet, unthreatening heat of the Thai capital in mild December.

On the other side of a barrier gate, a handsome Harry Jarsdel stood out among a thick mob of loud, wily Thai drivers hustling their services. Wes edged around the commotion, waving away the big mouths shouting fixed rates for taxis without meters. Wes waded through the suits and signs to get to Harry. When he finally was able to approach him, they hugged, and the mob of drivers got the message to back off.

Harry wheeled the suitcase into the back of his massive utility vehicle, a buffer against fleets of yellow taxis howling for the business of disoriented arrivals getting their bearings in a new tropical heaven. Wes had never been so grateful for a safe ride with a familiar friend.

Beyond the highway gleamed a skyscraper horizon, gold-tinted like an open treasure chest. For Wes, the city had changed in the six months he was away. The air smelled sweeter, somehow less sooty than the hotter seasons. As Harry steered off a highway exit, he pointed out the window at a row of abandoned food carts that once belonged to street chefs who'd since boarded buses bound for provinces upcountry, returning to the rice fields from whence they'd came.

Harry's ride rumbled like a tank into Khao San Road, formerly one of Bangkok's biggest rice markets turned backpacker ghetto. Harry maneuvered the boxy utility vehicle between the standing market umbrellas, double-parking it on the curbside of vendor tables still covered in tarps. At a guesthouse with a neon "No Vacancies" sign, a girl behind the counter looked a little young for the job, but sounded like a grown-up when she congratulated Wes for having snapped up the last ground floor suite.

"So," Wes said to Harry. "Are you going to back to London?"

"Not for a while," Harry replied, helping Wes lift the suitcase through the hatch. "I'm helping Wan's parents set up a business in Buriram. Hope it'll bring more revenue into the province."

"Let's not become strangers," Wes said as they hugged once again. "You're one hell of an Englishman, Harry. It's an honor to know you."

"When you're settled and feeling up to it, let's go scuba diving in Phuket," Harry suggested. "Word on the wire is that's where your old man has been hiding out."

"Foo-kit?" Wes mispronounced. "And he's supposed to be hiding out there?"

"From what I've heard, anyhow."

"That makes sense," Wes added. "As a kid, I went scuba diving with my dad a couple times. That was his thing, really."

"Beautiful island," Harry said. "I'll be in Thailand for just a few more weeks."

"Take care of yourself, Harry."

"I always do. Let's chat soon, Wes."

"Thanks again for the ride," Wes said as they shook hands.

Harry climbed back into driver's seat, and steered past a fleet of bicycle taxis parked in the morning sun. The touristy strip stirred to life as a rider revved up a motorcycle that spewed exhaust fumes at the sidewalk cooks toiling with tongs over crackling oil. The vehicles parked along the curb rattled a collective saber, roaring back as Harry's ride rolled in the other direction. Something about the SUV on the street seemed to piss off some of the locals.

Wes retreated to the sparse, monastic quarters. The tiny suite was a mattress in a box, a single bed under a squeaky ceiling fan. A cockroach squirmed out of a hole in the corner, flitting across the dusty floor as a green Tokay gecko scaled the wall. The little lizard slithered outside through the barred window. Wes watched, more curious than distressed, allowing a meditative minute to pass before dozing off.

He woke up sweaty, oblivious to time. The humid, uncirculated air in the room felt hotter inside than out. Wes knew he had to take a walk, to breathe and stretch his legs.

On a walk down the road, Wes happened upon a barber pole. Behind the window, a hairdresser swept up clippings beside his swiveling hydraulic chair. The barber only spoke Thai and laughed for no apparent reason as Wes came in and took an empty seat. He kept laughing as he snipped Wes's tufts with little scissors. Then, with precise, gentle scrapes, the barber took off the little curls with an open razor, straight-edged like those Wes used when sharpening his scribing quills in Amsterdam. But now, that seemed like it had happened so long ago. Standing beardless and clean before the mirror, Wes finally could see the angles of his own face.

After the shave, Wes cut through a narrow alley back to Khao San, feeling the cool breeze on his exposed facial skin. The road had turned into a sea of people flooding in from every direction. Wes spotted more than a few Star of David necklaces as they charged through the crowd like bulls, an entourage of young Israelis cutting loose in Bangkok after their military service. Still favoring his good leg as he limped into a tourist district teeming with slow-strolling guys and girls in tank tops and three-quarter shorts, Wes kept his head down. No one on the street looked a day over thirty, and despite his own youth, he still felt a bit old and weatherworn.

Khao San was a dead-end in the search for his now sixty-year-old father. Feeling a temporary sense of defeat, Wes went back to his room to rest in bed, the buzz of a persistent fly taunting him during an attempted nap. Wes then felt another buzz, but this time, it came from his front pants pocket. On an incoming call, Sao's name flashed on the Nokia screen.

"Hello, *sawasdee-khap*," Wes opened the call on a diplomatic note. By habit, he answered his calls in two languages.

"Welcome back to Thailand. I just got your e-mail about Amsterdam."

"It was quite an experience."

"When I went to university in France," Sao began, piquing Wes's interest as she paused. "My mates and I took the train into Amsterdam to blow off steam after exams."

"I miss Amsterdam already. I couldn't stay, but I miss it. There was a Jewish community, which I've never found here in Bangkok."

"Funny timing, then," Sao laughed. "I was just about to ask you if you'd like to meet me at the coffee shop at the new Jewish Community Center downtown."

"There's a J.C.C.?" Wes asked. "In Bangkok?"

"It opened soon after you went to New Zealand. Tell the taxi driver to take you to Siam Square, and I'll meet you there."

"What brought you to the J.C.C.?" Wes asked.

225

"I've been taking Hebrew classes. After you showed me your sketchbook, that became my focus. Now, thanks to you, I'm seriously thinking about becoming a scribe."

"Wow," Wes replied, admiring the student who would potentially follow his own path. "I'm speechless. Mazel tov."

"Thanks. I'll call you when I get to the square downtown."

Wes arrived early. Straight off the bus, he bought a little box of facial towels for ten baht from a wizened, haunching old woman peddling wares from a plastic blanket outside of the *Mahboonkrong* shopping mall. He patted down his sweaty forehead with tissues that turned to mush upon contact. Wes then found a bench and took a seat in front of the downtown bustle, the air thick from car exhaust and charcoal grills.

Sao texted him to say she was running a few minutes late. Wes waited for her on a traffic-facing bench beside an open garbage can. Five minutes felt like forever, and then, like a mirage, Sao turned up at the bottom of a stairwell to a sky bridge that connected the massive downtown mall to an overground subway station. Her black hair was longer and shinier than the pixie style Wes remembered from when they'd last met.

Sao touched Wes on the shoulder and stood from behind, wrapping him in her arms. While still in the embrace, she asked about his leg, and he, her foray into Hebrew.

"I've been spending too much time in my head," Sao said of her language studies.

"I understand. That's kind of how I hurt my leg," Wes said. Sao gave Wes a soft but polished smile before they proceeded into yet another narrow *soi* where slow-moving, underfed dogs wagged their pointy tails in a mixture of anticipation and defeat.

Sao led Wes to a fenced gate of the community center, an unmarked unit amid bright blazing marquees. Once inside, Sao led Wes through an aerobics studio padded with mirrors, echoey and empty save for a treadmill between rolled-up yoga mats stacked like pyramids. A daycare center was also in the works. Thai parents walked with their children through a narrow library and into a more spacious lounge with sofa chairs. On the face of it, the arched Hebrew letters looked similar to Thai, but flowed in opposite directions. The self-serve counter brimmed with Nescafé instant packets and a basket of granola bars and tea bags. Sao deposited some Thai baht into a wooden *tzedakah* box. Everything was on an honor system.

"I'm glad you came to meet me today," Sao said as they sat down at a small table. "Are you planning to scribe another Torah?"

"Not any time soon. For me, scribing was like sprinting through a marathon."

"But you had a good time in Amsterdam, no?"

"Well," Wes began, "I had as good of a time as one can have while completing a Torah in just three months. There were terrible headaches and sleepless nights, and other tedious circumstances. I'm not sure if I ever want to touch a quill again."

"There's always teaching," Sao suggested.

"At least in the classroom, everything happens at a more comfortable pace," Wes agreed. "Conjugating verbs on the board isn't so bad after all."

"You know, Wes. I stopped taking classes after you left. The other instructors didn't have a pleasant voice like you."

"I enjoyed having you in that class, but you were so ahead of everyone else. Did it ever seem kind of basic to you?"

"Naturally," Sao answered, tilting her head. "I'm already fluent in English."

"Before leaving the branch…" Wes stopped as though embarrassed over an unpleasant truth. "I tried talking to the head teacher about assigning you to a more advanced class."

Sao's perceptive eyes locked into a patient stare from across the table. "Can I be completely honest with you?"

"What's on your mind?"

"I only pretended to be a beginner," Sao admitted.

"Why? Were you auditing the class or something?"

"No, I was a student. One who took the quizzes and filled in all those basic crossword puzzles."

"I imagine that might have been a little boring, no?"

"My goals are fluency and accent reduction," Sao pointed out. "The advanced classes involved studying with a grammar nazi who didn't inspire me to speak the language. Besides, I liked your accent better than the German or Filipino teachers'."

"Humbled and honored," Wes replied sincerely.

Sao sipped her coffee. "I'm so sorry about Kayla," she said. "I couldn't stop crying after reading your e-mail about what happened."

"It was pretty devastating. It still is."

"I was seeing this guy for a while," Sao said halfheartedly. "He's getting ready to go to Antarctica to study climate change. Long distance relationships don't do it for me."

Wes nodded. "Me either."

"So, are you planning to stay in Thailand?"

"Yes, I am. Just haven't decided yet if I want my old job back."

Sao reached across the table, touching Wes on the hand. "Let me show you to the lounge. There's a bulletin board where you can leave your name, phone number, and whatever type of work you're looking to do."

Most postings were Thai-Hebrew business cards from synagogues in Bangkok, the names and phone numbers of actual people from Jewish congregations Wes never knew existed. Random clusters of yellow sticky notes on the corkboard shone brightly on thumbtack tips, with everything handwritten in Hebrew and Thai transliterations. On one slip, Stanley stood out as the only English name on the board:

Hi, I'm Stanley, the note began. *10+ years experienced scuba diving instructor in Mexico. Would love to learn more about starting a business here in Thailand. Native English speaker from the U.S. I'm also willing to teach English, Spanish or Hebrew.*

"I can't believe it," Wes said, joy and disbelief coming to him in rapid waves. "My father posted this." He quickly dialed the number into his Nokia.

"Hello?" answered the distant-sounding voice. "Who's calling?"

"Hi," Wes returned, the muscles in his throat tightening. "Um, is this Stanley Levine?"

"That depends on who's asking for him."

"It's Wes," he said, recognizing the tone of that voice. "Dad, I'm in Thailand. I've been looking everywhere for you."

"Wes?" Stanley returned, his voice changing quickly from threatened to warm. "Tell me, what are you doing here?"

"I came here to find you."

"How did you get my number?" Stanley now sounded more shocked than guarded.

"I'm at this new community center, in Bangkok. I got your number from that job bulletin in the lounge."

"Are you okay? Do you need anything?"

"Everything's fine. Can't believe I finally found you, that's all. How have you been?"

"Been better, been worse. Still bouncing around the world trying to figure out what to do with my life."

"I know the feeling," Wes replied. "But maybe I can help you find something."

"That would be great. What are you up to these days?"

"I'm an English teacher, mostly. But I did some work in Europe. When I visited my friend, Dave Sterling, in Auckland, he gave me your wedding *mezuzah,* which blew me away."

"What a small world! How did you meet the Sterlings?" Stanley asked.

"Let's talk more about later," Wes said, hoping to change the subject and lock down a chance to see his father. "I was about to ask what drew you to New Zealand?"

"I painted houses and came back to Bangkok when my visa ran out. Now I'm a scuba instructor down in Phuket."

"Phuket?" Wes asked, calculating the distance in his head. "Which part?"

"Kamala Beach. West side of the island."

"Can you give me an address?"

"I don't have a mailbox. Just call me when you land at the main airport."

"So, you probably didn't have a mailbox in Mexico, either?" Wes asked, his doubt-filled voice tinged with disappointment. "It's all still a mystery to me, Dad. Why did you have to leave me and Mom?"

"Come on, son. Your mom didn't want to move to Mexico, you knew that. I moved away for your safety."

"It seemed like a really shitty thing to do," Wes replied, counting on his fingers. "At least most of my friends thought so."

"For what it's worth, I'm sorry. I am. What do I really have to show for myself? I'm just a sixty-year-old bum still sniffing around for some honest work."

"I know you're sorry," Wes said. "It just feels a bit hollow right now."

"It's not. I promise you. But tell me something," Stanley diverted. "How did you know Dave Sterling?"

"I thought we could talk more about that in person. But the short answer is that we taught English together in Bangkok. You know, they're always looking to put warm bodies in classrooms here. If you go full time, they'll cover all your permits and provide health coverage."

"Well, that might be something," Stanley returned with a folksy drawl.

Wes flipped open his pocket watch, forgetting it hadn't ticked since he was on Central European Time. "I need a minute," Wes groaned, refastening the Velcro straps on his open-toe boot. "I broke my leg in Amsterdam. It's still healing."

"Did you get high in one of those coffeeshops and fall into a canal?" Stanley mused, his voice ringing loud and comical over the phone.

"No," Wes shot back, certain that he'd been misunderstood. "I really broke it. I fell down some steep stairs in the house where I stayed. I didn't tell Mom. Guess I didn't want her to worry."

"You told me, and now I'm worried," Stanley's voice trembled, and Wes felt a slight thrill at the hint of parental concern. "Wes, are you doing okay now?"

"I'm fine," Wes said as the battery on his Nokia lost another bar. "But my phone's about to die. Can I come see you in Phuket?"

"Any time, son," Stanley responded as the call blinked out. Wes looked at the phone, still a bit stunned by the interaction. After all the years, the countries, and the continents, he was finally within reach of his father.

"Sao," Wes called across shelves of books to Sao in the café. "Do you know of any hotels in Phuket?"

"I know some hippies," Sao returned. "They live in Phuket's capital city, on the east side."

"I'll start there. My dad says he doesn't have a permanent address."

Sao pulled a pen from her Kate Spade purse as Wes opened his sketchbook, flipping to some Hebrew lines going halfway across the page. "I'll tear some of this out for you, if you'd like," he said.

"Wait," Sao insisted, clasping Wes around his wrist. "Those are your letters. All that work you put into it."

"Back when I did those drawings, I didn't even know what work was," Wes confessed.

"Would you make photocopies of these for me?" Sao asked.

"No need to. Consider it yours." Wes looked down at the sketchbook, already sure he was ready to let it go.

Sao's mouth dropped open. "Wes, are you really giving me your sketchbook?"

"Yeah, don't mention it," he answered. "I was hoping we could catch up some more before your trip. But I've got to go."

"Wes? I think this is yours," Sao said as Wes began to leave. She held out a postcard that slipped from the sketchbook.

"I'll keep that one," Wes said, reaching for the postcard that went around the world with him. Needle-thin wrinkles ran across the faded palm tree horizon, a picture aging like human skin. The words in Stanley's message looked rubbed out and barely legible from years of wear and tear as a sketchbook marker.

"This means a lot to me," Sao told him. "Are you sure?"

"Definitely. It's already served me well," Wes added. "Hope it serves you well, too."

"Okay, then," Sao replied, standing expectantly straight as she collected her belongings. "I'll send you a text message with the location in Central Phuket."

"And who do I ask for?"

"They don't use their real names," Sao replied. "There's Flower Child, her on-and-off boyfriend Moonbeam, and the one I'm closest with is Sunshine."

"If you're still here when I get back to Bangkok," Wes suggested. "Let's do coffee again."

"Safe travels," Sao said, holding him in her gaze.

"Are you doing anything for New Year's Eve?"

Sao smiled warmly. "My cousins from Paris are staying at my house until after Christmas. After that, I'm planning to meet up with Sunshine and the whole crew. Maybe I'll see you there?"

"Stoked. Let's stay connected," Wes said, and then smiled as a taxi stopped to the curb while they exited the building.

Back at the guesthouse, Wes sorted through the clothes he no longer wanted, making them into neatly folded offerings to orange-robed monks treading softly across a local village. He packed what remained into a pointy rucksack scored from a table merchant who, quite gleefully, traded it straight-up for the sizeable piece of luggage.

Wes grabbed another taxi to the airport, boarding the southbound flight with all his remaining belongings strapped on his shoulders like a turtle to its shell. He left behind his dull walking stick, now rendered practically useless from constant grinding on the concrete, and looked forward, his eyes focused, into the unknown future.

From sprawling Bangkok, the flight touched down in the greener, balmier pastures of Phuket's international airport. Taxiing into town in the breezy afternoon heat, Wes took passing glimpses through the window at amulet shops and gold Buddha statues in shrines. Phuket's main street looked like Rainbow Row, with each tenement unit adding a different color to the spectrum.

Wes twice checked the address on Sao's most recent text message. He slipped the Nokia into his back pocket, and the door in front of him opened before Wes could knock. Sunshine stood in the entrance, her fingers twirling the ends of her flowing, sun-kissed blonde curls.

Wes grinned amiably, like a friendly professor on the first day of class. "I'm Wes. Sao's old teacher."

"Well, if it's okay with you, Sao's Old Teacher, I'd like to call you Love Child instead."

"Sunshine," Wes affirmed her preferred name. "My parents didn't get married until a year after I was born. How about something else?"

"Okay, then." The mystic in a tie-dyed dress sugared it up. "I'll just call you Love."

Wes forced himself to smile. "Why not just call me Wes, like everyone else does?"

"We prefer not to use our legal names," Sunshine said. She led him into the plant-filled living space where, on the cramped couch, three shirtless blond surfer dudes huddled around a giant bong.

Wes lingered around the doorway, nervously scoping out the pointy green leaves. The plants looked like ticking time bombs. The same cannabis smoke that smelled so sweet and inviting in Amsterdam now reeked like the devil's breath in a more forbidding tropical locale. Blond dude Moonbeam offered Wes a toke. Despite his reservations, and not wanting to turn down newfound hospitality, Wes lowered his head upon the bong's still-smoky rim and took a hit.

"We're plant-sitting," Moonbeam commented, his inflection mildly sarcastic and dead serious.

Sunshine took a seat on the sectional sofa. With longing eyes, she looked to Wes, and then patted the cushion beside her. Wes slowly came forward to sit down with the stoners, surrounded as they were by pounds of an illicit plant that, in much of the equatorial world, had led its purchasers and consumers into packed prison cells or early graves. The greenhouse aroma calmed his nerves and kept his worst thoughts at bay, if only for a moment.

"Sao said you might be able to help me find my dad," Wes said, picking at his fingernails. "He's a scuba diving instructor in Kamala Beach."

"The west side," Sunshine replied cheerily. "Lovely. Where exactly is your dad staying?"

"He doesn't have an address. Lives in a bungalow by the beach."

"Hmm." Sunshine gave him a pensive look. "Your dad might be trying to stay under the radar, too."

"His name is—"

"Ah, no no," Sunshine shushed Wes, playfully laying a finger across his lips. "You don't have to say his real name. A lot of *farangs* who live here long term prefer being known only by a chosen name. What do you think your dad's might be?"

"He's never had one," Wes said bluntly. "And if he does now, I wouldn't know. I haven't seen him in ten years."

"Phuket is where *farangs* come to disappear," Moonbeam stated, mildly suspicious. "Are you sure he even wants to meet you?"

"We've talked on the phone," Wes replied, checking his Nokia screen for a returned call that wasn't there. "I'm supposed to meet him somewhere on the beach. But he doesn't always pick up his phone. Maybe he's out diving."

"Yeah, maybe," Moonbeam said, patting Wes on the shoulder. "You're welcome to stay in our guest room."

"Thanks. I appreciate it."

"We haven't been going to the beach much," Moonbeam added, steadying his lips on the rim of the bong for another hit. "Something about the weather has been off lately."

"Think about it, Wes," Sunshine said, taking him by the hand and tracing the lines on his palm. "Try to come up with a hippie-sounding name for your dad."

"He was never much of a hippie to begin with."

Sunshine tapped Wes's palm like a fortune teller pointing out a revelation in the lines. "Would you say he was a lucky person?"

"For a while," Wes replied, staring at his palm as though he had all the answers. "He had a lucky streak."

"Lucky Streak!" Sunshine exclaimed through a knowing smile. "I went out scuba diving a few times last summer with Lucky Streak."

"So, do you think it might be him?"

"It's quite possible. I didn't know that he lived in Kamala Beach, but that was where we went diving."

"Can you give him a call?" Wes asked.

"Look, this is getting a little sketchy," Sunshine said as she climbed off the couch. "I don't know."

"Then maybe you can just tell me where you last went out to sea with him?"

"No worries," Sunshine returned, plugging a text message into her cell phone. "That's the address. A driver can get you there in an hour."

"If it's okay, I'd like to venture out now, while there's still daylight." Wes stood up and placed his bag in a corner of the room. "Cool if I keep this here?"

From the couch, Moonbeam grinned savvily. "We're sitting on upwards of fifty pounds of Mary Jane. Your bag is safe here."

"It's nice meeting everyone," Wes said, pressing his palms together in gratitude. "Is there a housekey I could borrow?"

"Here's the spare, Love," Sunshine quickly popped out of the room and returned to hand Wes a little keychain. "Just call me when you're at the door. Don't knock. We hate surprises."

From the front door, Wes stared into the living room, still a little subdued at the pot plants sprouting like a bamboo forest. "Cheers, then. I'll keep you posted."

For most of the ride, Wes was the only passenger on the *songthaew,* save for a few Thai kids in Primary school uniforms who came and went from the open-air benches under the hatch. Eventually, the driver stopped in front of a shop window with a faceless mannequin in a bridal dress. As he hopped from the bench and off the bumper, Wes scanned the Thai roadway signs for English translations.

"Is this Kamala?" Wes asked uncertainly.

"Yes, yes," the driver insisted, his raspy voice jovial but restive.

"Where's the shore?"

"Kamala Beach." The driver pointed a thick finger at a scant row of shaggy palm trees standing lopsidedly between the town and the surf. "Over there."

Beyond the ocean-facing hotel terraces and the spicy aromas of food markets, Wes glimpsed a patch of white sand. The aquamarine sea emerged in the spaces between heaving palm fronds. With a sandal on one foot and a Velcro boot fastened firmly against the other, he trudged forward onto the beach. At the water's edge, Wes dipped his sandaled foot into a gently surging tide, recoiling as soon as he felt the warm water foaming on his toes. He found it strange that even the birds wanted no parts of the placid Andaman Sea, watching aghast as the flock scattered into different directions.

As the receding tidewater continued to ebb, Wes walked along the shore in search for other signs of life. Under one umbrella, a mom and dad with two toddlers greeted Wes, their tiny voices guttural yet lilting as they spoke in a Scandinavian language. He approached a lifeguard, an older-looking Thai man sporting a teeny mustache and red cross tank top. Before Wes could get a word out, the lifeguard clicked his first aid kit shut, making his way off the beach as though an emergency awaited his attention at the hotel. Without considering the receding tide, Wes situated himself upon the soft sand of an irregular beachfront.

Wes stared into the bluest water he'd ever seen, wondering about his surroundings. He found it strange that no fish or other markers of marine life stood between the ocean's surface and its floor. What did the creatures know that he did not?

After a few minutes of sitting idly, the warm sand turned hot on his butt. Wes dusted off his cargo shorts as the lifeguard dashed off once again, heading in the other direction with a life preserver ring around each arm.

Wes headed back into town, abandoning the vacant beachfront to search for a diving instructor. He scanned the bulletin boards at an Internet café, a laundromat, a local coffee shop. All the ads were in Thai, except for one with two English words jumping off the page: Lucky Streak. *Sunshine's guy!* In a moment of impulse, Wes yanked the paper from the thumbtack and walked up to the counter.

"Can you help me to translate this?" Wes asked the barista, smoothing the flyer over the countertop.

The barista's radiant smile beamed with familiarity. "Yes, of course. I'm Ayesha, by the way."

"Hi, Ayesha," Wes spoke her name with warmth and discretion. "I'm Wes."

"Lucky Streak," Ayesha read, running a finger across the Thai print. "I can call this number for you. He's a *farang* who comes in for coffee almost every day."

Wes brushed his hair away from his eyes. "Well, the thing is, I'm not really looking for diving lessons."

"Oh yeah?" Ayesha returned, appearing guarded and skeptical. "Then what are you looking for?"

"My father. He lives in Kamala Beach and he's a scuba diver. On the phone, he said something about giving lessons. I'm just trying to find him."

"Okay, so, why don't you just give him a call?" Ayesha said, banging out espresso grinds from the portafilter basket.

"He doesn't always pick up the phone. I just tried to find him. Maybe he's out on the water?"

Ayesha frowned. "Not likely. It's low season; the water's too unpredictable. Most of my diver friends tend to hang it up until around February."

"Does Lucky Streak go by another name?"

"That I couldn't tell you," Ayesha replied from behind the bar. "This is Thailand. Most people here have nicknames. But I'll send Lucky Streak a text."

"Thanks for your help," Wes said as he held a hand over his chest.

Ayesha typed rapidly on the keypad of her cell phone. "No worries," she answered a moment later, smiling at Wes. "Lucky answered quickly. He's on his way."

A motorcycle roared from sidewalk, but the man who dismounted wasn't Stanley Levine. The salt-and-pepper-haired shaman came closer, shaking his head to loosen the strands of hair that had been matted by his helmet. Lucky Streak then staggered to the café counter in a wrinkled silk palm tree shirt and stonewashed jeans.

"Lucky Streak?" Wes asked. "I'm looking for my dad. He's also a diving instructor in West Phuket."

"Nice. So, I just wasted my time coming out here," Lucky Streak fired back, turning to Ayesha. "Why didn't you tell me he wasn't looking for a diving instructor?"

"What I told you is true," Ayesha declared. "He's looking for his father who is also a diving instructor. Maybe you can help him."

"For what it's worth," Wes said, his voice humble as he implored Lucky to listen. "Back on the east side of the island, I heard that you give good lessons."

"And if you're interested in that, call me when we're further into the high season." Lucky said, flipping out a business card from his back pocket. "The weather's been too damn unpredictable lately."

"My dad hasn't been picking up his phone all day," Wes added, growing concerned as he scanned his Nokia's empty message inbox. "I figured he might be busy underwater somewhere."

"Probably not. Strange winds are blowing all over Kamala and West Phuket," Lucky explained. "Every diver I know here is laying low. Except for this one oddball."

"And who's that?" Wes asked.

"I'll take you there on the back of my bike if you want."

Wes nodded and watched as Lucky walked out, quickly hopping on the motorcycle's saddle to rev up the engine. As Wes departed, he smiled a thank-you to Ayesha and hopped on the bike, feeling the motor growling beneath him like an enraged animal. Clutching uncomfortably around Lucky's waist, Wes held fast while the motorcycle whizzed up and down rolling hills that eventually leveled out. Dusty streets became a sand dune shore, with grains blowing down the leeward side.

"Look. Way out there." Lucky propped up the motorcycle and sprang for the shore, pointing to a wetsuit floating almost too far beyond the current to be seen from land. "He's one of the other *farang* diving instructors in town. The oddball I was telling you about. Still out at sea."

Wes looked on, with one hand shielding his eyes from the sun. "He may be odd, but is he any good?"

"Honestly, the best," Lucky replied. "No matter the weather, he's in the water every day."

From the shore, Wes gazed out at the black-clad diver who, in the distance, looked more like the tip of a whale's tail. Finally, a body started to take shape as this mystical "oddball" man of the sea paddled toward the shore with a cylindrical tank of oxygen reserves strapped to his back. Wes gasped as the form became clear.

Stanley Levine hopped through the shallow waters, treading to the shore with big, plastic fins on his feet. Wes kicked through sand as Stanley chucked his yellow breathing tank into a dune, and father and son looked at each other for no more than a second before embracing at long last.

CHAPTER EIGHTEEN

"Ten years," Wes uttered, feeling the gravity of time as he looked over Stanley's wrinkles and creases, taking in his father for the first time in a decade. "Look at you now."

"Son, I've changed," Stanley said, peeling out of his scuba gear like a seal shedding skin. "Over the years, I've relinquished all my bad habits. In Mexico, gambling became impossible since I couldn't speak Spanish. Here in Thailand, I stopped drinking to improve my oxygen levels for deep sea diving. Three months without a drop."

Wes nodded acceptingly. "I'm proud of you, Dad. You look great."

"I missed you and Mom every single day. But I knew that by staying, I'd only be putting all of us in danger."

"I was sixteen when you left," Wes said. "I knew things weren't going well when you got hooked on that phone psychic who convinced you to move to Mexico."

Wes tried to picture his dad in a sombrero, living some clichéd Mexican lifestyle. "Besides whatever some phone psychic told you, why did you go to Mexico?"

Stanley looked ashamed and turned his eyes to the sand. "When I started falling deeper into the hole, I tried to bet my way out, again and again. Before I knew it, everyone was coming to collect."

As Stanley slithered out of the wetsuit top, Wes couldn't take his eyes off his dad's trim physique. "You've really slimmed down," Wes remarked. "What's your secret?"

Stanley didn't answer right away. Then he looked down at his washboard torso and shrugged. "I got out of the restaurant business and started taking better care of myself. Lots of exercise right out there in that water."

"Maybe we could go back to Bangkok and get jobs with my old employer, the largest language learning company in the entire kingdom."

"Now that I'm a scuba diving instructor by trade," Stanley stated with conviction. "I've got to stay near a beach."

"But what about that little flyer you put up at the J.C.C. in Bangkok? It said that you were looking for work anywhere in Thailand."

"I posted that six months ago. Now that I've stopped choking on that Bangkok air, it's kind of hard to think about going back. Besides, you found me. Maybe you'll like it here."

After they reached a small outdoor restaurant and took their seats, Wes reached over and placed the postcard from Playa del Carmen on the middle of the table, rendering it visible against candlelight. "Dad, do you remember sending me this?"

"Sure," Stanley answered, tears welling in his eyes. "It was years ago on your birthday."

"It got me through some tough times. But there's something I need to tell you about Bubbie and Zayde. I should start with Amsterdam. While living there for a few months, I scribed the *Sefer* Torah that Zayde always wanted to write for himself."

A server set a steaming ceramic bowl of bubbling green curry on the table. Strong, fiery spices wafted from the table as Stanley covered his face. "It's only because I'm proud of you," he returned as Wes watched him. "I've already cried a million rivers for my mom and dad."

Wes's eyes widened as he sat for a moment in dumbstruck silence. Then the words found him. "You knew?"

"When I was living in Mexico, I'd pop into the Chabad houses from time to time. A rabbi there kept me informed when they both passed. He had some connections in Baltimore."

"I thought you had no idea," Wes said, his jaw slung in utter disbelief. "I looked everywhere for you. Mom wasn't so happy when I went to Mexico for Spring Break in my second year of college. I met a girl named Nayeli. We ended up spending the whole time in the hotel. I was ready to marry her."

"Did you ever see her again?" Stanley asked, his eyes now brighter.

Wes shook his head regretfully. "We e-mailed for a few months until she stopped responding."

"How did you feel about that?"

"At first, I was devastated. Mom, of course, said she saw it coming. But at least, finally, I had something new to be all bent out of shape about. In a strange way, I think that was what helped me get over my dad running out on me like that."

"Son, wait," Stanley cut in. "We're here now. Let's focus on that. But back to your time in Amsterdam for a minute. Are you telling me that your grandparents now have a Torah dedicated to them in the same place where they lived during the Shoah?"

"Yep, a hundred percent," Wes confirmed. "The gold-plated inscription has both of their full names on it, Hebrew and English."

"I'd love to see that," Stanley said, laying a hand on top of Wes's arm.

"Later on, I'll show you some pictures. They're in my backpack."

"And where's your backpack?" Stanley asked with concern in his voice.

"At a friend's place in the Phuket capital, all the way on the east side."

Wes dialed for Sunshine while behind him, a jangly pipe organ wailed over an electronic drumbeat, and the dancers dipped and swayed as an orange sky faded into nightfall. Cars roared in both directions, and each mobile ringtone passed like eternity.

"Hello?" Sunshine finally answered, her voice sounding anything but hopeful.

Wes figured she might be stoned. "Hey, Sunshine," he said cheerily. "Lucky Streak helped me find my dad. I'm with him right now. Do you think I can come over to get my bag?"

"Now's not a good time," Sunshine said slowly. "The owner of the apartment got busted with the pot plants."

"Oh, no," Wes said, feeling his chest rise and fall like a stormy ocean wave. "Is everyone okay?"

"All of us were out to lunch when it happened," Sunshine replied. "A neighbor rang Moonbeam and told him that cops confiscated mostly everything in the place."

"Do you think my backpack is still there?"

"Can't say for sure. All I know is the front door is now a wall of yellow police tape."

Wes suddenly felt naked, stripped of what vestiges remained from his already-downsized possessions.

"My passport and clothes, all my photos. Everything I own in the world is in that bag. Can I go back there and check?"

"We're staying in a hotel just outside of the city. None of us are going near there, at least not while the crime scene is still hot. You're welcome to join us if you still need a place to stay."

"I might take you up on that," Wes returned. "Can you give me the location? I left the damn cell phone charger in my bag, and my battery's about to die."

Sure enough, the call ended in silence before Wes could get the hotel address. Slipping the useless phone back into his pocket, Wes pondered the worst of his fears—namely, that the backpack had turned him into a fugitive, while the band of hippies who weren't home when cops busted in might elude the law.

"Where are you staying these days?" Wes asked his dad, nervous and expectant.

"Son, if you're in some kind of trouble," Stanley said, his voice soothing as the caramel sunset. "I know the police in Phuket. Give them a few hundred baht a month, and you'll never have a problem here."

"Those hippies I was staying with in the heart of town thought they had the local P.D. in their back pockets, too," Wes quipped. "Their apartment looked like an episode of *COPS* waiting to happen."

"You can stay with me tonight," Stanley offered protectively. "Just so you know, my place isn't that big. But you're my son. Of course, my door is open."

A white, gray-winged seagull perching on the thatched straw roof of Stanley's beachfront bungalow flew away as they approached. An old *mezuzah* with a nail missing turned upside down as Wes merely touched the scroll case dangling from a crooked, cracked doorpost. As Wes ducked to enter, Stanley held back the bohemian door beads sparkling like candy over the threshold. The micro-home was all wood slats with an exposed toilet and bathroom sink in the only room. Humbly, Stanley pointed to the mattress on the floor, a bedsheet, and two coffee-stained pillows.

Wes scanned all the empty space in the one-room shack. A beachfront hut, really, of weathered straw and warped wood baking into dilapidation at the mercy of a dominant equatorial sun. He held his tongue instead of telling Stanley what he really thought, that the bungalow was on the brink of collapse and smelled like a sewer.

"It's just what I have right now," Stanley confessed. "I use public showers."

Wes shook his head and frowned, turning his nose at the foul smell inside of a dwelling made from nature's shingles. "Any other bathing options?"

"There's a massage parlor in town." Stanley's eyes perked up wistfully. "Pretty girls. They'll soap you up real good on this little table shower before giving you a full body rub. We're talking *full* body."

"Dad," Wes responded with mild disappointment. "There's something unnerving about a human being getting hosed down like cattle. When I lived in Amsterdam, I'd go to museums in the Jewish Quarter. And quite vividly, I recall seeing something in the National Holocaust Museum that really stayed with me."

Stanley leaned closer to Wes with great interest. "Tell me, what did you see?"

"A picture of some Nazi asshole in a brown suit spraying water at full force on twenty, maybe thirty children being carted to a camp."

"My son," Stanley replied shakily, wrapping an arm around Wes's shoulders. "One day we'll go to Amsterdam, just the two of us. I've got to see that Torah."

"I'd like that," Wes replied, nervous and distracted. "But before I can go anywhere, can you ask your cop friends if my passport was seized?"

"Now, Wes," Stanley cautioned. "I've been on the run for long enough to know what *not* to do in a situation like this. Remember that we're not citizens or civilians in Thailand. We're *farangs.* Given the language barrier here, it's all too easy to say the wrong thing. A question that's asked at the wrong time can easily be mistaken for an admission of guilt."

"Okay, this is turning into a Criminal Justice 101 class," Wes quipped. "I just want my belongings back."

"Give it a few days to cool down," Stanley suggested, drawing together a white tablecloth curtain to cover an open window facing the beach. "Then I'll ring the central department to see what they have."

"Can we call tomorrow?" Wes negotiated. "Everything I own is in that bag."

Stanley shrugged. "It's Christmas. Let the holiday pass, and give the cops a chance to separate you from your friends who just got busted. Trust on me this."

"They're friends of my student, Sao. She's studying to become a scribe."

"Your grandmother always wanted to scribe. Did Zayde ever do anything with his letters?"

"Zayde's eyesight started fading before he had a chance to really get into it," Wes continued. "If it wasn't work, it was something else that always kept him from putting the time in. I immersed myself in it when I was eighteen. Instead of going to college straight out of high school, I took a gap year to learn the *Sofrut."*

"That was my father's vision for himself. His greatest aspiration was to become a scribe."

"Then we should go to Amsterdam," Wes said. "I know someone who says we can get European citizenship, and he can probably also help with the passport issue."

"Who's that?" Stanley asked with mild interest.

"Harry Jarsdel. His dad's a big-time lawyer in London. And his steel magnate great-grandfather Alfred had financed the ocean liner that took Bubbie and Zayde across the Atlantic. Harry sponsored me to scribe the Torah."

"How did you meet him?" Stanley asked, astonished.

"His aunt is a rabbi in Auckland," Wes quickly followed up. "By the way, what were you doing Down Under?"

"Painting houses," Stanley said after a long pause.

"I was thinking to stay here and finish my teaching contract," Wes said. "In Bangkok, I mean. I guess living there suits me. There's a Jewish community in the city, you know."

"I've been all around Bangkok," Stanley said dismissively. "But I've never been to Amsterdam, and would love to go. What sort of work can we take up in Europe?"

"Maybe I could scribe another Torah if I got a sponsor," Wes answered. "What are your interests these days?"

"This is it," Stanley replied, shaking the sand off his wetsuit. "Scuba diving is my whole life. I go out to sea every morning. Got an extra wetsuit and oxygen tank if you'd like to join me?"

"Dad," Wes said with reservation in his voice. "I'm glad I found you. Glad that you found yourself. But what if I don't want to stay in Phuket forever?"

"Are you kidding? This place is paradise. I've been here for months, and it still feels like I'm on vacation. Every day is pure fun."

"Bangkok might be a little more convenient," Wes spoke with all the politeness he could muster as he tried not to look around the ramshackle bungalow.

"But here the sand and sea are practically all ours," Stanley spoke sermonically, like a pulpit preacher selling eternal life on the beach.

Wes looked his dad up and down. "I'll have to think about it."

"Let me know when you do." Stanley whiffed himself under his T-shirt. "I need two things right now. A shower and a massage. See you in an hour or so."

Through the cracked-open door, Wes glimpsed as the sun fully set itself down, somewhere far off into the sea proper. Before long, the bungalow's damp rot no longer reeked. The lingering stench of decaying wood smelled something like the magic mushrooms he'd taken in Amsterdam, where no one got arrested for possessing or consuming. Wes smiled for a moment, and then drifted off to the sweet sound of low tide waves lapping softly on the shore.

He was startled awake to no sign of Stanley in the one-room shack. An eerie silence prevailed as Wes treaded lightly across the bungalow's unsteady floorboard. A faint thatch of emerald-green foliage stood between Wes and the ocean. No one else was on the beach, and every bird in the sky was flying crooked, looking lost or left behind by their flocks.

For a split second, Wes figured he'd yet again been abandoned by his father. Stanley had left him ten years before in a leafy Baltimore suburb, and would probably have no qualms about letting history repeat itself in a Thai mud hut.

But that wasn't the case. Standing on the broken steps of Stanley's bungalow, Wes looked beyond the palm tree fronds at a pair of big fins sticking out of the sea. His dad didn't have a pot to piss in, but did have a forehead light and prescription goggles, and that was all he needed.

"I didn't see you last night," Wes told his dad like they hadn't missed a beat in ten years apart. "What's going on out there?"

"The ocean is just about empty," Stanley replied with excitement. "Can you even believe that?"

"Are you trying to follow in Jacques Cousteau's footsteps?" Wes joked.

Stanley shot him a cross look, all eyes and no neck, not extending the dignity of a response. "I'd like to fill my oxygen tank and go out again. You're welcome to join."

"Doesn't it seem odd to you that there's no one out on the beach right now?" Wes voiced a concern that had been eating at him since the day before. "We're the only ones here."

"It's Christmas," Stanley announced, and it was news to Wes's ears. "Did you call your mother?"

Wes shook his head. "I don't want to worry her. I need to get my own house in order first."

"Then let's get you that other tank behind the shed." Stanley reached under the cracked open porch for an air compressor.

"Dad," Wes reasoned. "It's also Shabbat. Shouldn't we take it easy today?"

Stanley stopped rummaging through the clinking pile of appliances and trinkets, turning urgently around to face his son. "Are you kidding? This is perfect diving weather."

"I don't know," Wes doubted, eyeing the shifting clouds on the horizon. "If it's so perfect, then why are we the only ones here?"

Stanley shrugged. "It's always touch and go. This place is swamped with tourists one week and it's a ghost town the next."

"The last time I went diving," Wes began, rolling his eyes in thought. "I was maybe ten or eleven."

Stanley cracked a slow, patient smile. "It'll be just like old times, son."

"Sure," Wes agreed, his wistful eyes turning somber with nostalgia. "I was the coolest kid in school that year because you took me diving. Thank you for that."

Stanley gazed at Wes, clear-eyed and clearly proud. "Those early experiences made you into the confident, courageous person you are today."

Wes smirked at the praise, having not yet taken it to heart. "You know, Boone's dad bought him a night with a call girl when he was thirteen. That gave him an edge in high school. By then, the fact that I'd seen the bottom of the Atlantic was no longer all that impressive to anyone."

Stanley's face lit up. "The Atlantic Ocean's floor always looked so barren and gray. There's so much more color here in the Andaman Sea. I didn't see many fish this morning, which can only mean they'll be out later."

"Maybe the fish have left for a reason," Wes dropped a hint, a tear welling in his eye as he remembered Kayla advising him to watch what animals do. "I just thought there'd be more wildlife in Phuket."

"It's all right," Stanley assured him. "There's more for us to enjoy."

As Christmas morning slipped into the afternoon, Wes and Stanley went for brunch. At the same café where Wes stumbled on a flyer from diving instructor Lucky Streak, Ayesha was working behind the espresso bar. From the register, she handed them plastic laminated menus, written in English with Thai subtext. After retrieving their mugs from the coffee bar, Wes pointed to big, blooming muffins in the pastry case.

"You know something," Stanley said between bites of his banana nut muffin. "This little breakfast cost us forty baht each."

"That's like, what, two dollars?" Wes asked.

"Yes. I feel very lucky to be here," Stanley added. "It's a simple way of life."

Wes nodded in agreement, not wanting to ruin the moment by telling his dad he sounded like a walking travel brochure. "Yeah, it's really nice here," Wes chimed in.

"It's everything I've ever wanted," Stanley spoke with finality.

"If I stayed, though, what could I do for work around here?" Wes asked.

"I could help you become a diving instructor. You'll make enough in the high season to get you through the whole year."

"Aren't we in the high season now?"

"It's just getting started. Look, if you want to keep teaching, there's a day school on the island. I know the headmaster."

"A teaching job might be good for the time being," Wes replied, tapping his fingers on the teak wood tabletop. "Meanwhile, maybe we can think about launching a business. Father and son scuba diving instructors. That's pretty catchy. But do you think you'll ever get tired of taking people scuba diving?"

"Not a chance," Stanley answered straight away. "It's what I should've been doing all along."

"I mean," Wes began. "You may want to become a researcher or something."

"Research doesn't pay well," Stanley stated plainly. "And besides, what I do is much more fun. I've got clients on a waiting list through March. That's a big enough bankroll to stop working for the year by Passover."

"If this is your home, then, have you ever thought about fixing up the bungalow a little?"

"It's temporary," Stanley insisted. "I've got my eye on a roomier space in a little village closer to the pier."

"If you go out diving, pay attention to the current," Ayesha interjected, cautioning Wes and Stanley as she stowed a tray of donuts into the pastry case. "Lately the weather's been strange."

Clear skies prevailed as Wes and Stanley stood before the foamy water's edge in full scuba gear, the giant fins on their feet leaving trails in the sand. At the shoreline, Stanley adjusted the straps on Wes's aqualung, fastening the cylindrical yellow oxygen tank on his back. They swam into the sea together and then drifted apart as Wes paddled his way through underwater ruins. From the little castle on the ocean floor, Wes saw his dad floating his way to the water's surface, chasing tails of the scant marine life still present in the mostly vacant sea. As Stanley waved for Wes to swim closer, three or four tiny goldfish striped like zebras swam among three or four hundred specimens every color of the rainbow. On his dad's shoulder, Wes watched the fish wriggle for their lives in a race against the current, like sperm cells racing for a viable egg.

Stanley eventually emerged from the water, cradling a chubby mackerel long as his arm. The fish looked like a silvery torpedo. It squirmed as they trudged through shallow water. Back at the bungalow, Stanley passed the fish to Wes as he spread an old newspaper across the floor. With pulsating gills taking in its dying breaths, the water creature writhed on the yellowing pages of *The Nation*. Wes recoiled from the dampened wood floor, watching from the porch as Stanley intervened with a granite pestle, ending the fish's suffering with a quick blow to the head.

Together they filled a little pit with tinder, lighting a fire under an old, corroded wok. Stanley coated the skillet with olive oil, pouring from a big jug and letting the catch sizzle until it blackened. He spiced up their plates, sprinkling paprika from his palm before squeezing out a lemon to its last drops.

"Don't let it sit," Stanley recommended, setting the plate in Wes's lap. "Mackerel doesn't keep well for long."

"Dad, I'm not kidding," Wes said, picking ravenously at the finer bones. "Best fish ever."

"And this might be the best Shabbat of my life," Stanley returned, his face glowing with embers flickering in the pit. "Can't wait to do this again tomorrow."

"I'm spent, Dad. If we're going diving again tomorrow, I'd like to turn in early."

"Deal," Stanley concluded, winking surreptitiously as he poured water over the flickering fireplace. "Crash whenever you like. I'm going to see my girlfriend tonight."

"Well, I never expected you to wait around for Mom to take you back," Wes conceded.

Stanley didn't answer. He opened a shoebox, plucking out a stream of Thai baht. "Two thousand, three thousand," Stanley counted out loud.

"Hey Dad," Wes began, puffing his cheeks as Stanley returned the shoebox of cash to an unstable shelf over the wardrobe. Then he stopped himself. "Never mind. I guess you probably know what you're doing with your life by now."

"I'm putting most of my money into that new bungalow," Stanley announced, prompting from Wes a stoic, well-wishing smile.

"Have fun tonight," Wes replied, resigning himself to the mattress on the floor.

They came together for a hug. Wes was cautious, reluctant to slather fish oil from his fingers onto the thermoplastic rubber of Stanley's wetsuit.

"Love you," Stanley told his only son, sliding out of the embrace to shed the last of his scuba gear. "We'll do this again bright and early tomorrow. Rest up."

"You, too, Dad. Love you," Wes said, pulling back the bedsheets on the floor mattress.

In the morning, Wes opened his eyes to a silent breeze lifting the makeshift curtain, a cloth blowing in the soundless wind. Only one of Stanley's two scuba wetsuits still hung on the door rack. He rubbed his eyes and checked the time on his cell phone, thankful his dad had a charger he could use, and saw that it was a quarter past nine. As he focused once more on the one remaining wetsuit hanging on the door rack, Wes dialed for his dad, thinking maybe he'd stayed overnight with his girlfriend and took the scuba gear with him. It didn't make sense, and Wes was certain that by now he would've heard his dad stumble back into the creaky bungalow. When the call dropped, Wes tried the antique-looking rotary on Stanley's dresser. It didn't produce a dial tone. Stanley rarely picked up his calls, didn't do e-mail.

"What the fuck is wrong with that asshole?" Wes muttered to himself, thumbing on his Nokia for his dad's number a second time. Nothing.

Out on the porch, Wes found one pair of rubber fins where two giant duck feet once stood at the ramshackle door. One of the oxygen tanks was missing, though the face goggles were where Wes had left them, the elastic strap still dangling from a loose doorknob.

But none of that mattered nearly as much as what Wes noticed when he glanced out at the horizon: the sea had receded far enough to reveal the muddy ocean floor they'd scaled during yesterday's dive. Seemingly overnight, the beach had at least doubled in size. A hissing gust of wind did surprisingly little to stir the tranquil ocean.

He paced around the bungalow, scanning the scattered mess of clothes on the floor for a pair of cargo shorts. His first impulse was to look for his dad at Ayesha's café, and so Wes crossed through a maze of palm trees bent down like nails from the wind. From across the street, Wes noticed steel shutters running down the café entrance, a mirror to every other door on that block. He peered through a shop window at enlarged images of the Thai Royal Family. Through the palm trees whipping in the wind, Wes could see the shoreline had eroded further still, the tide having turned the horizon of five minutes ago into a hinterland.

And then, at the base of a resort near the beach, there were piercing screams. Wes originally heard it from off the shore, dismissing what he thought had been the cries of wayward seagulls. But the sound was shrill and fast, too human to be mistaken for anything else, and fear slammed into his body just as the biggest wave he'd ever seen walloped the shoreline near the huts and bungalows.

"Reo, reo, reo!" Wes could hear an urgent Thai voice somewhere on the other side of a hotel swimming pool. "Hurry!"

"I'm looking for my father," Wes pleaded from the bottom of the steps to a resort. "Can you help me out?"

"This way," urged a woman with a British accent. "Take my hand."

With outstretched arms, she pulled Wes to higher ground. As the wood patio steps opened into a poolside pavilion, they dodged a second wave, higher and faster than the preceding one that walloped Stanley's little beach shack. Through the windows of the hotel bar, Wes could see the vengeful sea overtaking every inch of the vacant horizon. Waves crashed upon the bungalows and palm trees standing in the way. Soon enough, the hotel's ocean-facing side was hit, smacked with such force that it tipped ten or more poolside guests off the ledge.

"Dad, where are you?" Wes screamed at the raging Andaman Sea that faced him.

"I'm so sorry, love," the British woman returned. "If your dad's out there, he isn't going to be making it back here."

Before Wes could respond, a wall of water turned the hotel into an island. Working people in the lobby down below paddled for their lives. Most of them weren't going to make it, either. Wes lost touch with the Brit as a new cast of frantic characters piled upon the poolside bar, hopeful that the sea would impose its wrath on other quarters.

But nothing on the balcony overlooking the ocean stood a chance against the rising sea. Wes watched in horror as a wave moved into the manmade basin, drowning out the hotel's hourglass-shaped swimming pool.

Stanley couldn't have been in that water, Wes told himself, second-guessing his own denial. *He might've been doing something else. Anything else. Best case, Stanley's girlfriend's apartment was far enough from the beach, and they'd made love the whole night through and slept in.* A lot of ifs and ands. He had to consider the possibilities, no matter what his heart was telling him.

At close range, palm trees snapped as easily as toothpicks, close enough for Wes to feel the watery branch's impact within his bones. Feverishly, he scrolled through the inbox on his Nokia and found a text he had not seen until now, time stamped eight-thirty-two a.m. Wes took a moment to process his father's fate:

Wes, you were sleeping, so I went out for a dive. Let's try again in the afternoon. Love, Dad.

Wes unglued his eyes from the pixels on his Nokia screen, looking up from the last words he'd ever receive from Stanley Levine, the absentee father who followed his truest passion into the depths of a sea where now, he likely lay dead.

From a distance, Wes could see a wave moving in on the British woman who'd lifted him to the platform. He couldn't remember when the previous wave had hit, or what happened to the hotel swimming pool that plunged under the sea while guests clung to the edge, falling from the deck like dominoes. In the distance, plaintive ambulance sirens wailed like answers to prayers. It took him a moment to realize that he, too, had been pushed under by the wave. Wes touched his forehead and squinted before looking around; he had resurfaced, sputtering and surviving, but he didn't see that woman.

With no currency or identification in his pockets, he stuttered on the letters of his first and last name. Wes Levine harnessed every working cell in his brain to not forget his own name. It was all he had left.

"Do you remember me?" a woman's voice called from across the flooded sidewalk. "Wes? It's Ayesha."

"Ayesha?" Wes asked, dazed. "You helped me find my dad, didn't you? You've got to help me locate him."

"Wes, I'm so sorry that your dad is gone," Ayesha spoke through the tears in her eyes. "This morning at the café, Stanley told me he was going out to dive."

Wes focused all his energy on the vanishing horizon, trying to see beyond the water without end. "Are you sure?"

She clasped his hand, squeezing it urgently. "Let's try to stay together."

"What's happening?" Wes asked.

Ayesha wrapped an arm around his waist. "You've been hurt, and we must hurry. The ocean's catching up to us too quickly."

259

They stood ahead of the sea as another rush of water gained more ground. Wes turned around in hope of seeing a trace of the sand or the shore, finding neither. Ayesha helped Wes lift an arm around her shoulder as the purple headwrap slipped from her crown. He stopped to stare into the river that had now replaced the shore, washing away the prospect of Stanley's survival.

"Try not to look back, Wes," Ayesha gently suggested as she purposefully repeated Wes's first name. "Keep your eyes on the land. All we have is here and now."

Here and now infused Wes with hope as floodwater drowned out more parked cars and road signs. Wes, a secular Jewish scribe, stood closely beside Ayesha, a faithful Muslim barista. They shed the same tears, spoke the same words. Wes repeated after her just to get his bearings.

"Here and now," Wes echoed, his eyes fixed on the bodies floating like driftwood in the gushing current. Closer to their feet, the incoming floodwater picked up all sorts of debris, collecting the trash and claiming everything except for the patchwork forests further offshore.

"Where do go from here?" Wes asked.

"There's only one way we can go." Ayesha nodded at the woodland. "Forward."

Ayesha knew the heavily wooded village well. The enchanted forest sparkled with bungalows bigger and better kept than Stanley's shack on the fringes of a shore that no longer existed. They climbed into a hatch, gripping wooden bench seats as the *songthaew* driver steered against the wind in search of survivors.

They found only one. Ayesha and Wes helped lift an eight-year-old Thai boy out of shallow water. As they checked the child for injuries, he cried, explaining through gasping exhalations that he had been separated from his parents, who were working at one of the beachfront hotels. Wes shook his head and looked to Ayesha, who turned away, covering her eyes.

After hours of sweat and oceans of tears, the boy's parents didn't turn up. Neither did Stanley. Wes kept his composure as he felt a keen, biting truth: Stanley may not have been the world's best father, but he was a man who had suffered, fighting his own complexities and demons until he found peace in the water. He died doing what he loved.

Is anyone else fortunate enough to say the same?

ACKNOWLEDGMENTS

Tracy C. Gold rescued the first incarnation of this novel from absurdity. Stormi Messenger helped give the story substance, while Melissa Ringsted made it sparkle. A special thanks to Lexa Hayes for giving a final sendoff to these complex characters who shine brighter because of your kindness and care.

By believing in the manuscript, Susan Ingram gave it a chance. Thanks to everyone in the Johns Hopkins University alumni writers' group for the many Saturday afternoons of creativity and friendship.

As the son and grandson of rabbis, my friend Henry Lefkowitz is like my minister of information. Portions of the novel relating to Judaica are no doubt more authentic with Henry as a guiding light.

Whalen Nash, a former Amsterdam street musician, lent a touch of local authenticity to chapters set in the Netherlands. Special thanks to Beit Ha' Chidush in Central Amsterdam and Beth El Congregation in Baltimore County.

Back in 2004, Nick Price welcomed me as a guest at his house in New Zealand's North Island. There, the first seeds of this novel were planted. Years later, my former student and close friend Adil Yousuf watered those seeds. At twenty-eight, Adil passed suddenly at home in Karachi, Pakistan. Adil's humor, and his love of travel and adventure are alive in these pages.

Thank you to my daughters, Jacqui and Zoey, for giving me four years to slay this beast.

Made in the USA
Middletown, DE
21 August 2023